**Everyone has fallen in love
with *The Keeper of Lost Things*.**

You will be next . . .

'This is the first book I read in 2017 – and if another
as good comes along in the next 12 months,
I'll eat my special gold reviewing spectacles.
Hogan's touching, funny and romantic debut
is that rare and precious thing: a real story with
brilliant characters . . . Wonderful stuff'
Daily Mail

'An exquisite, absorbing novel, a potent cocktail
of insightful psychological realism, whimsy and
glittering magic, where hopes and new beginnings
glint off the sharp edges of grief and loss. It grabs
you right from its intriguing opening scene'
The Lady

'I was hugely impressed by this flawlessly
written, most humane novel'
Ronald Frame, *Sunday Herald* (Books of the Year)

'A charming story of fresh starts and self-
discovery that warms the cockles'
Woman & Home

'A warm and heartfelt debut'
Prima

THE KEEPER OF LOST THINGS

OF

RUTH HOGAN

TWO
ROADS

www.tworoadsbooks.com

First published in Great Britain in 2017 by Two Roads
An imprint of John Murray Press
An Hachette UK company

First published in paperback in 2017

1

A CIP catalogue record for this title is
available from the British Library

Paperback ISBN 978 1 473 63548 7
Ebook ISBN 978 1 473 63549 4
Audio Digital Download ISBN 978 1 473 63566 1

Printed and bound by CPI Group (UK) Ltd, Croydon, CR0 4YY

Hodder & Stoughton policy is to use papers that are
natural, renewable and recyclable products and made
from wood grown in sustainable forests. The logging and
manufacturing processes are expected to conform to the
environmental regulations of the country of origin.

Hodder & Stoughton Ltd
Carmelite House
50 Victoria Embankment
London EC4Y 0DZ

www.hodder.co.uk

To Bill, my faithful wingman,
and Princess Tilly Bean

But he, that dares not grasp the thorn
Should never crave the rose.

Anne Brontë

1

Charles Bramwell Brockley was travelling alone and without a ticket on the 14.42 from London Bridge to Brighton. The Huntley & Palmers biscuit tin in which he was travelling teetered precariously on the edge of the seat as the train juddered to a halt at Haywards Heath. But just as it toppled forward towards the carriage floor it was gathered up by a safe pair of hands.

He was glad to be home. Padua was a solid redbrick Victorian villa with honeysuckle and clematis framing the steeply pitched porch. The cool, rose-scented, echoing space of the entrance hall welcomed the man inside from the relentless glare of the afternoon sun. He put down his bag, replaced his keys in the drawer of the hall table and hung his panama on the hat stand. He was weary to the bone, but the quiet house soothed him. Quiet, but not silent. There was the steady tick of a long-case clock and the distant hum of an ancient refrigerator, and somewhere in the garden a blackbird sang. But the house was untainted by the tinnitus of technology. There was no computer, no television, no DVD or CD player. The only connections to the outside world were an old Bakelite telephone in the hall and a radio. In the kitchen, he let the tap run until the water was icy cold and then filled a tumbler. It was too early for gin and lime, and too hot for tea. Laura had gone home for the day, but she had left a note and a ham salad in the refrigerator for his supper. Dear girl. He gulped the water down.

Back in the hall, he took a single key from his trouser pocket and unlocked a heavy oak door. He retrieved his bag from the floor and entered the room, closing the door softly behind him. Shelves and drawers, shelves and drawers, shelves and drawers. Three walls were completely obscured and every shelf was laden and every drawer was full with a sad salmagundi of forty years gathered in, labelled and given a home. Lace panels dressed the French windows and diffused the brash light from the afternoon sun. A single shaft from the space between them pierced the gloom, glittering with specks of dust. The man took the Huntley & Palmers biscuit tin from his bag and placed it carefully on a large mahogany table, the only clear surface in the room. Lifting the lid, he inspected the contents, a pale grey substance the texture of coarse-grained sand. He had scattered the like many years ago in the rose garden at the back of the house. But surely these could not be human remains? Not left on a train in a biscuit tin? He replaced the lid. He had tried to hand them in at the station, but the ticket collector, cocksure that it was just litter, suggested that he put it in the nearest bin.

'You'd be amazed at the rubbish people leave on trains,' he said, dismissing Anthony with a shrug.

Nothing surprised Anthony any more, but loss always moved him, however great or small. From a drawer he took a brown paper luggage label and a gold-nibbed fountain pen. He wrote carefully in black ink; the date and time, and the place – very specific:

Huntley & Palmers biscuit tin containing cremation remains?
Found, sixth carriage from the front, 14.42 train from London Bridge to Brighton.
Deceased unknown. God bless and rest in peace.

He stroked the lid of the tin tenderly before finding a space on one of the shelves and gently sliding the tin into position.

The chime of the clock in the hall said time for gin and lime. He took ice cubes and lime juice from the refrigerator and carried them through to the garden room on a silver drinks tray with a green cocktail glass and a small dish of olives. He wasn't hungry but he hoped they might awaken his appetite. He didn't want to disappoint Laura by leaving her carefully prepared salad. He set the tray down and opened the window into the garden at the back of the house.

The gramophone player was a handsome wooden affair with a sweeping golden horn. He lifted the needle and placed it gently onto the liquorice-coloured disc. The voice of Al Bowlly floated up through the air and out into the garden to compete with the blackbird.

The very thought of you.

It had been their song. He released his long, loose limbs into the comfort of a leather wing-backed chair. In his prime, his bulk had matched his height, and he had been an impressive figure, but old age had diminished the flesh, and now skin lay much closer to bones.

His glass in one hand, he toasted the woman whose silver-framed photograph he held in the other.

'Chin-chin, my darling girl!'

He took a sip from his drink and lovingly, longingly kissed the cold glass of the photograph before replacing it on the side table next to his chair. She was not a classic beauty; a young woman with wavy hair and large dark eyes that shone, even in an old black and white photograph. But she was wonderfully striking, with a presence that still reached out from all those years ago and captivated him. She had been dead for forty years, but she was still his life, and her death had given him his purpose. It had made Anthony Peardew the Keeper of Lost Things.

2

Laura had been lost; hopelessly adrift. Kept afloat, but barely, by an unhappy combination of Prozac, Pinot Grigio and pretending things weren't happening. Things like Vince's affair. Anthony Peardew and his house had saved her.

As she pulled up and parked outside the house, she calculated how long she had worked there – five, no almost six years. She had been sitting in her doctor's waiting room anxiously flicking through the magazines when an advertisement in the *Lady* had caught her attention:

Housekeeper/Personal Assistant
required for gentleman writer.
Please apply in writing to Anthony
Peardew – PO Box 27312

She had entered the waiting room intending to plead for more drugs to make her unhappy existence more bearable, and left it determined to apply for a position that would, it turned out, transform her life.

As she turned her key in the lock and stepped through the front door, the peace of the house embraced her as it always did. She went through to the kitchen, filled the kettle and set it on the hob. Anthony would be out on his morning walk. She hadn't seen him at all yesterday. He had been to London to see his solicitor. Waiting for the kettle to boil, she leafed through the neat pile of paperwork he had left for her to deal with: a few bills to pay, some letters to answer on his behalf and a request to make an appointment with his doctor. She felt a prickle of anxiety. She had tried not to see him fading over the past months, like a fine portrait left too long in harsh sunlight, losing clarity and colour. When he had interviewed her all those years ago, he had been a tall, muscular man with a full head of dark hair, tanzanite eyes and a voice like James Mason. She had thought him much younger than his sixty-eight years.

Laura had fallen in love with both Mr Peardew and the house moments after stepping through the door. The love she felt for him was not the romantic kind, but more the love of a child for a favourite uncle. His gentle strength, tranquil manner and immaculate urbanity were all qualities that she had learned, albeit a little late, to appreciate in a man. His presence always lifted her spirits and made her value her life in a way that she hadn't for a very long time. He was a comforting constant, like Radio 4, Big Ben and 'Land of Hope and Glory'. But always very slightly distant. There was a part of himself which he never revealed; a secret always kept. Laura was glad. Intimacy, both physical and emotional, had always been a disappointment to her. Mr Peardew was the perfect employer who had become Anthony, a dear friend. But one who never came too close.

As for Padua, it was the tray cloth that made Laura

fall in love with the house. Anthony had made her tea at her interview. He had brought it into the garden room; teapot with cosy, milk jug, sugar bowl and tongs, cups and saucers, silver teaspoons, tea strainer and stand. All set out on a tray with a tray cloth. Pure white, lace-edged linen. The tray cloth was definitive. Padua was clearly a house where all these things, including the tray cloth, were part of everyday life; and Mr Peardew was a man whose everyday life was exactly the kind that Laura longed for. When they were first married, Vince had teased her about her attempts to introduce such things into their own home. If he was ever forced to make his own tea, he abandoned the used teabag on the draining board, no matter how many times Laura asked him to put it in the bin. He drank milk and fruit juice straight from the carton, ate with his elbows on the table, held his knife like a pen and spoke with his mouth full. Each on its own was a small thing, like the many other small things he did and said that Laura tried to ignore, but nonetheless chafed her soul. Over the years, their accumulation in both number and frequency hardened Laura's heart and stymied her gentle aspirations for even modest fragments of the life she had once sampled in the homes of her school friends. When Vince's teasing eventually curdled into mocking, a tray cloth to him became an object worthy only of derision. And so did Laura.

The interview had taken place on the day of her thirty-fifth birthday and had been surprisingly brief. Mr Peardew had asked her how she took her tea and then poured it. There had been precious few other questions from either party before he had offered Laura the job and she had accepted. It had been the perfect present, and the beginning of hope for Laura.

The whistle of the kettle pierced her reminiscence. Laura took her tea, along with a duster and some polish, through to the garden room. She hated cleaning at home, especially when she had shared a home with Vince. But here it was an act of love. When she had first arrived, the house and its contents were gently neglected. Not dirty or shabby, just vaguely overlooked. Many of the rooms were unused. Anthony spent most of his time in the garden room or his study, and never had any guests to stay in the extra bedrooms. Softly, gently, room by room, Laura had loved the house back into life. Except the study. She had never been in the study. Anthony had told her at the start that nobody went into the study except him, and when he wasn't in there it was kept locked. She had never questioned it. But all the other rooms were kept clean and bright and ready for anyone to enjoy, even if no one ever came.

In the garden room, Laura picked up the silver-framed photograph and buffed the glass and silver until it shone. Anthony had told her that the woman's name was Therese, and Laura knew that he must have loved her very much because hers was one of only three photographs on display throughout the whole house. The others were copies of a picture of Anthony and Therese together, one of which he kept on a small table next to his bed, and the other on the dressing table in the big bedroom at the back of the house. In all the years she had known him she had never seen him look as happy in life as he did in that photograph.

When Laura left Vince, the last thing she had done was to chuck the large framed photograph of their wedding into the bin. But not before she had stamped on it, grinding the smashed glass into his smirking face with her heel. Selina from 'Servicing' was welcome to him. He was a complete and utter arsehole. It was the first time she had really admitted it, even to herself. It didn't make her feel any better. It just made her sad that she had wasted so many years with him. But with an unfinished education, no real work experience and no other means of supporting herself, there had been little choice.

When she had finished in the garden room, Laura went through to the hallway and started up the stairs, stroking a golden gleam from the curved wooden banister with her duster as she went. She had often wondered about the study; of course she had. But she respected Anthony's privacy as he respected hers. Upstairs, the largest bedroom was also the handsomest and had a bay window that overlooked the back garden. It was the room Anthony had once shared with Therese, but now he slept in the smaller room next door. Laura opened the window to let in some air. The roses in the garden below were in full bloom; undulating ruffles of scarlet, pink and creamy petals, and the surrounding borders frothed with fluttering peonies punctuated with sapphire lances of larkspur. The scent of the roses floated upwards on the warm air and Laura breathed deeply, taking in the heady perfume. But this room always smelled of roses. Even in mid-winter when the garden was frozen and asleep, and the windows sealed with frost. Laura straightened and stroked the already perfect bedcovers and plumped the cushions on the ottoman. The green glass dressing-table set sparkled in the sunlight, but was lovingly dusted nonetheless. But not everything in the room was perfect. The little blue enamelled clock had stopped again. 11.55 and no ticking. Every day it stopped at the same time. Laura checked her watch and reset the hands on the clock. She carefully wound the small key until the soft ticking resumed, and then returned it to its place on the dressing table.

The sound of the front door closing signalled Anthony's return from his walk. It was followed by the unlocking, opening and closing of the study door. It was a sequence of sounds with which Laura was very familiar. In the kitchen she made a pot of coffee that she set out on a tray with a cup and saucer, a silver jug of cream and a plate of digestive biscuits. She took it through to the hall and knocked gently on the study door and when it was opened passed the tray to Anthony. He looked tired; etiolated rather than invigorated by his walk.

'Thank you, my dear.'

She noticed unhappily that his hands shook slightly as he took the tray from hers.

'Is there anything in particular that you'd like for lunch?' she asked coaxingly.

'No, no. I'm sure whatever you decide will be delicious.'

The door closed. Back in the kitchen, Laura washed up the dirty mug that had appeared in the sink – left, no doubt, by Freddy, the gardener. He had started working at Padua a couple of years ago but their paths rarely crossed, which was disappointing for Laura, as she had the feeling that she might like to get to know him better. He was tall and dark, but not so handsome as to be a cliché. He had a faint scar which ran vertically between his nose and top lip, and puckered his mouth a little on one side, but somehow its effect was to add rather than detract, giving his smile a particular lopsided charm. He was affable enough when they did bump into one another, but no more so than politeness demanded, giving Laura little encouragement to pursue his friendship.

Laura started on the pile of paperwork. She would take the letters home with her and type them on her laptop. When she had first worked for Anthony, she used to proofread his manuscripts and type them on an old electric typewriter, but he had stopped writing several years ago now and she missed it. When she was younger, she had thought about writing as a career; novels, or maybe journalism. She had had all sorts of plans. She was a clever girl with a scholarship to the local girls' school followed by a place at university. She could have – should have – made a proper life for herself. But instead she met Vince. At seventeen she was still vulnerable, unformed; unsure of her own worth. She was happy at school, but the scholarship meant that she was always slightly displaced. Her factory worker father and shop assistant mother were so proud of their clever daughter. Money was found – scraped together – to buy every item of her expensive school uniform; unheard-of unnecessaries like indoor and outdoor shoes. Everything had to be new. Nothing second-hand for their girl, and she was grateful, truly she was. She knew only too well the sacrifices that her parents had made. But it wasn't enough. Being bright and beautifully presented was never quite enough for her to slip seamlessly into the society of those who formed the rank and file of the school's assembly. Girls for whom holidays abroad, trips to the theatre, supper parties and sailing weekends were commonplace. Of course she made friends, girls who were kind and generous, and she accepted their invitations to stay at grand houses with their kind and generous parents. Grand houses where tea was served in pots, toast in racks, butter in dishes, milk in jugs and jam with a silver spoon. Houses with names instead of numbers that had terraces, tennis courts and topiary. And tray cloths. She saw a different kind of life and was enchanted. Her hopes were raised. At home, the milk in a bottle, the marge in a tub, the sugar in a bag and the tea in a mug were all stones in her pockets, weighing her down. At seventeen she had fallen into the space between the two worlds and there was nowhere left she truly belonged. And then she met Vince.

He was older; handsome, cocksure and ambitious. She was flattered by his attentions and impressed by his certainty. Vince was certain about everything. He even had a nickname for himself: Vince the Invincible. He was a car dealer and drove a red Jaguar E-Type; a cliché on wheels. Laura's parents were quietly distraught. They had hoped that her education would be the key to a better life for her; better than theirs. A life with more living and less struggling. They may not have understood about tray cloths, but they knew that the kind of life they wished for Laura was about more than just money. For Laura, it was never about the money. For Vince the Invincible, it was only ever about money and status. Laura's father soon had his own private nickname for Vince Darby: VD.

Unhappy years later, Laura often wondered what it was that Vince had seen in her. She was a pretty girl, but not beautiful, and certainly not the teeth, tits and arse combination he usually favoured. The kind of girls Vince normally dated dropped their knickers as naturally as they dropped their aitches. Perhaps he had seen her as a challenge. Or a novelty. Whatever it was, it was enough for him to think that she would make him a good wife. Eventually, she came to suspect that his marriage proposal was driven as much by his desire for status as it was by physical desire. Vince had plenty of money, but alone it wasn't enough to get him into the Freemasons or elected chair of the golf club. With her beautiful manners and private school education, Laura was intended to bring a sheen of social sophistication to his brass. He was to be bitterly disappointed. But not as much as Laura.

When she first found out about Vince's affair, it had been easy to blame him for everything; to cast him as some Austen-esque cad about town with Laura as the virtuous heroine left at home to knit spare toilet-roll covers or sew ribbons on her bonnet. But somewhere deep down Laura knew that that was really fiction. Desperate for refuge from an unsatisfactory reality she had asked her doctor for antidepressants, but he had insisted that she see a counsellor before handing over the drugs. For Laura it was a means to an end. She fully expected to run rings round a mousey, middle-aged, polyester Pamela to procure her prescription. What she got was a sassy, sharp-suited blonde called Rudi who forced her to face some rather unpalatable facts. She told Laura to listen to the voice inside her head; the one that pointed out inconvenient truths and raised uncomfortable arguments. Rudi called it 'engaging with her internal linguistics' and said that it would be 'a very gratifying experience' for Laura. Laura called it consorting with the Truth Fairy and found it as gratifying as listening to her favourite record with a deep scratch in it. The Truth Fairy had a very suspicious nature. She accused Laura of buckling under the weight of parental expectations, of marrying Vince in part to avoid going to university. In her opinion, Laura was afraid of going to university in case she failed; afraid to stand on her own two feet in case she fell flat on her face. She also raised the unhappy memory of Laura's miscarriage and subsequent, almost obsessive and ultimately unsuccessful quest for a baby. In truth, the Truth Fairy unsettled Laura. But when she got her Prozac she had stopped listening.

The clock in the hallway struck one and Laura began gathering ingredients for lunch. She beat eggs and cheese together with fresh herbs from the garden, tipped the mixture into a hot pan on the stove and watched it froth and bubble and then settle into a fluffy, golden omelette. The tray was set with a crisp, white linen napkin, a silver knife and fork and a glass of elderflower cordial. At the door of the study, she swapped it with Anthony for the remains of his morning coffee. The biscuits had not been touched.

3

Eunice

Forty years earlier . . . May 1974

She had decided on the cobalt blue trilby. Her grand-mother had once told her that one could blame ugliness on one's genes and ignorance on one's education, but there was absolutely no excuse whatsoever for being dull. School had been dull. Eunice had been a clever girl, but restless; too bored in lessons to do well. She wanted excitement; a life less lifeless. The office where she worked was dull, full of dull people, and so too was her job: endless typing and filing. Respectable, her parents called it, but that was just another word for dull. Her only escape was in films and books. She read as though her life depended on it.

Eunice had seen the advertisement in the *Lady*:

Assistant required for established publisher.
Wages woeful but work never dull!

The job was obviously meant for her and she applied the same day.

Her interview was at 12.15 p.m., and she had allowed herself plenty of time to get there, so now she could walk the remainder of the way at her leisure, gathering in the sights and sounds of the city to furnish future memories. The streets were crowded and Eunice drifted through the homogeneous flow of humanity, occasionally struck by a figure who, for some reason, bobbed above the surface of the indeterminate tide. She nodded at the whistling waiter sweeping the pavement outside The Swish Fish restaurant, and swerved to avoid an unpleasant collision with a fat and sweaty tourist too busy studying her *A–Z* to watch where she was going. She noticed and smiled at the tall man waiting on the corner of Great Russell Street because he looked nice, but worried. In the moment she passed him, she gathered in everything about him. He was well built and handsome with blue eyes and the bearing of a good man. He was anxiously checking his watch and looking up and down the street. He was clearly waiting for someone, and they were late.

Eunice was still early. It was only 11.55 a.m. She strolled on. Her thoughts drifted to the approaching interview and interviewer. She hoped that he would look like the man she had left waiting on the corner. But perhaps it would be a woman; a sharp, spiky unfolded paperclip of a woman with black bobbed hair and red lipstick. As she reached the glossed green door of the address she had been given on Bloomsbury Street she barely noticed the crowd gathered on the pavement opposite and the distant keen of a siren. She pressed the buzzer and waited; back straight, feet together, head held high. She heard the sound of footsteps bounding down stairs and the door was flung open.

Eunice fell in love with the man as soon as she saw him. His physical components were individually unremarkable: medium height, medium build, light brown hair, pleasant face, two eyes and ears, one nose and mouth. But in composition they were magically transformed into a masterpiece. He grasped her hand as though to save her from drowning and pulled her up the stairs behind him. Breathless with exertion and enthusiasm he greeted her on the way up with: 'You must be Eunice. Delighted to meet you. Call me Bomber. Everyone does.'

The office that they burst into at the top of the stairs was large and light and very well organised. Shelves and drawers lined the walls and three filing cabinets stood beneath the window. Eunice was intrigued to see that they were labelled 'Tom', 'Dick' and 'Harry'.

'After the tunnels,' Bomber explained, following her gaze and registering the query on her face. The query remained.

'*The Great Escape*? Steve McQueen, Dickie Attenborough, bags of dirt, barbed wire and a motorbike?'

Eunice smiled.

'You *have* seen it, haven't you? Bloody marvellous!' He began whistling the theme music.

Eunice was resolute. This was definitely the job for her. She would chain herself to one of the filing cabinets if necessary to secure it. Fortunately it wasn't. The fact that she had seen *The Great Escape* and was a fan was apparently enough. Bomber made them a pot of tea in the tiny kitchen that adjoined the office to celebrate her appointment. A strange rolling rattle followed him back into the room. The sound was made by a small tan and white terrier with one ear at half mast and a brown patch over his left eye. He was seated on a wooden trolley affair with two wheels and pulled himself along by walking with his front legs.

'Meet Douglas. My right-hand man. Well, dog.'

'Good afternoon, Douglas,' Eunice greeted him solemnly. 'Bader, I presume.'

Bomber thumped the table with delight. 'I knew right away that you were the one. Now, how do you like your tea?'

Over tea and biscuits (Douglas drank his from a saucer) Eunice learned that Bomber had found Douglas abandoned as a puppy after he had been hit by a car. The vet had advised that he be put to sleep, but Bomber had brought him home instead.

'I made the jalopy myself. It's more Morris 1000 Traveller than Mercedes, but it does the job.'

They agreed that Eunice would start the following week on a salary that was perfectly adequate rather than 'woeful', and that her duties would include just about anything that needed doing. Eunice was euphoric. But just as she was gathering her things to leave, the door burst open and the unfolded paperclip woman strode into the room. She was an inelegant zigzag of nose, elbows and knees; unsoftened by any cushioning flesh and with a face which had, over the years, sunk into a permanent sneer.

'I see that deformed little rat of yours is still alive,' she exclaimed, gesturing at Douglas with her cigarette as she flung her bag down onto a chair. Catching sight of Eunice, a twisted smile flitted across her face.

'Good God, brother! Don't tell me that you've found yourself a paramour.' She spat the word out as though it were a grape pip.

Bomber addressed her with weary patience. 'This is Eunice, my new assistant. Eunice, this is my sister, Portia.'

She looked Eunice up and down with her cold grey eyes, but didn't offer her hand. 'I should say that I'm pleased to meet you, but it would probably be a lie.'

'Likewise,' Eunice replied. It was barely audible and Portia had already turned her attention to her brother, but Eunice could have sworn that she saw the tip of Douglas's tail wag. She left Bomber to his odious sister and tripped downstairs into the bright afternoon sunshine. The last thing she heard as she closed the door behind her was from Portia, in an altogether changed, but still unpleasant, wheedling tone:

'Now, darling, when are you going to publish my book?'

At the corner of Great Russell Street she stopped for a moment, remembering the man she had smiled at. She hoped that the person he was meeting hadn't left him waiting for too long. Just then, in amongst the dust and dirt at her feet, the glint of gold and glass caught her eye. She stooped down, rescued the small, round object from the gutter and slipped it safely into her pocket.

4

It was always the same. Looking down and never turning his face to the sky, he searched the pavements and gutters. His back burned and his eyes watered, full of grit and tears. And then he fell; back through the black into the damp and twisted sheets of his own bed. The dream was always the same. Endlessly searching and never finding the one thing that would finally bring him peace.

The house was filled with the deep, soft darkness of a summer night. Anthony swung his weary legs out of bed and sat shrugging the stubborn scraps of dream from his head. He would have to get up. Sleep would not return tonight. He padded down the stairs, their creaking wood echoing his aching bones. No light was needed until he reached the kitchen. He made a pot of tea, finding more comfort in the making than the drinking, and took it through to the study. Pale moonlight skimmed across the edges of the shelves and pooled in the centre of the mahogany table. High on a shelf in the corner, the gold lid of the biscuit tin winked at him as he crossed the room. He took it down carefully and set it in the shimmering circle of light on the table. Of all the things that he had ever found, this troubled him the most. Because it was not a 'something' but a 'someone'; of that he was unreasonably sure. Once again, he removed the lid and inspected the contents, as he had done every day for the past week since bringing it home. He had already repositioned the tin in the study several times, placing it higher up or hidden from sight, but its draw remained irresistible. He couldn't leave it alone. He dipped his hand into the tin and gently rolled the coarse, grey grains across his fingertips. The memory swept through him, snatching his breath and winding him as surely as any punch to the gut. Once again, he was holding death in his hands.

The life they could have had together was a self-harming fantasy in which Anthony rarely indulged. They might have been grandparents by now. Therese had never spoken about wanting children, but then they had both assumed that they had the indubitable tenure of time. A tragic complacency, as it turned out. She had always wanted a dog. Anthony had held out for as long as he could, blustering about damage to the rose garden and excavations in the lawn. But she had won him round in the end, as she always did, with a fatal cocktail of charm and sheer bloody-mindedness. They were due to collect the dog from Battersea the week after she died. Instead Anthony spent the day wandering through the empty house desperately gathering in any traces of her presence; the indent of her head on a pillow; Titian strands in her hairbrush and a smudge of scarlet lipstick on a glass. Paltry but precious proof of a life now extinguished. In the miserable months that followed, Padua fought to keep the echoes of her existence within its walls. Anthony would come into a room feeling that she had, only moments before, left it. Day after day he played hide-and-seek with her shadow. He heard her music in the garden room, caught her laughter in the garden and felt her kiss on his mouth in the dark. But gradually, imperceptibly, infinitesimally she let him be. She let him make a life without her. The trace that lingered, and still remained to this day, was the scent of roses in places where it could not be.

Anthony brushed the grey powder from his finger-tips and replaced the lid on the tin. One day this would be him. Perhaps that was why the ashes troubled him so much. He must not be lost like this poor soul in the tin. He had to be with Therese.

Laura lay wide awake with her eyes clenched shut in fruitless pursuit of sleep. The worries and doubts that daytime activity kept at bay came sneaking back under cover of darkness, unpicking the threads of her comfort-able life like moths on a cashmere sweater. The slam of a front door and loud voices and laughter from the neighbouring flat crushed any fragile hope of sleep that remained. The couple who had moved in next door enjoyed a busy and rowdy social life at the expense of their fellow residents. Within minutes of their return, accompanied by a dozen or so fellow party animals, the thin walls of Laura's flat began to pulse to the relentless throb of drum and bass.

'Sweet Jesus – not again!'

Laura swung her legs out of bed and drummed her heels against the side of the divan in frustration. It was the third time this week. She had tried reasoning with them. She had threatened them with the police. In the end, and rather to her shame, she had resorted to yelling expletives. Their response was always the same: gushing apologies laced with empty promises followed by no change whatsoever. They simply ignored her. Perhaps she should consider letting down the tyres on their Golf GTi or shoving horse manure through their letter box. She smiled to herself in spite of her anger. Where on earth would she get horse manure from?

In the kitchen, Laura warmed milk in one saucepan to make hot chocolate, and with another she beat an exasperated tattoo on the party wall. A chunk of plaster the size of a dinner plate dislodged and smashed onto the floor.

'Shit!'

Laura scowled accusingly at the saucepan still clenched in her hand. There was a hiss of burning milk as the contents of the other saucepan boiled over.

'Shit! Shit! Shit!'

Having cleared up the mess and heated some more milk, Laura sat at the table cradling her warm mug. She could feel the clouds gathering about her and the ground slipping beneath her feet. There was a storm coming, of that she was certain. It wasn't just the neighbours who were troubling her; it was Anthony, too. Over the past weeks something had changed. His physical decline was gradual; inevitable with age, but there was something else. An indefinable shift. She felt as though he was pulling away from her like a disenchanted lover secretly packing a suitcase, preparing to leave. If she lost Anthony, then she would lose Padua too, and together they offered her asylum from the madness that was the real world.

Since her divorce, the precious few bearings that had set her course through life had drifted away. Having given up university and the chance of a writing career to marry Vince, she had hoped for children and all that motherhood would bring and later, perhaps, an Open University degree. But none of these had happened. She had fallen pregnant just once. The prospect of a child had temporarily shored up their already crumbling marriage. Vince had spared no expense and completed the nursery in a single weekend. The following week Laura had miscarried. The next few years were spent doggedly trying to replace the child that was never born. The sex became grim and dutiful. They subjected themselves to all the necessary invasive and undignified medical interventions to determine where the problem lay, but the results were all normal. Vince became angry more than sad that he couldn't have what he thought he wanted. Eventually, and by then to Laura's relief, the sex stopped altogether.

It was then that she began to plan her escape. When she had married Vince, he insisted that there was no need for her to work, and by the time it became clear that she was not going to be a mother, Laura's lack of experience and qualifications were a significant problem when she began looking for a job. And she had needed a job, because she needed money. She needed money to leave Vince. Laura just wanted enough to get a flat and be able to keep herself; to slip away one day when Vince was at work and then divorce him from a safe distance. But the only job she could get was part-time and low paid. It wasn't enough and so she started writing, dreaming of a bestseller. She worked on her novel every day for hours, always hiding any evidence from Vince. In six months it was complete and with high hopes Laura began submitting it to agents. Six months later, the pile of rejection letters and emails was almost as thick as the novel itself. They were depressingly consistent. Laura's writing had more style than substance. She wrote 'beautifully' but her plot was too 'quiet'. In desperation, she answered an advertisement in a women's magazine. It guaranteed an income for writers who could produce short stories to a specific format for a niche publication which was enjoying a rapidly expanding readership. The deposit for Laura's flat was eventually paid for by an embarrassing and extensive catalogue of cloying erotica written for *Feathers, Lace and Fantasy Fiction* – 'a magazine for hot women with burning desires'.

When she began working at Padua, Laura stopped writing. The short stories were, thankfully, no longer necessary to provide an income and her novel ended up in the recycling bin. She had lost all confidence to begin another. In her darkest moments, Laura wondered to what extent she had engineered her own failures. Had she become a habitual coward, afraid to climb in case she fell? At Padua with Anthony she didn't have to think about it. The house was her emotional and physical fortress, and Anthony her shining knight.

She poked with her fingertip at the skin forming on the surface of her hot chocolate as it cooled. Without Anthony and Padua she would be lost.

5

Anthony swirled the gin and lime round in his glass and listened to the ice cubes tinkling in the colourless liquid. It was barely noon, but the cold alcohol woke what little fire was left in his veins, and he needed it now. He took a sip and then set the glass down on the table amongst the labelled bric-a-brac which he had taken from one of the drawers. He was saying goodbye to the things. He felt small in the gnarled oak carver, like a boy wearing his father's overcoat, but aware as he was of his own diminution he was not afraid. Because now, he had a plan.

When he had started gathering lost things all those years ago, he hadn't really had a plan. He just wanted to keep them safe in case one day they could be reunited with the people who had lost them. Often he didn't know if what he had found was trash or treasure. But someone somewhere did. And then he had started writing again; weaving short stories around the things he found. Over the years he had filled his drawers and shelves with fragments of other people's lives, and somehow they had helped to mend his, so cruelly shattered, and make it whole again. Not picture perfect, of course not, after what had happened – a life still scarred and cracked and misshapen, but worth living nonetheless. A life with patches of blue sky amidst the grey, like the patch of sky he now held in his hand. He had found it in the gutter of Copper Street twelve years ago, according to its label. It was a single piece of a jigsaw puzzle; bright blue with a fleck of white on one edge. It was just a scrap of coloured cardboard. Most people wouldn't even have noticed it, and those who did would have dismissed it as rubbish. But Anthony knew that for someone, its loss could be incalculable. He turned the jigsaw piece over in the palm of his hand. Where did it belong?

Jigsaw puzzle piece, blue with white fleck.
Found in the gutter, Copper Street, 24 September . . .

They had the wrong names. Maud was such a modest little mouse of a name, quite unlike the woman who owned it. To have called her strident would have been a compliment. And Gladys, so bright and cheery sounding; it even had the word 'glad' in it. But the poor woman it described seldom had any reason to be glad now. The sisters lived unhappily together in a neat terraced house in Copper Street. It had been their parents' house and the place where they had both been born and brought up. Maud had entered the world as she had meant to carry on in it: loud, unattractive and demanding attention. Her parents' firstborn, she had been indulged until it was too late to salvage any sensitivity or selflessness in her character. She became and remained the only person of any significance in her world. Gladys was a quiet, contented baby, which was just as well as her mother could barely accommodate her basic needs whilst coping with the inexhaustible demands of her four-year-old sister. When, at eighteen, Maud found a suitor almost as disagreeable as herself, the family breathed a collective and only very slightly guilty

*sigh of relief. Their engagement and marriage were enthusiastically
encouraged, particularly when it transpired that Maud's fiancé
would have to relocate to Scotland for his business interests. After
an expensive, showy wedding, chosen and then criticised by Maud
and entirely paid for by her parents, she left to inflict herself upon
an unsuspecting town in the far west of Scotland, and life at
Copper Street became gentle contentment. Gladys and her parents
lived quietly and happily. They ate fish and chips for supper on
Fridays, and salmon sandwiches and fruit salad with tinned cream
for Sunday tea. They went to the pictures every Thursday night and
to Frinton for a week each summer. Sometimes Gladys went dancing
at the Co-op with her friends. She bought a budgerigar, named him
Cyril and never married. It wasn't her choice; simply a consequence
of never being given the choice. She had found the right man for her,
but unfortunately the right woman for him had turned out to be one
of Gladys's friends. Gladys had made her own bridesmaid dress and
toasted their happiness with champagne and salty tears. She
remained a friend to them both and became godmother to their two
children.*

*Maud and her husband had no children. 'Bloody good job too,'
her father remarked quietly to Cyril if the topic were ever raised.*

*As her parents grew older and frailer, Gladys took care of them.
She nursed them, fed and washed them, kept them comfortable and
safe. Maud stayed in Scotland and sent the occasional useless gift.
But when they eventually died, she found the funerals very
upsetting. The contents of the Post Office savings account were
divided equally between the two sisters, and in recognition of her
devotion her parents left their home to Gladys. But the will had a
catastrophic codicil. It stated that if Maud should ever become
homeless, she could live in the house in Copper Street until her
circumstances improved. It had been kindly meant to make
provision for a circumstance that her parents had believed to be*

most unlikely, and more easily included for that reason. But 'most unlikely' is not impossible, and when Maud's husband died he left her homeless, penniless and speechless with rage. He had gambled away every asset they possessed and, rather than face Maud, he had then deliberately died.

Maud returned to Copper Street an old-woman-shaped vessel of vitriol. The peaceful, happy life that Gladys enjoyed was destroyed the moment Maud arrived at the front door demanding money from her sister to pay the taxi driver. Untempered by any trace of gratitude, Maud invited misery as a permanent house guest. With her accomplished repertoire of tiny tortures she tormented her sister at every turn. She put sugar in her tea, knowing full well that Gladys didn't take it, overwatered the house plants and left a trail of mess and chaos in her wake. She refused to lift a finger to help with any of the chores, and sat all day growing fat and flatulent, eating fudge, doing jigsaw puzzles and listening to the radio at full blast. Gladys's friends stopped coming to the house and she went out as often as she dared. But her return was always met with a punishment; a precious ornament 'accidentally' smashed or a favourite dress inexplicably burned with the iron. Maud even frightened away from the garden the birds that her sister had lovingly fed by leaving out scraps for the neighbour's cat. Gladys could never disregard her parents' wishes, and any attempts to reason or remonstrate with her sister were met with disdain or violence. To Gladys, Maud was a death-watch beetle; an unwelcome parasite who had invaded her home and turned her happiness into dust.

And she tapped. Just like a death-watch beetle she tapped. Pudgy fingers tapping on the table, the arm of the chair, the edge of the sink. The tapping became the worst torture of all: incessant and invasive, it haunted Gladys day and night. Macbeth may have murdered sleep, but Maud murdered peace. That day she sat at the dining-room table tapping as she contemplated the huge half-completed jigsaw puzzle in front of her. It was Constable's The Hay Wain – *a monstrous reproduction of one thousand pieces and the largest she had ever attempted. It was going to be her masterpiece. She squatted toad-like in front of the puzzle, a surplus of buttocks spilling over the edges of a chair groaning under her weight, and tapped.*

Gladys closed the front door quietly behind her and set off down Copper Street, smiling as the wind whisked and twirled the crispy autumn leaves along the gutter. In her pocket her fingers felt around the edges of a small scrap of cardboard, machine cut, blue with a tiny fleck of white.

Anthony's fingers traced the edges of the jigsaw piece in the palm of his hand and he wondered whose life it had once been a tiny part of. Or perhaps not so tiny. Perhaps its loss had been disproportionately disastrous to its size, causing tears to flow, tempers to flare or hearts to break. So it had been with Anthony and the thing that he had lost so long ago. In the eyes of the world it was a gimcrack, small and worthless; but to Anthony it was precious beyond measure. Its loss was a daily torment tapping on his shoulder: a merciless reminder of the promise he had broken. The only promise that Therese had ever extracted from him, and he had failed her. And so he had started to gather the things that other people lost. It was his only chance for atonement. It had worried him greatly that he had not found a way to reunite any of the things with their owners. Over the years he had tried: advertisements in the local press and newsletters, and even entries in the personal columns of the broadsheets, none of which had produced any response. And now there was very little time left. But he hoped that he had at last found someone to take over: someone young enough and bright enough to have new ideas; someone who would find a way to return the lost things to where they belonged. He had seen his solicitor and made the necessary adjustments to his will. He leaned back into his chair and stretched, feeling the hard wooden struts press into his spine. High on its shelf, the biscuit tin gleamed, burnished by early-evening sun. He was so tired. He felt that he had overstayed his time, but had he done enough? Perhaps it was time for him to talk to Laura, to tell her that he was leaving. He dropped the jigsaw piece onto the table and took up his gin and lime. He had to tell her soon, before it was too late.

6

Eunice

June 1974

Eunice dropped the keys of the petty cash tin back into their rightful place and closed the drawer. Her drawer. In her desk. Eunice had worked for Bomber for a whole month now, and he had sent her out to buy iced buns for the three of them so that they could celebrate. The month had flown past with Eunice arriving earlier and leaving later each day, stretching her time in a place and with company that made her feel ignited with exciting possibilities. In those four short weeks she had learned that Bomber was a fair and generous boss, passionate about his job, his dog and films. He was also her matinée idol. He had a habit of quoting lines from his favourite films and Eunice was beginning to follow suit. Her taste was more contemporary, but he was teaching her to appreciate some of Ealing Studios' finest, and already she had piqued his interest sufficiently for him to see a couple of newer releases at the local cinema. They agreed that *Kind Hearts and Coronets* was utterly marvellous and *Brief Encounter* tragic; *The Exorcist* was shocking but the spinning-head bit hilarious; *The Wicker Man* chilling, *The Optimists of Nine Elms* magical and *Don't Look Now* atmospheric and haunting, but with rather excessive exposure of Donald Sutherland's naked buttocks. Eunice was even considering the purchase of a red duffle coat like the one worn by the dwarf in the film and doing some haunting of her own. And, of course, *The Great Escape* was perfection. Bomber said that the wonderful thing about books was that they were films that played inside your head. Eunice had also learned that Douglas liked to go for a little stroll at 11.00 a.m., particularly if it took him past the bakery that sold such delicious iced buns, and that he always ate the icing first and then the bun. And finally, she had learned that poisonous Portia was every bit as odious as a bowl of rotting offal.

Bomber was in the kitchen making the tea and Douglas was chivvying him along by dribbling on his conker-coloured Loake brogues in anticipation of an iced bun. From the window, Eunice watched the street below, today bustling with life, but only recently paralysed by a death; pedestrians and traffic stopped in their tracks by a heart stopping forever before their very eyes. According to Mrs Doyle in the bakery, Eunice had been there. But she hadn't seen a thing. Mrs Doyle recalled the exact date and time, and every detail of what had happened. As an ardent fan of police dramas on the television she prided herself on being an excellent potential eyewitness, should the occasion ever arise. Mrs Doyle inspected unfamiliar customers carefully, committing to memory lazy eyes, thin moustaches, gold teeth and left-sided partings, all of which she believed to be signs of a questionable moral character. And women with red shoes and green handbags were never to be trusted. The young woman who had died had had neither. Dressed in a powder blue summer coat with matching shoes and handbag, she had collapsed and died right there outside the bakery against a backdrop of Mrs Doyle's finest cakes and pastries. It had happened on the day of Eunice's interview at 11.55 a.m. exactly. Mrs Doyle was sure of the time because she'd had a batch of Bath buns in the oven that was due out at twelve.

'They were burned to buggery hell,' Mrs Doyle told Eunice. 'I was too busy phoning the ambulance to remember the buns, but I don't blame her. It wasn't her fault that she went and dropped dead, poor love. The ambulance came quick enough, but she was already gone when it got here. Not a mark on her, mind you. Heart attack I 'spect. My Bert says it could have been an annualism, but my money's on a heart attack. Or a stroke.'

Eunice could remember a crowd gathered and a distant siren, but that was all. She was sad to think that the best day of her life so far had been the last day of someone else's, and all that had separated them had been a few feet of tarmac.

'Tea up!' Bomber plonked the tray down on the table. 'Shall I be mother?'

Bomber poured the tea and dished out the iced buns. Douglas settled down with his bun gripped between his paws and set to work on the icing.

'Now, my dear girl, tell me what you think of old Pontpool's latest offering. Is it any good or shall we chuck it on the slippery slope?'

It was Bomber's name for the slush pile of rejected manuscripts. The scrap-heap of stories invariably grew so high, so quickly, that it avalanched onto the floor before anyone transferred it to the bin. Percy Pontpool was an aspiring children's author and Bomber had asked Eunice to look at his latest manuscript. Eunice chewed thoughtfully on her iced bun. She didn't need any time to decide what she thought, but simply how honest to be. However amiable Bomber was, he was still her boss and she was still the new girl trying to deserve her place. Percy had written a book for little girls called *Tracey Has Fun in the Kitchen*. Tracey's adventures included washing up with Daphne the dish-cloth, sweeping the floor with Betty the broom, cleaning the windows with Sparkle the sponge and scrubbing the oven with Wendy the wad of wire wool. Sadly, he had missed the opportunity of having Tracey unblock the sink with Portia the plunger, which might have proved to be some small redemption. Tracey had about as much fun as a pony in a coal pit. Eunice had a horrible feeling that Percy would be working on a sequel called *Howard Has Fun in the Shed*, with Charlie the chisel, Freddy the fretsaw and Dick the drill. It was a load of sexist codswallop. Eunice translated her thoughts into words.

'I'm struggling to envisage an appropriate audience for it.'

Bomber nearly choked on his bun. He took a swig of tea and rearranged his face into a suitably serious expression.

'Now tell me what you really think.'

Eunice sighed. 'It's a load of sexist codswallop.'

'Quite right!' said Bomber as he snatched the offending manuscript from Eunice's desk and hurled it through the air towards the corner where the slippery slope skulked. It belly-flopped onto the pile with a dull thud. Douglas had finished his bun and was sniffing the air hopefully in case any crumbs remained on the plates of his friends.

'What's your sister's book about?' Eunice had been dying to ask ever since her first day, but before Bomber could answer, the downstairs door buzzer sounded.

Bomber leaped to his feet. 'That'll be the parents. They said they might pop in for a visit while they were up in town.'

Eunice was eager to meet the couple who had produced such contradictory offspring and Godfrey and Grace were a double delight. Bomber was a perfect mix of their physical characteristics, with his father's aquiline nose and generous mouth and his mother's shrewd grey eyes and colouring. Godfrey was resplendent in salmon pink jumbo corduroy trousers, teamed with a canary yellow waistcoat, matching bow tie and a rather battered but still decent enough panama. Grace was wearing a sensible cotton frock with a print that might have looked more appropriate on a sofa, a straw hat with several large yellow flowers attached to the brim and smart shoes with a small heel but comfortable for walking in. The brown leather handbag which was tucked firmly into the crook of her arm was large and sturdy enough to biff any would-be muggers, whom Grace was convinced were lurking in every alley and doorway of the city, waiting to pounce on country folk like her and Godfrey.

'This must be the new girl, then.' Grace pronounced 'girl' to rhyme with 'bell'. 'How do you do, my dear?'

'Very pleased to meet you.' Eunice took the hand that was offered; soft but with a firm grip.

Godfrey shook his head. 'Good God, woman! That's not the thing at all now with the young 'uns.' He grabbed Eunice with both arms and squeezed her tight, almost lifting her feet from the floor, and then kissed her firmly on both cheeks. She felt the scratch of whiskers he'd missed when shaving and caught a hint of eau de cologne. Bomber rolled his eyes and grinned.

'Pops, you're shameless. Any excuse to kiss the girls.'

Godfrey winked at Eunice. 'Well, at my age you have to take any chance you can get. No offence intended.'

Eunice returned his wink. 'None taken.'

Grace kissed her son affectionately on the cheek and then sat down purposefully to address him, waving away offers of tea and iced buns with a dismissive hand.

'Now, I promised that I would ask, but I refuse to interfere . . .'

Bomber sighed. He knew exactly what was coming.

'Your sister has apparently written a book that she would like you to publish. I haven't read it – haven't even seen it, come to that – but she says you're being deliberately mulish and refusing to give it proper consideration. What have you got to say for yourself?'

Eunice was agog and intrigued by the hint of a smile that skittered across Grace's mouth as she delivered her words in such a stern tone. Bomber strode across the room to the window in the manner of a defence barrister preparing to address the jury.

'The first point is undoubtedly true. Portia has written something that she calls a book and she does indeed want me to publish it. The second point is a wicked falsehood which I deny with every fibre of my being.'

Bomber slammed the palm of his hand onto his desk

to emphasise his apparent indignation, before laughing out loud and slumping into his chair.

'Listen, Ma, I have read it and it's bloody awful. It's also been written by someone else first and they made a damn sight better fist of it than she did.'

Godfrey furrowed his brows and tutted in disapproval. 'You mean she's copied it?'

'Well, she calls it an "ommage".'

Godfrey turned to his wife and shook his head. 'Are you sure that you brought home the right one from the hospital? I can't think where she gets it from.'

Grace bowled a rather desperate attempt at a defence for her daughter's sticky wicket.

'Perhaps she didn't realise that her story resembled someone else's. Perhaps it was simply an unfortunate coincidence.'

It was a no-ball.

'Nice try, Ma, but it's called *Lady Clatterly's Chauffeur* and it's about a woman called Bonnie and her husband Gifford, who's been paralysed playing rugby. She ends up having an affair with her chauffeur, Mellons, a rough yet strangely tender northerner with a speech impediment who keeps tropical fish.'

Godfrey shook his head in disbelief. 'I'm sure that girl was dropped on her head.'

Grace ignored her husband but didn't contradict him and turned to Bomber.

'Well, that's cleared that up. Sounds perfectly dreadful. I'd chuck it in the bin if I were you. I can't abide laziness and if she can't even be bothered to think of her own story she can't expect anything else.'

Bomber winked gratefully at her.

'A boy's best friend is his mother.'

Grace stood up and re-armed herself with her hand-bag. 'Come along, Godfrey. It's time for Claridge's.' She kissed Bomber goodbye and Godfrey shook his hand.

'We always have tea there when we come up to town,' she explained to Eunice. 'Best cucumber sandwiches in the world.'

Godfrey tipped his hat to Eunice. 'The gin and lime's not bad either.'

7

The ruby droplet glistened on her fingertip before splashing onto the pale lemon skirt of her new dress. Laura cursed, sucked her finger angrily and wished she had worn her jeans. She loved filling the house with fresh flowers, but the beauty of the roses came at a price and the tip of the thorn was still embedded in her finger. In the kitchen, she stripped the lower leaves from the stems she had cut and filled two large vases with tepid water. One arrangement was for the garden room and one for the hall. As she trimmed and arranged the flowers, she fretted over the conversation that she had had with Anthony that morning. He had asked her to 'come and have a chat' with him in the garden room before she went home for the day. She checked her watch. She felt as though she had been summoned to the headmaster's office. It was ridiculous; he was her friend. But . . . What was the 'but' that kept prickling Laura's skin? Outside, the sky was still blue, but she could smell a storm in the air. She picked up one of the vases, took a deep breath and carried it out into the hall.

In the rose garden, it was hushed and still. But the air was heavy with the coming storm. In Anthony's study nothing moved or made a sound. But the air was thick with stories. A blade of light from the cloud-streaked sun sliced through the barely breached curtains and fired a blood-red glint onto a crowded shelf just beside the biscuit tin.

Red gemstone
Found in St Peter's churchyard, late afternoon, 6 July . . .

The smell of gardenias always reminded Lilia of her mother in her lilac Schiaparelli gown. St Peter's was awash with their waxy blooms and their perfume filled the cool air that welcomed friends and relations in from the fierce afternoon sun outside. At least the flowers had been Eliza's choice. Lilia was glad to sit down. New shoes were pinching her toes, but her vanity made no concession to arthritis and old age. The woman in the ridiculous hat had to be his mother. Half the occupants of the pew behind her would miss the entire wedding. An announcement from the vicar brought the rustling congregation to its feet as the bride arrived in her ugly mushroom of a dress, clinging desperately to her father's arm. Lilia's heart winced.

She had offered Eliza the Schiaparelli. She loved it, but the groom wasn't keen.

'Good God, Lizzie! You can't get married in a dead woman's dress.'

Lilia had never liked Eliza's intended. Henry. She could never trust a man who shared his name with a vacuum cleaner. The first time they met, he had looked down his shiny, bulbous nose at her in a fashion that clearly intimated that women over sixty-five don't count. He spoke to her with the exaggerated patience of someone housetraining a recalcitrant puppy. In fact, at that first family lunch, so lovingly prepared and so kindly intended, Lilia got the distinct impression that none of the family passed muster – except, of course, Eliza. And her greatest assets, in his eyes, were her beauty and her tractability. Oh, he was complimentary enough about the food. The roast chicken was almost as delicious as his mother's, and the wine was 'really quite good'. But Lilia watched him registering with disdain a slight mark on his fork and an imaginary smudge on his wine glass. Eliza was already, even then, gently explaining and excusing his behaviour, like an anxious mother with an unruly toddler. Lilia thought that what he needed was a jolly good slap on the back of his chubby legs. But she wasn't really worried, because she never dreamed it would last. Henry was an irksome addition to the family, but she could cope because he was temporary. Surely?

Eliza had been such a spirited child; determined to follow her own path. She wore her party frock with wellingtons to go fishing for newts in the stream at the bottom of the garden. She liked banana and tuna fish sandwiches and once spent the whole day walking everywhere backwards 'just to see what it feels like'. But everything changed when her mother, Lilia's daughter, died when Eliza was just fifteen. Her father had remarried and provided her with a perfectly serviceable step-mother. But they were never close.

Lilia's own mother had taught her two things: dress for yourself, and marry for love. Her mother had managed the first but not the second, and regretted it her whole life. Lilia learned this lesson well. Clothes had always been her passion; it had been a love affair that had never disappointed. And so it was with her marriage. James was a gardener for her parents at their country house. He grew jewel-hued anemones, pompom dahlias and velvet roses that smelled of summer. Lilia was astonished that such a man, sinewy and strong, with hands twice the size of hers could coax into life such delicate blooms and blossoms. She fell in love. Eliza had adored her grandfather, but Lilia was widowed when she was still a little girl.

Years later, she once asked Lilia how she had known that he was the man she should marry, and Lilia told her: because he loved her anyway. Their courtship was long and difficult. Her father disapproved and she was strong-willed and impatient. But no matter how ill her temper, how sunburned her face, how dreadful her cooking, James loved her anyway. They were happily married for forty-five years, and she still missed him every day.

When her mother died, Eliza's sense of purpose faded away and she became lost, like an empty paper bag being blown this way and that in the wind. And so she remained, until one day the bag got caught on a barbed-wire fence: Henry. Henry was a hedge fund manager and everyone knew that that was not a proper job. He was a money gardener; he grew money. For Christmas, Henry bought Eliza cordon bleu cookery lessons, and took her to his mother's hairdresser. Lilia waited for it to be over. For her birthday, in March, he bought Eliza expensive clothes that made her look like someone else and replaced her beloved old Mini with a brand new two-seater convertible she was too afraid to drive in case it got scratched. And still Lilia waited for it to be over. In June he took her to Dubai and proposed marriage. She wanted her mother's ring, but he said that diamonds were 'so last year'. He bought her a new one set with a ruby the colour of blood. Lilia always felt it was a bad omen.

Eliza would be there soon. Lilia thought that they'd sit under the apple tree. It was shady there and she liked to listen to the sleepy buzzing of the bees and smell the warm grass, like hay. Eliza always had tea with Lilia on Saturday afternoons. Salmon and cucumber sandwiches and lemon curd tarts. Thank heavens the tuna fish and banana had fallen out of favour eventually. It was a Saturday afternoon when she had brought Lilia's wedding invitation, and she had asked Lilia then what her mother would have thought of Henry; would she have liked him and would she approve of their marriage? Eliza had looked so young in spite of her overdone hair and her stiff new clothes, so anxious for approval and so keen for someone to reassure her that this would be the 'happy ever after' that she was longing for. Lilia had been a coward. She had lied.

Henry turned and saw Eliza creeping nervously down the aisle and smiled. But there was no tenderness softening his face. It was the smile of a man taking delivery of a smart new car; not that of a groom melting at the sight of his beloved bride. As she arrived at his side and her father placed her hand in his, Henry looked smug; he approved. The vicar announced the hymn. As the congregation struggled through Guide Me, Oh Thou Great Redeemer, *Lilia could feel the panic bubbling inside her like jam in a saucepan about to boil over.*

Lilia always used the best china tea things on a Saturday, and the lemon curd tarts always perched on a glass cake stand. The sandwiches were ready and the kettle had boiled, ready to warm the pot. It was their own little tea party and they had been keeping this ritual since Eliza's mother died. Today Lilia had a present for her.

A hush is a dangerous thing. Silence is solid and dependable, but a hush is expectant, like a pregnant pause; it invites mischief, like a loose thread begging to be pulled. The vicar started it, poor chap. He asked for it. When Lilia was a little girl during the war, they had a house in London. There was an Anderson shelter in the garden, but they didn't always use it. Sometimes they just hid under the table; madness, she knew, but you had to be there to understand it. When the doodlebugs were raining down, the thing they all feared most was not the bangs and the crashes and the ear-splitting explosions, but the hush. The hush meant that that bomb was for you.

'If any person here present knows of any reason why . . .'

The vicar launched the bomb. There was a hush, then Lilia detonated it.

As the bride swept back down the aisle alone, her face was lit by a beaming smile of relief. She looked truly radiant.

Eliza had given him back the ring. But the ruby had fallen out on the day of the wedding and they never found it. Henry was livid. Lilia imagined his face the colour of the lost stone. They should be in Dubai now. Eliza would have preferred Sorrento, but it wasn't swanky enough for Henry. In the end, he took his mother with him instead. And Eliza was coming to tea with Lilia. On her seat was her present. Nestled in silver tissue paper and tied with a lilac ribbon was the Schiaparelli. He'd never loved her anyway.

Anthony picked up the framed photograph from Therese's dressing table and gazed at her image. It had been taken on the day of their engagement. Outside, lightning crazed the charcoal sky. From the window of her bedroom, he stared out at the rose garden, where the first plump raindrops were splashing onto velvet petals. He had never seen Therese wearing the dress, but over the long years without her he had often tried to picture their wedding day. Therese had been so excited. She had chosen flowers for the church and music for the ceremony. And, of course, she had bought the dress. The invitations had been sent. He imagined himself nervously waiting at the altar for her arrival. He would have been so happy and so proud of his beautiful bride. She would have been late, of that there was no doubt. She would have made quite an entrance in her cornflower silk chiffon gown; an unusual choice for a wedding dress, but then she was an unusual woman. Extraordinary. She had said that it matched the colour of her engagement ring. Now the dress was shrouded in tissue paper and buried in a box in the attic. He couldn't bear to look at it; nor could he part with it. He sat down on the edge of the bed and buried his face in his hands. He had still been in church on the day that should have been their wedding day. It was the day of Therese's funeral. And even now, he could almost hear her saying that at least his new suit had been put to good use.

Laura threw her keys onto the hall table and kicked off her shoes. Her flat was hot and stuffy and she opened the window in the poky sitting room before pouring herself a large glass of white wine, icy cold from the fridge. She hoped that the wine would soothe her dishevelled mind. Anthony had told her so many things that she hadn't known, and the knowledge had swept through her head like a wild wind through a field of barley, leaving it mussed and disarranged. She could picture him waiting there all those years ago, checking his watch and searching for Therese's face in the crowd or a glimpse of her powder blue coat. She could feel the sickening panic blooming in his stomach like a drop of ink in a bowl of water, as the minutes ticked by and still she didn't come. But she could never know the blood-freezing, gut-twisting, breath-choking anguish he must have felt when he followed the wailing ambulance and found her crumpled and dead on the pavement. He had remembered every detail: the girl in the bright blue hat who had smiled at him on the corner of Great Russell Street; 11.55 a.m. on his watch when he'd first heard the siren; the smell of burning from the bakery, and the rows of cakes and pastries in the window. He could remember the sound of the traffic, the hushed voices, the white blanket that covered her face, and that even as the greatest darkness fell on him, the merciless sun kept shining. The details of Therese's death, once shared, forged an intimacy between Anthony and Laura that both honoured and unsettled her. But why now? Why, after almost six years, had he told her now? And there was something else, she was sure. Something that had been left unsaid. He had stopped before he had finished.

Anthony swung his legs onto the bed and lay back, staring at the ceiling, remembering the cherished nights he had spent there with Therese. He turned onto his side and formed his arms in an empty embrace, willing himself to remember when the space had been filled with her warm, living flesh. Outside, the thunder cracked and growled as the silent tears he so rarely allowed streamed down his cheeks. He was finally exhausted by a lifetime of guilt and grieving. But he could not regret his life without Therese. He would a million times rather have spent it with her, but to give up when she died would have been the greatest wrong; to throw away the gift that had been snatched from her would have been an act of appalling ingratitude and cowardice. And so he had found a way to carry on living and writing. The dull ache of dreadful loss had never left him, but at least his life had a purpose which gave him a precious, if precarious, hope for what might follow it. Death was certain. Reunion with Therese was not. But now, at last, he dared to hope.

He had spoken to Laura that afternoon, but he still hadn't told her that he was leaving. He'd meant to, but one look at her worried face and the words had dissolved in his mouth. Instead, he had told her about Therese and she had wept for them both. He had never seen her cry before. It wasn't at all what he had intended. He wasn't looking for sympathy or, God forbid, pity. He was just trying to give her a reason for what he was about to do. But at least her tears were testament to the fact that he had made the right choice. She was able to feel the pain and joy of others and recognise their value. Contrary to the impression that she often gave, she wasn't a mere spectator of other people's lives; she had to engage. Her capacity to care was instinctive. It was her greatest asset and her greatest vulnerability; she had been burned and he knew it had left a mark. She had never told him, but he knew anyway. She had made a different life, grown a new skin, but somewhere there was a hidden patch, still red and tight and puckered, and sore to the touch.

Anthony stared at the photograph that lay on the pillow next to him. There were no smudges on the glass or frame. Laura saw to that. She cared for every part and piece of the house with a pride and tenderness that could only be born from love. Anthony saw all of this in Laura and knew that he had chosen well. She understood that everything had a value far greater than money; it had a story, a memory and, most importantly, a unique place in the life of Padua. For Padua was more than just a house; it was a safe place to heal. A sanctuary for licking wounds, drying tears and rebuilding dreams – however long it took. However long it took a broken person to be strong enough to face the world again. And he hoped that by choosing her to finish his task, it might set Laura free. For he knew she was in exile at Padua – one that was comfortable and self-imposed, but an exile nonetheless.

Outside, the storm was spent and the garden washed clean. Anthony undressed and for one last time crept beneath the cool embracing covers of the bed that he had shared with Therese. That night, the dream stayed away and he slept soundly until dawn.

8

Eunice

1975

Bomber grabbed Eunice's hand and gripped it tightly as Pam recoiled in horror at the rather unusual furniture. It appeared to be made from human bones. She turned to flee but the grumpy Leatherface caught her, and just as he was about to impale the poor girl on a meat hook Eunice woke up.

They had been to see *The Texas Chainsaw Massacre* at a local film club the previous evening and had both been truly horrified. But it wasn't a nightmare that had broken Eunice's sleep. It was a dream come true. She climbed out of bed and hurried to the bathroom, where she smiled happily at her slightly rumpled reflection. Bomber had held her hand. Only for a moment, but he had actually held her hand.

Later that morning, on the way to the office, Eunice warned herself to be careful. Yes, Bomber was her friend, but he was also her boss, and she still had a job to do. At the green door on Bloomsbury Street Eunice paused for a moment and took a deep breath before galloping up the stairs. Douglas rattled over to greet her with his usual enthusiasm, and Bomber called out from the kitchen, 'Tea?'

'Yes please.'

Eunice sat down at her desk and began sorting studiously through the post.

'Sleep well?'

Bomber thumped a steaming mug down in front of her, and to her horror Eunice felt herself blushing.

'That's the last time I let you choose the film,' he continued – oblivious to, or perhaps kindly ignoring, her embarrassment. 'I didn't sleep a wink last night, even though I had Douglas to protect me, and I kept the bedside lamp on!'

Eunice laughed as she felt her red face returning to its usual colour. Bomber always managed to make her feel comfortable. The rest of the morning passed as easily as usual and at lunchtime Eunice went out to fetch sandwiches from Mrs Doyle's. As they sat together eating cheese and pickle on granary bread and looking out of the window, Bomber remembered something.

'Didn't you say that it was your birthday next Sunday?'

Eunice suddenly felt hot again. 'Yes. It is.'

Bomber passed a piece of cheese to Douglas, who was drooling hopefully at his feet.

'Are you doing anything fabulous?'

That had been the original plan. Eunice and Susan, her best friend from school, had always said that to celebrate their twenty-first birthdays, which were only days apart, they would go to Brighton for the day. Eunice had never been fond of parties, and her parents were happy to pay for the trip instead of hiring a hall with a bar and hirsute disco DJ. But Susan had found herself a boyfriend, a David Cassidy doppelgänger who worked in Woolworths, and he had apparently planned a surprise for her birthday. She had been very apologetic, but chose new love over her oldest friendship nonetheless. Eunice's parents had offered to come with her instead, but that wasn't quite what she'd had in mind. Bomber was distraught on her behalf.

'I'll come!' he volunteered. 'That is, if you don't mind your aged boss tagging along.'

Eunice was thrilled. But tried very hard not to show it.

'Okay. I suppose I could cope with that.' She grinned. 'I just hope you'll be able to keep up with me!'

On Saturday morning Eunice went to the hairdresser for a cut and blow dry, and then for a manicure. In the afternoon, having checked Sunday's weather forecast for the umpteenth time, she tried on virtually every item of clothing in her wardrobe, in every conceivable combination. She eventually decided on a pair of purple high-waisted flared trousers, a flower-printed blouse and a purple hat with a huge, floppy brim to complement her newly purpled nails.

'How do I look?' she asked her mum and dad, as she paraded up and down the living room, intermittently blocking their view of *The Two Ronnies* on the television.

'You look lovely, dear,' her mum replied.

Her dad nodded in agreement but said nothing. He had learned, over the years, that it was wiser to leave opinions on fashion to the ladies of the house.

That night Eunice hardly slept at all, but when she did, she dreamed of Bomber. Tomorrow was going to be an extraordinary day!

9

It had seemed like a perfectly ordinary day. But in the weeks that followed, Laura scoured her memory, searching for missed clues and portents that might have gone unheeded. Surely she should have known that something terrible was going to happen? Laura often felt that she should have been a Catholic. She did guilt so well.

That morning, Anthony went for his walk as usual. The only thing that was different was that he didn't take his bag. It was a beautiful morning and when he returned Laura thought how happy he looked; more relaxed than she had seen him in a long time. He didn't go into the study, but asked Laura to bring his coffee to the garden where she found him chatting to Freddy about the roses. As Laura placed the tray down on the garden table she deliberately avoided catching Freddy's eye. Perhaps it was because she found him attractive that being in his presence made her uncomfortable. He had an easy confidence and was blessed with both charm and good looks, which Laura found rather unsettling. He was too young for her in any case, she thought, and then immediately ridiculed herself for even considering that it would ever be an issue.

'Morning, Laura. Lovely day.'

Now she had to look at him. He was smiling at her,

and held her eyes in a steady gaze. Her embarrassment made her sound clipped and unfriendly.

'Yes, lovely.'

And now she was blushing. Not a flattering, rosy tint, but a vivid, scarlet mottling that made her look as if she had just had her head in the oven. She hurried back into the house. The cool, calm of Padua soon restored her equilibrium and she went upstairs to change the flowers on the landing. The door to the master bedroom was open, and Laura went in to check that everything was all right. The smell of roses was overpowering that day, even though the windows were closed. The clock downstairs in the hall began chiming midday, and Laura automatically checked her watch. The long-case clock had been gaining time, and she had been meaning to arrange to get it fixed. Her watch said 11.54 a.m. and suddenly a thought struck her. She picked up the blue enamel clock from Therese's dressing table and watched as the second hand ticked rhythmically round the dial. When it reached the twelve it stopped. Dead.

Anthony had his lunch in the garden room, and when Laura collected the tray she was delighted to see that he had eaten almost everything. Perhaps whatever it was that had been troubling him in recent months had been resolved, or perhaps his visit to the doctor had resulted in some improvement to his health. She also wondered if finally sharing his story about Therese with her had helped in some way. Whatever it was, she was glad. And relieved. It was wonderful to see him looking so well.

She spent the afternoon sorting through Anthony's accounts. He still received some royalties from his writing and would occasionally be asked to do a reading for some local book group or branch library. After a couple of hours poring over the paperwork, Laura leaned back in her chair. Her neck was sore and her back ached. She rubbed her tired eyes and made a mental note, for the hundredth time, to get them tested.

The lure of the study eventually proved irresistible for Anthony, and Laura heard him go in and shut the door behind him. She slipped the sheets of paper in front of her into their respective files and then went out into the garden to stretch her legs and feel the sun on her face. It was late afternoon, but the sun was still hot and the sound of bees on the honeysuckle throbbed in the sultry air. The roses looked magnificent. Blooms of every shape, size and hue combined to create a shimmering sea of scent and colour. The lawn was a perfect square of lush green and the fruit trees and bushes at the bottom of the garden burgeoned with the promise of late-summer bounty. Freddy clearly had a gift when it came to growing things. When Laura had first come to work for Anthony, the only part of the garden that was lovingly cared for was the rose garden. The lawn had been patchy and ragged with weeds, and the trees had been left to outgrow their strength, with branches too spindly to bear the weight of fruit. But in the two years since Freddy had come to work at Padua, the garden had been brought back to life. Laura sat down on the warm grass and hugged her knees. She was always reluctant to leave Padua at the end of the day, but on days like this it was even harder. Her flat held little attraction in comparison. At Padua, even when she was alone, she never felt lonely. In her flat she only ever felt that way.

Since Vince, there had been no other long-term relationships. The failure of her marriage had knocked her confidence and mocked her youthful pride. The wedding had been arranged so quickly that her mother had asked her if she was pregnant. She wasn't. She was simply swept away by a handsome Prince Charming who promised her the world. But the man she married was a flashy rogue who, instead of the world, delivered insipid suburbia. Her parents had done their very best to persuade her to wait; until she was older, knew better her own mind. But she'd been young and impatient, stubborn even, and marrying Vince had seemed like a shortcut to growing up. She could still remember the sad, anxious smile which her mother had fixed on her face as she watched her daughter walk down the aisle. Her father was less able to hide his misgivings, but fortunately most of the congregation assumed his tears were ones of happiness and pride. The worst thing of all was that, on her wedding day, she too had feared for the first time that she was making a mistake. Her doubts were buried in a barrage of confetti and champagne, but she had been right. Her love for Vince was a callow, fanciful love, formed as quickly as the silver-edged invitations had been issued and as frothy as the dress that she had worn down the aisle.

That evening, Laura picked at her supper in front of the television. She wasn't really hungry and she wasn't really watching the flickering screen. Giving up on both, she unlocked the door and stood out on the cramped balcony of her flat looking up at the inky sky. She wondered how many other people in the world were looking up at the same vast sky at that exact moment. It made her feel small and very much alone.

10

The midnight summer sky was a watercolour wash of darkness with a glitter of tiny stars thrown across it. The air was still warm as Anthony walked down the path towards the rose garden, inhaling the rich perfume of the treasured blooms that he had planted all those years ago for Therese, when they first moved into the house. He had been to the post box, his footfalls echoing softly through the empty streets of the village. The letter posted was the final full stop to his story. His solicitor would pass it on to Laura when the time came. And now he was ready to leave.

It had been a Wednesday when they had moved into the house. Therese had found it.

'It's perfect!' she had said.

And it was. They had met only months earlier, but they had not needed an 'approved' passage of time to bind them to one another. The attraction was instant; illimitable like the sky that hung above him now. At first it had frightened him, or rather the fear of losing it had. It was surely too potent, too perfect to last. But Therese had absolute faith. They had found each other and that was exactly as it was meant to be. Together they were sacrosanct. She was named after St Therese of the Roses and so he planted the garden as a gift to her.

He spent October in wellingtons trenching the ground in the new beds and digging in well-rotted manure, while Therese brought him cups of tea and unstinting encouragement. The roses arrived on a dank, foggy November morning, and their fingers, toes and noses froze as Anthony and Therese spent the day setting out and planting the garden around a perfect patch of lawn. But the washed-out palette that painted the November landscape was rainbow-tinted by the descriptions Therese read aloud from the labels that named every rose. There was pink and fragrant 'Albertine' to climb over the trellis archway leading to the sundial; the blood red velvet 'Grand Prix', the pure white 'Marcia Stanhope', the flushed copper 'Gorgeous', the silvery pink 'Mrs Henry Morse', the dark red 'Etoile de Hollande', 'Melanie Soupert' with pale yellow petals suffused with amethyst, and the vermilion and old gold of 'Queen Alexandra'. At the four corners of the lawn they planted weeping standard roses – 'Albéric Barbier', 'Hiawatha', 'Lady Gay' and 'Shower of Gold' – and when it was all done and they stood close together in the spectral drear of a winter twilight, she kissed him softly on the lips and placed something small and round into his cold-bruised hand. It was a picture of St Therese of the Roses framed in gold metal and glass in the shape of a medallion.

'It was a gift for my first Holy Communion,' she said. 'It's for you, to say thank you for my beautiful garden and to remind you that I will love you forever, no matter what. Promise me you'll keep it with you always.'

Anthony smiled. 'I promise,' he solemnly declared.

Tears scored Anthony's cheeks once again as he stood alone amongst the roses on a beautiful summer night. Alone and bereft as he remembered her kiss, her words and the feel of the medallion pressed into his hand.

He had lost it.

It had been in his pocket as he stood waiting for Therese on the corner of Great Russell Street. But she never came, and by the time he got home that day he had lost them both. He went back to look for the medallion. He searched the streets and gutters, but he had known that it was a hopeless task. It was as though he had lost her twice. It was the invisible thread that would have connected him to her even after she was gone, but now it was broken along with his promise to her. The contents of his study were testament to the reparation he had tried to make. But had he done enough? He was about to find out.

The grass was still warm and smelled like hay. Anthony lay down and stretched out his long, dwindled limbs towards the points of an imaginary compass, ready to set his final course. The scent of roses washed over him in waves. He looked up at the boundless ocean of sky above him and picked a star.

11

She thought he was asleep. Ridiculous, she knew, but the alternative was unthinkable.

Laura had arrived at her usual time and finding the house empty, assumed that Anthony had gone for his walk. But an insistent unease was tapping on her shoulder. She went to the kitchen, made coffee and tried to ignore it. But the tapping grew faster, louder, harder. Like her heartbeat. In the garden room, the door to the outside was open and she went out, feeling as though she were walking the plank. Anthony lay covered in rose petals, spread-eagled on the dew-soaked grass. From a distance he could have been asleep, but standing over him, there was no such comfort. His once blue eyes, still open, were milky veiled, and his mouth gaped breathless, hemmed by purpled lips. Her reluctant fingertips brushed his cheek. The tallow skin was cold. Anthony had gone and left behind a corpse.

And now she was alone in the house. The doctor and the funeral directors had come and gone. They had spoken in hushed voices and dealt with death kindly and efficiently. It was their livelihood after all. She found herself wishing that Freddy had been there, but it wasn't one of his regular days at Padua. She sat at the kitchen table watching another cup of coffee grow cold, her face scorched red and tight by angry tears. This morning her whole world had blown away like feathers in the wind. Anthony and Padua had become her life. She had no idea what she was going to do now. For a second time she was completely lost.

The clock in the hall struck six and still Laura could not bring herself to go home. She now realised that she was already home. The flat was just somewhere to go when she couldn't be here. Tears spilled down her cheeks again. She had to do something; a displacement activity, a distraction, however short-lived. She would do her job. She still had the house and everything in it to take care of. For now. She would keep doing it until somebody told her to stop. She started a tour of the house; upstairs first, checking everything was in order. In the main bedroom she smoothed the covers and plumped the pillows, dismissing as ridiculous her suspicion that the bed had recently been slept in. The scent of roses was overwhelming and the photograph of Anthony and Therese lay face down on the floor. She picked it up and returned it to its place on the dressing table. The little blue clock had stopped as usual. 11.55. She wound the key until the ticking started, like a tiny heartbeat. She passed the bay window without looking out at the garden. In Anthony's room she felt awkward in a way that she had never done when he had been alive. It seemed too intimate; an inappropriate intrusion. His pillow still smelled of the soap he always used. She pushed away unwelcome thoughts of strangers pawing through his things. She had no idea who his next of kin might be. Downstairs, she closed the windows in the garden room and locked the door to the outside. The photograph of Therese lay flat on the table. Laura picked it up and gazed at the woman for whom Anthony had lived and died.

'I hope to God you find each other,' she said softly before replacing the picture in its usual upright position. Laura wondered to herself if that counted as a prayer.

In the hall she stood by the study door. Her hand hovered above the doorknob, fearful, as though it might burn her if she touched it, then she dropped it back down by her side. She was desperate to see what secrets the room might hold, but the study was Anthony's private kingdom, and one which she had never been invited to enter. She couldn't yet decide if his death had changed that or not.

Daring herself, she stepped outside from the kitchen door and into the garden. It was late summer and the roses were beginning to shed their petals like fragile, worn-out ballgowns coming apart at the seams. The lawn was perfect again. It bore no imprint of a corpse. Well, what had she expected? Not this. As she stood in the middle of the grass in the ebb and flow of the sun-warmed, rose-scented air, she felt lifted; strangely reassured.

On her way back down to the house, the glint of setting sun on tilted glass caught her eye. It was the study window, left open. She couldn't leave it. The house would not be safe. Now she would have to go into the study. When she reached the door, she realised she had no idea where Anthony kept the key when it wasn't in his pocket. As she tried to think where it might be her fingers closed around the cool wooden handle. It turned easily at her touch and the door to the study swung open.

12

Shelves and drawers, shelves and drawers, shelves and drawers; three walls were completely obscured. The lace panels at the French windows lifted and fell in rhythm with the evening air which breathed gently through the crack in the frame. Even in the half-light Laura could see that every shelf was packed, and without looking she knew that every drawer was full. This was a life's work.

She walked around the room peering at its contents in astonishment. So this was Anthony's secret kingdom: a menagerie of waifs and strays meticulously labelled and loved. Because Laura could see that these were so much more than things; much more than random artefacts arranged on shelves for decoration. They were important. They really mattered. Anthony had spent hours every day in this room with these things. She had no idea why, but she knew he must have had a very good reason, and somehow, for his sake, she would have to find a way to keep them safe. She slid open the drawer nearest to her and picked up the first thing she saw. It was a large dark blue button which looked as though it belonged on a woman's coat. Its label noted when and where it had been found. Memories and explanations began to coalesce in Laura's consciousness; tentacles grasping for connections that she could sense but not yet substantiate.

She reached for the back of a chair to steady herself. Despite the open window and the draughts, the room was stuffy. The air was thick with stories. Was that what this was all about? Were these the things that Anthony had written his stories about? She had read them all and she distinctly remembered one about a blue button. But where had all these things come from? Laura stroked the soft fur of a small teddy slumped forlornly against the side of a biscuit tin on one of the shelves. Was this a museum for the missing pieces of people's real lives or the furnishings for Anthony's fiction? Perhaps it was both. She picked up a lime green hair bobble that lay next to the teddy on the shelf. It would have cost only a few pence when new, and one of the flowers on the elastic was badly chipped, yet it had been carefully kept and properly labelled like every other object in the room. Laura smiled at the memory of herself as a schoolgirl with swinging plaits adorned with bobbles much the same as this one.

Lime green hair bobble with plastic flowers.
Found on the playing field, Derrywood Park,
2 September . . .

It was the last day of the summer holidays and Daisy's mum had promised her a special treat. They were going for a picnic. Tomorrow Daisy would start at her new school; big school. She was eleven now. Her old school had not been a success. Well, at least not for her. She was pretty enough, with beautiful long dark hair; clever enough, but not too clever; didn't wear glasses or braces on her teeth. But it wasn't enough to keep her camouflaged. She saw the world through a slightly different lens from other children; nothing too obvious, just a fraction out of kilter. The faintest fontanelle in her character. But Ashlyanne Johnson and her posse of apprentice bitches soon sniffed it out. They pulled her plaits, spat in her lunch, urinated in her school bag and ripped her blazer. It wasn't what they did that upset her the most; it was how they made her feel. Useless, weak, scared, pathetic. Worthless.

Her mum had gone mad when she had found out. Daisy had kept quiet for as long as she could, but when the bed-wetting started she had to come clean. But it only proved how pathetic she was; a big girl of eleven wetting the bed. Her mum went straight to the headmistress and scared her half to death. After that, the school did what they could, which wasn't much, and Daisy set her sights on the end of term with gritted teeth and her hair cut short. She had chopped the plaits herself with the kitchen scissors and when her mum saw her she had cried. But over the summer her hair had grown again; not long enough for plaits, but just about for ponytails. And today she had new hair bobbles for them, bright green with flowers on. 'Daisies for Daisy,' her mother had said. As she sat admiring them in the mirror, her stomach lurched like the gears slipping on a bicycle. What if tomorrow her new classmates looked at the face of the girl in the mirror and didn't like what they saw?

Annie zipped the cool bag closed, satisfied that she had included all her daughter's favourites in their picnic: cheese and pineapple sandwiches (brown bread with seeds), salt and vinegar crisps, custard doughnuts, Japanese rice crackers and ginger beer to drink. She could still feel the need for physical violence smouldering inside her, stoked rather than soothed by the reaction of that idiot fairy-fart of a headmistress who could barely control a basket of sleeping kittens, let alone a school full of chip-fed, benefits-bred kids, most of whom already believed that the world owed them a council flat, a baby and the latest pair of Nike trainers. After Daisy's dad had left, Annie had worked bloody hard as a single mother to bring Daisy up. She had two part-time jobs, and the flat they lived in might not be in the best area, but it was clean and homely and it was theirs. And Daisy was a good kid. But good was bad. In the world of school where Daisy had to survive, the things that Annie had taught her were not enough. Common decency, good manners, kindness and hard work were treated as peculiarities at best, but in gentle Daisy they were seen as weaknesses; faults for which she was cruelly punished. So Annie had one more lesson to teach her daughter.

The sun was already high and hot by the time they reached the park, and the grass was littered with groups of young women accessorised with pushchairs, wailing toddlers, mobile phones and Benson & Hedges. Daisy's mother took her hand and they walked straight across the grass playing field towards the woods at the back of the park. They weren't just strolling, they were striding; going somewhere specific. Daisy didn't know where, but she could feel her mother's sense of purpose. The woods were another world; cool and quiet and empty, save for the birds and the squirrels.

'I used to come here with your dad.'

Daisy looked up at her mother with innocent eyes. 'Why?'

Her mother smiled, remembering. She put down the cool bag and looked up towards the sky.

'We're here,' she said.

The cool bag was at the foot of a huge oak tree, which was bent and twisted like an old man racked with arthritis. Daisy looked up through its branches, glimpsing flecks and flashes of blue through the flickering canopy of leaves.

Twenty minutes later she was sitting in the canopy looking down at the cool bag.

When her mother had announced that they were going to climb the tree, Daisy thought she must be joking. In the absence of a punchline or a laugh, Daisy took refuge in fear.

'I can't,' she said.

'Can't or won't?'

Daisy's eyes filled with tears, but her mother was resolute.

'You don't know you can't until you try.'

The silence and the stillness that followed seemed eternal. Eventually her mother spoke.

'In this world, Daisy, we are tiny. We can't always win and we can't always be happy. But the one thing that we can always do is try. There will always be Trashcan Johnsons' – a twitch of a smile crossed Daisy's face – 'and you can't change that. But you can change how she makes you feel.'

Daisy wasn't convinced. 'How?'

'By climbing this tree with me.'

It was the scariest thing Daisy had ever done. But somewhere before they reached the top a strange thing happened. Daisy's fear blew away like feathers in the wind. At the bottom of the tree she was tiny, and the tree an invincible giant. At the top, the tree was still huge, but tiny though she was, she had climbed it.

It was the best day of the summer holidays. By the time they walked home across the playing field, the park was nearly empty and a man riding a mower was about to cut the grass. Her hair had come loose climbing the tree and she pulled out her hair bobbles and stuffed them into her pocket, but when she got home she realised one of them was missing. After the triumph of the afternoon she scarcely cared. When Daisy got ready for bed that night, with her new school uniform hanging on the wardrobe door, she noticed that the face in the mirror was a new face; happy and excited. Today Daisy had learned how to conquer a giant, and tomorrow she was going to big school.

*

Laura replaced the hair bobble on the shelf and came out of the study, closing the door behind her. Her reflection in the hall mirror was of the face that belonged to the old Laura before Anthony and Padua: hollowed out, defeated. The clock struck nine. She would have to go. She picked up her keys from the small Maling bowl on the hall table where she always left them. But there was one extra. Underneath her bunch of house and car keys was a large single internal door key. Suddenly Laura understood, and the face in the mirror was transformed by a slow smile. Anthony had left the door to his secret kingdom unlocked for her. His trust in her resurrected the resolve that his death had dissipated. Today she had been left a kingdom and tomorrow she would begin unravelling its secrets.

13

Eunice

1976

Arrogantly sprawled across Eunice's desk, Portia flicked cigarette ash into a pot of paperclips. Eunice had nipped across the road with Douglas to fetch doughnuts from Mrs Doyle's, and Bomber was seeing a client out. Portia yawned and then sucked greedily on her cigarette. She was tired, bored and hungover. Too many Harvey Wallbangers with Trixie and Myles last night. Or rather this morning. She hadn't got in until 3 a.m. She picked up a manuscript from the pile which she had carelessly toppled as she arranged her spiky limbs into a praying mantis posture.

'"*Lost and Found* – a collection of short stories by Anthony Peardew",' she read aloud, with sing-song derision. As she flipped over the title page it ripped free of its treasury tag.

'Oopsy!' she sneered, frisbee-ing it across the room. She peered at the first page as though she were sniffing milk to see if it had turned.

'Good God! What a load of drivel. Who wants to read a story about *a large blue button* which fell off the coat of a waitress called Marjory! And to think he wouldn't publish me, his own sister.'

She threw the manuscript back onto the desk with such violent disdain that it toppled a half-empty cup, soaking the pages with coffee-coloured scorn.

'Shag and shit a pig!' Portia cursed as she retrieved the soggy sheaf of papers and hastily hid it halfway down the precarious stack of the 'slippery slope' just before Bomber bounded back into the room.

'Absolutely tipping it down out there now, sis. You'll get soaked. Would you like to borrow an umbrella?'

Portia looked up and about as though trying to locate an irksome bluebottle, and then addressed the room in general.

'Firstly, do not call me "sis". Secondly, I don't do umbrellas, I do cabs. And thirdly, are you trying to get rid of me?'

'Yes,' called Eunice, bundling back up the stairs, a muddle of mackintosh, damp Douglas and doughnuts. She dumped Douglas on the floor, the doughnuts on Bomber's desk and hung up her dripping mackintosh.

'I think we might need a bigger boat,' she muttered, tipping her head ever so slightly in Portia's direction. Bomber bit back the laugh that threatened to escape. Eunice saw that he was teetering and started 'duh da-ing' the music from *Jaws*.

'What is that ridiculous girl going on about now?' Portia squawked from her perch.

'Just a cinematic reference to the inclement weather,' Eunice replied cheerfully.

Portia was unconvinced, but more concerned by the fact that Douglas had wheeled himself as close to her as he could manage and was about to shake his wet fur in her direction.

'Get that blasted rat away from me,' she hissed, retreating, and promptly fell backwards onto Eunice's desk, scattering pens, pots and paperclips in all directions onto the floor. Eunice swept Douglas into the kitchen and soothed his hurt feelings with a doughnut. But Portia's rudeness had finally toppled even Bomber's extraordinary equanimity. His customary geniality slipped from his face like a landslide after a storm. Thunderstruck, he grabbed Portia by the wrists and heaved her from Eunice's desk.

'Clear it up,' he commanded, gesturing at the mess she had made.

'Don't be silly, darling,' she replied, picking up her bag and searching inside it for her lipstick in an attempt to disguise her surprise and embarrassment. 'I have people to do that sort of thing.'

'Well, they're not here now, are they?' fumed Bomber.

'No, darling, but you are,' said his sister, applying a fresh slick of scarlet. 'Be a sweetie and call me a cab.'

Red-faced, she dropped her lipstick back inside her bag and clip-clopped downstairs in her ridiculous heels to wait for the car she knew her brother would order. Portia hated it when he was cross with her but she knew that she deserved it, and the fact that he was right made her worse. She was like a toddler stuck in an eternal tantrum. She knew that she behaved badly, but somehow couldn't seem to stop herself. She sometimes wished that they could go back to when they were children and he was the big brother who doted on her.

As Bomber watched her go, he tried and failed to recognise in this brittle woman even the faintest trace of the affectionate little girl that he had once loved so dearly. For years now he had mourned the sister he had lost so long ago, who had hung on his every word, ridden on the crossbar of his bicycle and carried his maggots when he went fishing. In return he had eaten her sprouts, taught her to whistle and pushed her 'as high as the sky' on her swing. But she belonged to the distant past, and his present was poisonous Portia. He heard the cab door slam and she too was gone.

'Is it safe to come in?' Eunice poked her head around the kitchen door.

Bomber looked up and smiled apologetically. 'I'm so sorry about this,' he said, gesturing at the floor around her desk.

Eunice grinned. 'Not your fault, boss. Anyway, no harm done.'

They gathered the things up from the floor and restored them to their proper places.

'I spoke too soon,' said Eunice, cradling a small object in her hand. It was a picture of a lady holding flowers, and the glass inside the gold-coloured frame was smashed. She had found it on the way home from her interview and had kept it on her desk from her first day. It was her lucky charm. Bomber surveyed the damage.

'I'll soon have that fixed,' he said, taking the picture from her and placing it carefully in an envelope. He disappeared downstairs without another word. Eunice finished rescuing her things from the floor and swept up the cigarette ash. Just as the kettle boiled, Bomber returned both in body and spirit; soaking wet again, but his broad smile and good humour restored.

'The watchmaker on Great Russell Street has assured me that the glass will be replaced by tomorrow afternoon at the latest.'

They sat down to their very belated tea and doughnuts, and Douglas, finally assured of Portia's departure, wheeled himself back into the room hoping for seconds.

'She wasn't always like this, you know,' said Bomber thoughtfully, stirring his tea.

'I know it's hard to believe, but as a little girl she was really quite sweet; and for a little sister, tremendous fun.'

'Really?' Eunice was understandably sceptical. 'What happened?'

'Great Aunt Gertrude's trust fund.'

Elevated eyebrows registered Eunice's curiosity.

'She was my mother's aunt; rich, pampered and cantankerous as hell. She never married but always longed for a daughter. Unfortunately Ma wasn't her idea of a girl at all; couldn't be bought with expensive dolls and pretty dresses. Might have had more luck with a pony or a train set, but anyway . . .' Bomber bit into his doughnut and squirted jam onto his chin.

'Portia was a different matter. Ma tried to intervene; withheld some of the more lavish gifts; remonstrated with the termagant Gertrude, face to gargoyle face. But as Portia grew up Ma's influence inevitably diminished. Furious at what she called Ma's jealous meddling, when the Great Gertie died she took her revenge. She left the lot to Portia. And it was a lot. Of course Portia couldn't touch it until she was twenty-one, but it didn't matter. She knew it was there. She stopped bothering to make a life for herself and started waiting for one to happen to her. You see Great Gertie's legacy was a tainted tiara; the worst gift of all. It made Portia rich, but robbed her of any sense of purpose.'

'Thank goodness I'm not filthy rich if that's what it does to a girl,' Eunice joked. 'Just how filthy, exactly?'

'Feculent.'

Eunice cleared away the tea things and went back to work.

Bomber was clearly still fretting over the effect of Portia's tantrum. 'I hope you're not sorry that you came to work here.'

Eunice grinned manically. 'I must be nuts to be in a loony bin like this office,' she said in her best Jack Nicholson voice.

Bomber laughed his relief as he picked up a loose sheet of paper from the floor by his desk and screwed it into a ball. Eunice leapt to her feet, arms in the air.

'Hit me, Bomber, I got the moves!'

They had been to see *One Flew Over the Cuckoo's Nest* that week for the third time. They spent so much time together now, both in and out of work, that Bomber couldn't imagine life without her. The film had made an indelible mark and the ending had had them both in tears. Eunice knew the script almost by heart.

'So you're not about to hand in your notice and leave me to the mercy of my sister?'

Bomber's eyes almost filled with tears again as she replied with a line from the end of the film.

'I'm not goin' without you, Bomber. I wouldn't leave you this way . . . You're coming with me.' And then she winked. 'Now, about my pay rise . . .'

14

The girl watched as the tiny scarlet dome on black legs crawled across the back of her hand towards the curl of her little finger.

'Ladybird, ladybird, fly away home, your house is on fire, your children have gone.

All except one, and she is called Anne, and sorry but she died.'

The ladybird opened her wings.

'It's not truth.' The girl spoke slowly, as though she were reciting a poem that she was struggling to remember. 'It's only a made-up sing-song.'

The ladybird flew off anyway. It was hot; September. The girl sat swinging her legs on the wooden bench that faced Padua from the small green. She had watched as the shiny black cars had arrived outside the house. The first one had big windows in the side and she could see a box for dead people inside with flowers growing out of its lid. A sad lady and an old man but not the man who lived there came out of the house. The girl didn't know who the old man was, but she had seen the lady lots of times before she was sad. The man in the black chimney-pot hat put them in the second car. Then he went to the front of the car with the box in and started walking. He had a stick, but not a limp. But he was walking slowly so perhaps he had a bad leg after all. She wondered who was in the box. Thinking was something she did slowly. She was quicker at feeling. She could feel happy or sad, or angry or excited in a wrinkling of the eye. And she could feel other things too which were more difficult to explain. But thinking took longer. Thoughts had to be put in the right order in your head and looked at properly so that your brain could do the thinking. Eventually she decided that it must be the man who lived in the house who was in the box, and she was sad. He had always been nice to her. And not everyone was. After a long time (she had a nice watch, but she hadn't quite worked out the time please Mr Wolf yet) the sad lady came back on her own. The girl scratched the back of her hand where the ladybird's feet had tickled. Now that the man was dead, the lady would need a new friend.

Laura closed the front door behind her and slipped out of her black court shoes. The cold tiles of the hall floor kissed her aching feet and once again the peace of the house enveloped her. She padded through to the kitchen and poured herself a glass of wine from the fridge. Her fridge. Her kitchen. Her house. She still couldn't quite believe it. The day after Anthony had died she had telephoned his solicitor, hoping he would know if there was anyone she should contact; a distant cousin that she didn't know about, or a designated next of kin. He sounded as though he had been expecting her call. He told her that Anthony had instructed him to inform Laura immediately after his death that she was his sole heir; everything he had owned was now hers. There was a will, and a letter for her, the details of which would be revealed after the funeral. But Anthony's first concern had been that she shouldn't worry. Padua would remain her home. His kindness made his death all the more unbearable. She had been unable to continue the telephone conversation, her words choked by tears. It was no longer grief alone that overwhelmed her, but relief for herself, chased by guilt that she could feel such a thing at such a time.

She took her wine through to the study and sat down at the table. She felt a strange solace surrounded by Anthony's treasures. She was now their guardian and they gave her a sense of purpose, even though she was as yet unsure as to what that might be. Perhaps Anthony's letter would explain, and then she might find a way to deserve his extraordinary generosity towards her. The funeral had been a revelation. Laura had expected there to be only a handful of people, including herself and Anthony's solicitor, but the church was almost full. There were people from the publishing world who had known Anthony as a writer and others who had only known him to say 'Good morning' to, but it seemed as though he touched the lives of everyone he met and left an indelible mark. And then, of course, there were the busybodies: stalwart members of the local residents' association, WI, Amateur Dramatics Society and general purveyors of the moral high ground, led by Marjory Wadscallop and her faithful deputy, Winnie Cripp. Their 'heartfelt condolences' – offered a little too enthusiastically as Laura left the church – had been accompanied by sad, well-practised smiles and unwelcome hugs that left Laura smelling of damp dog and hairspray.

The large blue button that Laura had taken from the drawer on her first visit to the study was still on the table, resting on its label.

Large blue button, from woman's coat?
Found on the pavement of Graydown Street,
11 November . . .

Margaret was wearing her dangerous new knickers. 'Ruby silk with sumptuous cream lace' was how the saleswoman had described them, clearly wondering what business Margaret had buying them. They were not even distant cousins of her usual Marks & Spencer utility wear. Downstairs her husband waited expectantly. Twenty-six years they had been married, and he had done his best to let Margaret know how much he loved her for every one of those years. He loved her with his fists and his feet. His love was the colour of bruises. The sound of breaking bones. The taste of blood. Of course, no one else knew. No one at the bank where he was assistant manager, no one at the golf club where he was treasurer, and certainly no one at the church where, in the first year of their marriage, he had been born again a Baptist bedlamite. Beating the crap out of her was God's will. Apparently. But no one else knew; just him, God and Margaret. His respectability was like a neatly pressed suit; a uniform he wore to fool the outside world. But at home, in mufti, the monster reappeared. They'd never had any children. It was probably for the best. He might have loved them too. So why had she stayed? Love, at first. She had truly loved him. Then fear, weakness, desolation? All of the above. Body and spirit crushed by God and Gordon.

'Where the fuck's my dinner!' a voice bawled from the sitting room. She could picture him, fleshy faced and florid; rolls of fat seeping over the belt of his trousers, watching the rugby on the

television and drinking his tea. Tea that Margaret had made; milk and two sugars. And six Tramadol. Not enough to kill him; not quite. God knows, she had enough. The last time she 'tripped' and broke her wrist, that kind doctor in A&E had given her a whole box. Not that she wasn't tempted. Manslaughter with diminished responsibility thrown in seemed like a fair trade. But Margaret wanted him to know. Her left eye was almost swollen shut and the colour of the Valpolicella Gordon was expecting to swill with his dinner. Touching it, she winced, but then she felt the whisper of soft silk brushing against her skin and smiled. Downstairs, Gordon wasn't feeling quite himself.

When she entered the sitting room, she looked him straight in the eyes for the first time in years. 'I'm leaving you.'

She waited to make sure that he understood. The rage in his eyes was all the confirmation she needed.

'Get back here, you stupid bitch!'

He tried to haul himself from his chair, but Margaret had already left the room. She heard him crash to the floor. She picked up the suitcase in the hall, closed the door behind her and walked down the drive without looking back. She didn't know where she was going, and she didn't care as long as it was away. The bitter November wind stung her bruised face. Margaret put down her suitcase for a moment to fasten the top button of her old blue coat. The worn-out thread snapped and the button spun through her fingers and onto the pavement. Margaret picked up her suitcase and left the button where it was.

'Sod it,' she thought. 'I'll buy a new coat. Happy Birthday, Margaret.'

Laura awoke to the sound of knocking. She had fallen asleep slumped over the table, and her cheek now bore the imprint of the blue button it had been resting on.

Still befuddled with sleep, she slowly realised that the knocking was coming from the front door. In the hall she passed her suitcase still waiting to be unpacked. She had decided that tonight would be the first night that she would stay at Padua. It had somehow felt right to wait until after the funeral. The knocking began again, insistent but not urgent. Patient. As though the person would wait for as long as it took for someone to answer. Laura opened the door to a young girl with a serious and beautiful moon face, set with almond-shaped eyes the colour of conkers. She had seen her many times before, sitting on the bench across the green, but never this close. The girl drew herself up to her full height of five feet and one and a quarter inches and then she spoke.

'My name is Sunshine and I can be your new friend.'

15

'When the sitter comes, shall I make the lovely cup of tea?'

Laura smiled. 'Do you know how?'

'No.'

It had been two weeks since Anthony's funeral and Sunshine had called every day apart from on Sundays when her mum had stopped her.

'Give the poor woman a day off, Sunshine. I'm sure she doesn't want you pestering her peace and quiet all the time.'

Sunshine was unfazed. 'I'm not a pester. I'm her new friend.'

'Hmm . . . whether she likes it or not,' her mum muttered as she peeled the potatoes ready for Sunday lunch. Her mum worked long hours as a carer for the elderly and was rarely at home during the day, and her dad worked on the trains. Sunshine's older brother was supposed to keep an eye on her, but he rarely noticed anything that didn't take place in high definition on a screen the size of a kitchen table that obscured most of his bedroom wall. Besides, she was nineteen. They couldn't keep her locked up like a child. To be honest she was pleased that Sunshine had found something else to do other than sit on a bench all day. But she was

81

always anxious about the response of strangers to her daughter's sudden and enthusiastic attachments. Sunshine was fearless and trusting, but her courage and good nature made her vulnerable. Her virtues were often her most serious handicap. Her mum had popped round to see the woman – Laura, she was called – who owned the big house, to check whether or not she minded Sunshine's visits. She also wanted to satisfy herself that Sunshine wouldn't come to any harm. The woman seemed nice enough, if a little stand-offish, and said that Sunshine was very welcome. But it was the house itself that reassured her the most. It was very beautiful, but more than that, it had a lovely feeling about it that she struggled to describe to her husband, Bert.

'It just feels *safe*,' was the best she could do to explain why she was happy to approve her daughter visiting Padua. For Sunshine, it was the highlight of her day, and now she sat at the kitchen table waiting patiently for Laura's answer. Laura paused, kettle in hand, and looked into Sunshine's serious face.

'I suppose I could show you how.'

Some days she found Sunshine an unwelcome intruder into her new and as yet uncertain life; a determined gatecrasher. Of course, she would never have admitted it. She had even told Sunshine's mum that she was very welcome. But some days Laura pretended not to be in, leaving Sunshine on the doorstep, patiently but persistently ringing the bell. Once she had even hidden in the garden behind the shed. But Sunshine had eventually found her and her beaming smile of delight had made Laura feel like a prize-winning idiot and a cold-hearted bitch.

Anthony's solicitor was coming today with the will and the letter. Laura had explained this to Sunshine, but could never be sure exactly how much she understood. She was watching Laura intently now as she set the kettle on the hob and took a fresh tray cloth from the drawer. Mr Quinlan was due at 2.30 p.m. Before that, Sunshine managed to squeeze in five practice runs, including the washing-up, and Laura, as Mr Quinlan's stand-in, had been forced to tip the last three cups into the aspidistra for the sake of her bladder.

Mr Quinlan arrived on time. Sunshine recognised him as the old man who had come out of the house with Laura on the day of Anthony's funeral. He was wearing a charcoal grey pinstripe suit and a pale pink shirt, and a gold watch chain could just be seen disappearing into his waistcoat pocket. He looked important. Uncertain how to greet a person of such standing, Sunshine bobbed a little curtsey and offered him a high five.

'I'm delighted to meet you, young lady. I'm Robert Quinlan, and who are you?'

'I'm Sunshine, the new friend for Laura. People sometimes call me Sunny for short.'

He smiled. 'Which do you prefer?'

'Sunshine. Do people ever call you Robber?'

'It's an occupational hazard, I'm afraid.'

Laura led them through to the garden room and Sunshine made sure that the sitter had the best chair. She looked at Laura meaningfully.

'Shall I go and make the lovely cup of tea now?'

'That would be very helpful,' Laura replied, secretly wishing that she had nipped to the loo just one more time before Mr Quinlan had arrived.

Mr Quinlan read the contents of the will to Laura while Sunshine was in the kitchen. It was clear and simple. Anthony thanked Laura for her work and friendship, but most particularly for her loving care of the house and everything in it. He wanted Laura to inherit all that he owned on the condition that she lived in the house and kept the rose garden exactly as it was. He knew that Laura loved the house almost as much as he had, and he had died content in the knowledge that she would continue to care for it and 'take the best possible advantage of all the happiness and peace it had to offer'.

'And so, my dear, it's all yours. As well as the house and its contents, there's also a sizeable sum in the bank, and any royalties from his writing will now come to you.' Mr Quinlan peered at her over the top of his horn-rimmed spectacles and smiled.

'Here's the lovely cup of tea.' Sunshine barged the door open with her elbow and inched her way into the room like a tightrope walker. Her knuckles were white from the weight of the tray she was carrying, and the tip of her tongue poked out of her tiny rosebud mouth in agonised concentration. Mr Quinlan leapt to his feet and relieved her of her burden. He set the tray down on a side table.

'Shall I be mother?' he asked.

Sunshine shook her head. 'I've got a mum. She's at the work.'

'Quite right, young lady. I meant shall I pour the tea?'

Sunshine considered carefully for a moment. 'Do you know how?'

He smiled. 'Perhaps you'd better show me.'

Three expertly poured cups of tea and two custard creams later, all consumed under Sunshine's unswerving observation, Mr Quinlan's visit was drawing to a close.

'Just one more thing,' he said to Laura. 'The third condition of the will.'

He handed Laura a sealed white envelope bearing her name in Anthony's handwriting.

'I believe this explains it in greater detail, but it was Anthony's wish that you should endeavour to return as many of the things in his study to their rightful owners as you possibly can.'

Laura recalled the groaning shelves and packed drawers and balked at the enormity of the task. 'But how?'

'I can't begin to imagine. But Anthony clearly had faith in you, so perhaps all you need is a little faith in yourself. I'm sure you'll find a way.'

Laura was less sure than hopeful. But then hope went well with faith, didn't it?

'She had wonderful red hair, you know.' Mr Quinlan had picked up the photograph of Therese.

'Did you ever meet her?' Laura asked.

He traced the outline of the face in the photograph wistfully with his finger.

'Several times. She was a magnificent woman. Oh, she had a wild streak, and a fiery temper when roused. Still, I think every man who met her fell just a little bit under her spell.'

Clearly reluctant to let her go, he put the photograph back on the table. 'But Anthony was the only chap for her. He was my friend as well as a client for many years and I never saw a man more in love. When she died it crushed his soul. It was the saddest thing . . .'

Sunshine sat quietly, listening to every word and gathering them all in so that she could try to sort them into the proper story later.

'Let me guess,' said Mr Quinlan, getting up and going over to the gramophone. '"The Very Thought of You", Al Bowlly?'

Laura smiled. 'It was their song.'

'Of course. Anthony told me the story.'

'I'd love to hear it.'

Since Anthony's death, Laura had been increasingly saddened by the realisation that she knew so little about him, and in particular about his past. Their relationship had been firmly fixed in the present, forged by daily routines and events and not by sharing the past or planning for the future. So now Laura was keen to find out anything she could. She wanted to better know the man who had trusted her and treated her with such kindness and generosity. Mr Quinlan returned to his seat in the best chair.

'One of Anthony's earliest and most precious memories was when he was a little boy dancing to that tune. It was during the Second World War and his father was home on leave. He was an officer in the RAF. That evening his parents were going to a dance. It was a special occasion and his father's last night so his mother had borrowed a beautiful lilac evening gown from a friend. It was a Schiaparelli, I believe. There was a photograph Anthony had . . . Anyway, they were having cocktails together in the drawing room when Anthony came in to say goodnight. They were dancing to that Al Bowlly song – his dashing father and elegant mother – and they gathered him up into their arms and danced with him between them. He said he could still remember the smell of his mother's perfume and the serge of his father's uniform. It was the last time they were together, and the last time he saw his father. He returned to his air base early the next morning before Anthony was awake. Three months later he was captured behind enemy lines and was killed attempting to escape from Stalag Luft III. Many years later, not long after they met, Anthony and Therese were having lunch in a wine bar in Covent Garden that favoured deco over Donny Osmond and David Cassidy. The pair of them always did seem to belong to another age. The Al Bowlly song started playing and Anthony told Therese the story. She took his hand and stood up and danced with him then and there, as though they were the only ones in the room.

Laura was starting to understand. 'She sounds like an amazing woman.'

Mr Quinlan's reply was heartfelt. 'Indeed she was.'

As he began packing his paperwork into his briefcase, the silent Sunshine stirred. 'Would you like the lovely cup of tea again?'

He smiled gratefully but shook his head. 'I'm afraid I must go or else I shall miss my train.' But in the hall he paused and turned to Laura.

'I wonder if I might use the loo before I go?'

16

The paper knife was solid silver with a handle in the form of an Egyptian pharaoh. Laura slid the blade between the folds of thick white paper. As the envelope split open she imagined Anthony's secrets escaping like a cloud of whispers into the air. She had waited until Sunshine had gone home before bringing the letter into the study. The garden room was more comfortable, but it felt more fitting to read it surrounded by the things it concerned. The mild summer evenings had slipstreamed imperceptibly into crisp autumn twilights and Laura was half tempted to light the fire in the grate, but instead she pulled the sleeves of her cardigan down to cover her knuckles and slid the letter out of the envelope. She unfolded the stiff sheets of paper and spread them on the table in front of her.

My dear Laura,

Anthony's deep and gentle voice sounded in her ears and the black writing disappeared into a blur, washed away by the tears which filled Laura's eyes. She sniffed loudly and wiped her eyes on her sleeve.

'For God's sake, Laura, get a bloody grip!' she

admonished herself, and was surprised by the smile that hijacked her lips.

My dear Laura,

By now you will know that Padua and everything in it is yours. I hope that you will be very happy living here and will forgive my foolish sentimentality about the rose garden. You see I planted it for Therese, who was named after St Therese of the Roses. When she died, I scattered her ashes amongst the roses so that I could always be near to her, and if you could possibly bring yourself to do it, I should like mine to be scattered there too. If you find it too gruesome, perhaps you could ask Freddy to do it. I'm sure he wouldn't mind; he has the constitution of a concrete cockroach, dear boy.

And now I must tell you about the things in the study. Once again, it starts with the rose garden. On the day I planted it, Therese gave me a gift. It was her first Holy Communion medal. She told me that it was to say thank you for the rose garden, and to remind me that she would love me forever, no matter what. She made me promise to keep it with me always. It was the most precious thing that I have ever owned. And I lost it. On the day that Therese died. I had it in my pocket that morning when I left Padua, but by the time I returned it was gone. It felt as though the last remaining thread that bound us together had been broken. Like a clock, unwound, I stopped. I stopped living and began existing. I breathed, ate, drank and slept. But only as much as I had to, and that was all.

It was Robert who eventually brought me to my senses. 'What would Therese think?' he said. And he was right. She had been so full of life and it had been stolen from

*her. I still had life, but was choosing a living death. She
would have been furious. 'And heartbroken,' said Robert. I
began walking; visiting the world again. One day I found a
glove; ladies', navy blue leather, right hand. I took it home
and labelled it – what it was, and when and where I'd
found it. And so it began, my collection of lost things.
Perhaps I thought that if I rescued every lost thing I found,
someone would rescue the one thing left in the world that I
really cared about and one day I might get it back and so
restore my broken promise. It never happened, but I never
gave up hope; never stopped gathering in the things that
other people had lost. And those tiny scraps of other
people's lives gave me inspiration for my stories and helped
me to write again.*

*I know it is likely that most of the things are worthless,
and no one will want them back. But if you can make just
one person happy, mend one broken heart by restoring to
them what they have lost then it will have all been
worthwhile. You may wonder why I kept all this secret;
kept the study door locked for all those years. I hardly know
myself except perhaps it was that I was afraid of being
thought foolish or even a little insane. And so this is the
task I leave you with, Laura. All I ask is that you try.*

*I hope that your new life is everything that you wish for
and that you find others to share it with. Remember,
Laura, there is a world outside of Padua and it is well
worth a visit now and then.*

*One final thing – there is a girl who often sits on the
bench across the green from the house. She seems to be
something of a lost soul. I have often wished that I could
do more for her than a few kindly words, but unfortunately
it is difficult for an old man to help a young lady nowadays*

*without being sadly misconstrued. Perhaps you could
'gather her in' and offer a little friendship? Do what you
think is best.*

With fondest love and grateful thanks,
God bless,
Anthony

By the time Laura stirred from her chair in the study,
her limbs were stiffened by cold. Outside, in a black
sky, hung a perfect pearlescent moon. Laura sought
warmth in the kitchen and set the kettle to boil as she
pondered Anthony's requests. The scattering of his
ashes she would do gladly. Returning the lost things
was not so simple. Once again she felt those stones in
her pocket, reminding her of who she really was. Laura's
parents had been dead for some years now, but she had
never been able to shake the feeling that she had let
them down. They had never said as much, but in all
honesty what had she ever done to repay their unfailing love and loyalty and make them proud? She had
dodged university, her marriage had been a disaster
and she had failed to give them a single grandchild.
And she had been eating fish and chips in Cornwall
when her mother died. The fact that it had been her
first holiday since she had left Vince wasn't any kind of
excuse. When her father had died just six months later,
Anthony filled some of the void that had remained,
and perhaps now the task that he had left her would be
her chance to make some sort of amends? Perhaps this
was her opportunity to finally succeed at something.

And then there was Sunshine. In this, at least, she
was ahead of Anthony, but she couldn't take any credit

for it. It was Sunshine who had offered her friendship first and even then Laura had been – was still – reluctant to reciprocate. She thought about all the times that she had seen Sunshine before Anthony had died, and done nothing. Said nothing. Not even 'Hello'. But Anthony had done what little he could even after his death. Laura was disappointed in herself, but she was determined to try and change. She took her tea upstairs to the rose-scented bedroom she had claimed for her own. Or rather that she had chosen to share with Therese. Because she was still there. Her things were still there. Not her clothes, of course, but her dressing-table set, the photograph of her with Anthony, which was inexplicably face down once more, and the little blue enamel clock. 11.55. Stopped again. Laura put down her cup and wound the clock until its gentle ticking resumed. She went to bed leaving the curtains wide open, and outside the perfect moon veiled the rose garden in a ghostly damask of light and shade.

17

Eunice

1984

'At Christmas time we da, di, da and we vanish shade . . .'

Mrs Doyle was in fine voice as she served the man in front of Eunice with two sausage plaits and a couple of squares of Tottenham cake. She paused for breath to greet Eunice.

'He's a great bloke, that Bob Gelding, getting all those pop singers to make a record for those poor blighters in Ethio . . .' the rest of the word slipped away from Mrs Doyle's lexical grasp. '– in the desert.'

Eunice smiled in agreement. 'He's almost a saint.'

Mrs Doyle began putting doughnuts in a bag. 'Mind you,' she continued, 'it's not as though that Boy George and Midget Ure and the like can't afford to do a bit of charity. And those Bananas – lovely girls, but not a hairbrush between them, by the looks of things.'

Douglas was undisturbed by Eunice's returning footsteps up the stairs. His grey and grizzled muzzle twitched and his front paws flicked gently as he dreamed of who knows what. But it must have been a happy dream, Eunice thought, because the corners of his mouth were turned up in a smile. Bomber was watching him from his desk like an anxious child from a window watching his snowman begin inevitably to melt. She wanted to reassure him, but there was nothing she could say. Douglas was getting old. His days were growing shorter in length and in number. He would die and hearts would break. But for now he was warm and content, and when he eventually woke, a cream doughnut would be waiting for him. The switch from jam to cream (which was actually jam *and* cream) was an effort to keep Douglas's old bones padded with a little of the flesh that seemed to mysteriously dissolve with each passing year.

Bomber, however, was experiencing the exact opposite. In the ten years or so that Eunice had known him he had eventually managed to grow a very modest tummy to add a little softness to his still rangy frame. He patted it affectionately as he said for the umpteenth time, 'We must stop eating so many doughnuts.' A comment completely unaccompanied by any sincerity or intent, and duly ignored by Eunice.

'Are your parents coming into town this week?'

Eunice had grown very fond of Grace and Godfrey and looked forward to their visits, which were unfortunately becoming less and less frequent. It was all too apparent that old age was an unforgiving wingman. Godfrey in particular was becoming less solid in both body and mind; his reason and robustness inexorably stealing away.

'No, not this week. They're feeling a bit out of sorts. Stoked up the Aga, stocked up on the single malt and secured the portcullis, I shouldn't wonder.' Bomber was frowning at a manuscript that was open on his desk.

'Why? What's up?' Eunice was concerned.

'Well, one of their good chums was caught up in that bomb in Brighton, and then there was the fire in the tube station a couple of weeks ago and that's on their normal route. I just think that they feel, in the words of that classic song favoured by teddy bears, "it's safer to stay at home".' Bomber slapped the manuscript shut. 'Probably just as well. I think that Ma might have felt duty bound to enquire about this.'

He waggled the manuscript at Eunice as though it were a rotting fish. Douglas finally stirred in his corner. He took in his surroundings through aged, opalescent eyes, and finding them safe and familiar summoned the energy to gently wag the tip of his tail. Eunice rushed over to kiss his sleep-warm head and tempt him with his doughnut, which was already cut and plated to his exacting requirements. But she hadn't forgotten the rotting fish.

'What is it?'

Bomber heaved an exaggerated sigh. 'It's called *Big Head and Bigot*.'

'Sounds intriguing.'

'Well, that's one word for my darling sister's latest *livre terrible*. It's about the five daughters of a bankrupt football manager. Their mother is determined to marry them off to pop stars or footballers or anyone who's rich. She parades them at the local hunt ball, where the eldest, Janet, is asked to dance by the special guest, a young, handsome owner of a country house hotel called Mr Bingo. Her sister, Izzy, is rather taken with his enigmatic friend, Mr Arsey, a world-famous concert pianist, but he thinks that the antics of the Young Farmers in attendance are rather vulgar and refuses to join Izzy in a karaoke duet. She calls him a snob and goes off in a bit of a huff. To cut a long and strangely familiar story short, the youngest daughter runs off to Margate with a second-rate footballer where they get matching tattoos. She falls pregnant, is dumped and ends up in a bedsit in Peckham. After some well-intentioned but rather pomp-ous interference from Mr Arsey, Janet eventually marries Mr Bingo, and after his agent forbids it, Mr Arsey ends up making sweet music with Izzy.'

Eunice had given up trying to keep a straight face by now, and was howling with laughter at Portia's latest literary larceny. Bomber continued regardless.

'The girls' cousin, Mr Coffins, a religious education teacher at an extremely expensive and completely incompetent private girls' school, offers to marry any of the sisters who will have him, but, to their mother's despair, none of them will on account of his bad breath and protruding belly button, and so he marries their other cousin, Charmaine, on the rebound. Charmaine is happy to have him as she has a slight moustache, and is on the shelf at twenty-one and a half.'

'Poor Charmaine. If she has to settle for bad breath and a protruding belly button at twenty-one and a half, what hope is there for me at almost thirty-one?'

Bomber grinned. 'Oh, I'm sure we could find you a nice Mr Coffins of your own if you really want one.'

Eunice threw a paperclip at him.

Later that evening, she wandered round the garden of Bomber's rambling flat while he cooked their supper, closely supervised by Douglas. She would never marry. She knew that now. She could never marry Bomber and she didn't want anybody else, so that was an end to it. In the past there had been the occasional date with some hopeful young man; sometimes several. But for Eunice it always felt dishonest. Every man came second best to Bomber, and no man deserved to be forever runner-up. Every relationship would only ever be friendship and sex, never love, and no friendship would ever be as precious as the one she shared with Bomber. Eventually she gave up dating altogether. She thought back to her birthday trip to Brighton all that time ago. It was almost ten years now. It had been a wonderful day, but by the end of it her heart had been broken. On the train home, sitting next to the man she loved, Eunice had fought back the tears, knowing that she would never be the right girl for Bomber. There would never be a right girl for Bomber. But they were friends; best friends. And for Eunice, that was infinitely better than not having him in her life at all.

As he stirred the Bolognese sauce in the kitchen, Bomber thought back to their earlier conversation. Eunice was a striking young woman with a fierce intelligence, a ready wit and an astonishing assortment of hats. It was unfathomable that she had never been courted or set one of her rather spectacular caps at any particular deserving young man.

'Does it bother you?' He was thinking aloud, albeit a little carelessly, rather than actually posing the question. It seemed a bit blunt to ask.

'Does what bother me?' Eunice appeared in the doorway waving a breadstick in the air like a conductor's baton and sipping a glass of red wine.

'Not having some handsome chap with a red sports car, a Filofax and a flat in Chelsea?'

Eunice bit the end off the breadstick decisively. 'What on earth would I want with one of those, when I have you and Douglas?'

18

'The lady doesn't want it back.'

Sunshine placed the cup and saucer on the table in front of Laura.

'You should keep it for the lovely cup of tea.'

The delicate cream bone china was almost translucent, and hand painted with deep purple violets speckled with gold. Laura looked up at Sunshine's serious face; into her treacle-dark eyes. She had brought Sunshine into the study that morning and explained in broad terms the content of Anthony's letter.

'He said that you and I should take care of each other,' she paraphrased.

It was the first time that she had seen Sunshine smile. Curious and eager, she had handled the things in the study without seeking permission, but with a gentleness and reverence which would have delighted Anthony as much as it reassured Laura. She cradled each object in her soft hands as though it were a baby bird with a broken wing. Laura's attention returned to the cup and saucer and its cardboard label. It was certainly a strange thing to lose.

'But we don't know that, Sunshine. We don't know whom it belonged to.'

Sunshine's conviction was immutable. 'I do. It was the lady and she doesn't want it back to her.'

Her words were delivered without a whisper of arrogance or petulance. She was simply stating a fact.

'But how do you know?'

Sunshine picked up the cup and held it close to her chest. 'I can feel it. I don't think it in my head, I just feel it.' She put the cup back in its saucer. 'And the lady had a bird,' she added, for good measure.

Laura sighed. The fate of the lost things hung over her; heavy, like a drowning man's clothes. Anthony had chosen her as his successor and she was proud and grateful, but also terrified of failing him; and if the cup and saucer were anything to go by, Sunshine's 'feelings' might prove to be more of a hindrance than a help.

Bone china cup and saucer.
Found on a bench in the Riviera Public Gardens,
31 October . . .

Eulalia finally stirred in her armchair, taking in her surroundings through age-opaqued eyes. Finding them familiar and herself quick rather than dead, a broad smile split her wrinkled brown face, revealing a haphazard assortment of still-white teeth.

'Praise Jesus for one more day this side of Heaven's gates,' she thought. 'And curse him too,' as arthritis shot shards of pain through her bony legs when she tried to stand up. Alive she might be, but quick she certainly wasn't. She had taken to sleeping downstairs in her chair more of late. Upstairs was fast becoming unattainable territory. Which was why she was moving. Sheltered accommodation they called it. She called it surrender. A defeated display of the lily-livered flag. But it couldn't be helped. One room with en-suite, a communal lounge, shared kitchen and meals prepared if you wanted. Plastic mattress cover in case you wet the

bed. Eulalia shuffled through to her kitchen, sliding in her slippers and gripping her sticks like a geriatric cross-country skier. Kettle on and teabag in the mug, she opened the back door and let the sunshine in. She had once been proud of her garden. She had planned and planted it, nurtured and cherished it for all these years. But now it had outgrown her, like an unruly teenager, and ran wild. The magpie appeared at her feet as soon as the door was opened. He looked as though he was having a bad feather day; a near miss with next door's cat, perhaps. But his eyes were bright and he chuck-chucked softly to Eulalia as he tipped his head this way and that.

'Good morning, Rossini, my friend' – it was their little joke – 'you'll be wanting your breakfast, I suppose.'

He hopped into the kitchen behind her and waited patiently for her to take a handful of raisins from a tin on the draining board.

'What will you do without me?' she asked, as she threw a couple onto the kitchen floor. The bird gobbled them up and looked to her for more.

'Outside now, my friend,' she said, scattering the rest of the raisins onto the doorstep.

She took her tea back into the sitting room, making precarious progress with a single stick, and gingerly lowered herself into her chair. The room was full of pretty things; weird and wonderful baubles and ornaments. Eulalia had been a magpie all her life, surrounding herself with sparkle and glister, twinkle and velvet, the magical and the macabre. But now the time had come to let them go. These were her treasures and she would decide their fate. She couldn't take them with her, but neither could she bear the thought of her precious things being picked over by a white van driver called Dave – 'House Clearances: no job too big or too small'. Besides, some of the things could get her into trouble. Some of the things weren't exactly . . . legal. Well, not here, anyway. There were skeletons in her cupboards. Truly.

By the time she had filled her tartan shopping trolley with the chosen objects it was almost midday. Her ratchety limbs, lubricated by activity, moved more freely now as she headed towards the public gardens by the park. She would give her things away. She would leave them where others would find them; as many things as she had been able to drag in her trolley. And as for the rest, no one would have them. It was a school day and the park and gardens were deserted save for a couple of dog walkers and a poor unfortunate soul still asleep in the bandstand. Eulalia was unobserved as she placed four snow globes, a rabbit's skull and a gold pocket watch on the little wall that encircled the ornamental fountain. Further into the park, two silver church candlesticks, a stuffed weasel and a set of gold-plated dentures were secreted in the niches of the war memorial statue. A mummified pig's penis and the ormolu music box from Paris were left on the steps by the pond, and the china bride doll with empty eye sockets on the seat of one of the children's swings. Back in the gardens the crystal ball wallowed in a stone bird bath and the bowler hat with a cockade of crow's feathers was perched on top of the sundial. The ebony cursing bowl was placed at the foot of a sycamore tree whose leaves were a molten kaleidoscope of scarlet, orange and yellow. And so she continued until, almost emptied, the trolley bounced along behind her on skittish wheels. She sat down on the wooden bench facing the park and breathed a sigh of contentment. A job well done – almost. The final item on the wooden slats beside her was a bone china cup and saucer painted with gold and violets. It rattled in the aftershock of an explosion two streets away that killed a postman and seriously injured a passer-by. A thick pall of smoke smudged a dark column into the afternoon sky and Eulalia smiled as she remembered that she had left the gas on.

*

'Put the gas on under the kettle, tea to the teapot, milk to the jug.'

Back in the kitchen Laura smiled as Sunshine talked herself through the tea-making as she always did with any task that required concentration. There was a knock at the back door and, without waiting for a reply, Freddy came in. Laura had spoken to him the night before to let him know that his job was still there if he wanted it, and to invite him for tea in the kitchen, rather than drinking it alone in the garden as he usually did. He had been away since the funeral, and when he had left the situation at Padua had still been uncertain.

She had surprised herself by issuing the invitation, but reasoned that the more often she came into contact with him, the less flustered she might be when she did. Because she couldn't help but find him rather increasingly attractive.

'Two sugars, please,' he said, winking at Sunshine, who blushed deeply and found something fascinating to look at on the teaspoon she was holding. Laura knew how she felt. There was something intriguing about this laconic man who tended the garden with such care, and did odd jobs around the place with quiet efficiency. Laura had learned scarcely anything about his life away from Padua; he gave so little away and she hadn't yet found the courage to ask. But she was building up to it, she promised herself. The only information he seemed to require was what needed doing, and if there were any biscuits.

'Freddy, this is Sunshine, my new friend and assistant. Sunshine, this is Freddy.'

Sunshine tore her gaze away from the teaspoon and tried to look Freddy in the eye.

'Hi, Sunshine. How's it going?'

'How's what going? I'm nineteen and I'm dancing drome.'

Freddy smiled. 'I'm thirty-five and three quarters and I'm a Capricorn.'

Sunshine placed a cup of tea in front of Freddy and then the milk jug and sugar bowl. Then a teaspoon and a plate of biscuits. And then a fork, a bottle of washing-up liquid, a packet of cornflakes and an egg whisk. And a box of matches. Freddy's slow smile split his handsome face, revealing a perfect set of white teeth. The smile burgeoned into a deep, throaty laugh. Whatever Sunshine's test was, he had passed it. She sat down next to him.

'Saint Anthony has left all the lost things to Laura and we have to get them back at the right people. Except the cup and saucer.'

'Is that right?'

'Yes it is. Shall I show you?'

'Not today. I'll finish my tea and washing-up liquid first, and then there's a job I have to go to. But next time I'm here, it's a date.'

Sunshine almost smiled. Laura was beginning to feel a little superfluous. 'Anthony was certainly a very good man, Sunshine, but strictly speaking, he wasn't a saint.'

Freddy drained his cup. 'Well now, he could have been. Have you never heard of Saint Anthony of Padua, the Patron Saint of Lost Things?'

Laura shook her head.

'I kid you not. It's true. Five years at Sunday school,' he added by way of explanation.

Sunshine smiled triumphantly. Now she had two friends.

19

Laura was throwing away her old life. It was going to be a messy business. She tipped a boxful of junk into the bin and slammed the lid shut, blowing a puff of dust and dirt into her face in the process. She had been sorting through the last of the things she had brought with her from the flat, many of which hadn't been unpacked since she had moved from the house she had shared with Vince. If she hadn't needed them in the last six or so years, she reasoned, she wasn't likely to need them now. The local charity shop might have been glad of some of her 'junk', but that would involve a trip into town which Laura wasn't keen to make. 'I'm too busy for that at the moment,' she convinced herself. Before the ink could dry on her words of excuse they were smudged with guilt as she remembered Anthony's letter: *there is a world outside of Padua and it is well worth a visit now and then.* 'Another day,' she promised herself.

She wiped the grime from her face with her hands, and then wiped her hands on her jeans. God, she was filthy; time for a shower.

'Hello. Do you work here?'

The question came from a leggy blonde who appeared down the path at the side of the house in skin-tight jeans and pale pink suede loafers which boasted tell-tale Gucci horse-bit trims and matched perfectly with her cashmere sweater. Laura's dumbfounded expression clearly caused the young woman to assume that she was either foreign, simple or deaf. She tried again, speaking very slowly and a little too loudly.

'I'm looking for Freddo – the groundsman.'

Thankfully, at that moment, the man himself appeared, sauntering down the garden carrying a wooden crate of freshly dug potatoes that he set down at Laura's feet.

'Darling Freddo!'

The young woman flung her arms around his neck and kissed him enthusiastically on the lips. Freddy gently untangled himself and took her hand.

'Felicity, what in God's name are you doing here?'

'I've come to take my darling boyfriend out to lunch.'

Freddy grinned. He looked a little uncomfortable. 'Felicity, this is Laura. Laura, this is Felicity.'

'So I gather.' Laura nodded, but didn't offer her hand, which was just as well because Felicity wasn't in the habit of shaking hands with 'the help'. The happy couple trotted off arm in arm and Laura took the potatoes into the kitchen and banged the crate down on the table.

'Sodding cheek!' she fumed. 'Do I look like I work here?'

Catching sight of herself in the hall mirror, Laura was forced to reconsider. With her unkempt hair scragged back under a spotted bandana, grime-streaked face and baggy, shapeless sweatshirt, she looked like a modern-day scullery maid.

'Bugger!'

She stomped upstairs and had a long hot shower, but afterwards, as she sat on her bed swathed in a towel, it was clear that the water had only succeeded in washing away the dirt and not her anger. She was jealous. She was mortified to admit it, but she was. The sight of that wretched woman kissing Freddy had thoroughly annoyed her. Laura raised her eyebrows at her own reflection in the dressing-table mirror and smiled sheepishly.

'*I* can go out to lunch if I like.'

That was it. She *would* go out to lunch. Anthony had wanted her to go out, and so she would. Today. Right now.

The Moon is Missing was a 'smart casual' pub with black-tie aspirations. Its proximity to St Luke's meant it was popular for post-funeral pick-me-ups and pre-wedding loin-girders. Laura ordered a whisky and soda, and 'herb-crumbed goujons of cod served with hand-cut wedges of King Edwards and a lightly frothed tartare sauce', and took a seat in one of the booths that lined the wall facing the bar. Her bravura had deserted her almost as soon as she had left the house, and what should have been a treat had become something to endure, like a visit to the dentist or a crawl through rush-hour traffic. Laura was glad she had arrived early enough to bag a booth, and that she had remembered to bring a book with her to hide behind, just in case anyone tried to talk to her. On her way here, it had suddenly and rather worryingly occurred to her that Freddy and the frisky Felicity might also be lunching in this particular pub, but much though the thought horrified her, she was too stubborn to turn back. And so here she was, drinking in the middle of the day, which was unheard of, and pretending to read a book she wasn't really interested in, whilst waiting for a lunch that she didn't really want. All in order to prove a point to herself and not let Anthony down. And to think that she could have been at home cleaning the cooker . . . Even Laura couldn't help but crack a wry smile at her own ridiculousness.

The pub was filling up and just as the waitress brought her posh fish fingers and chips, the booth next to Laura's was occupied with a great deal of huffing and puffing and shedding of coats and shopping bags. As her new neighbours began reading aloud from the menu, Laura recognised the imperious alto of Marjory Wadscallop accompanied by the dithering descant of Winnie Cripp. Having decided upon and ordered two 'poussin and portobello potages', the pair chinked their glasses of gin and tonic and began discussing the production of *Blithe Spirit* currently in rehearsal by their amateur dramatics group.

'Of course, technically, I'm far too young to play Madame Arcati,' asserted Marjory, 'but then the part does require an actor of extraordinary range and subtlety, so I suppose, considering the "dramatis personae" at Everard's disposal, I was the only real choice.'

'Yes, of course you were, dear,' agreed Winnie, 'and Gillian's an absolute pro at costumes and make-up, so she'll have you looking old in no time.'

Marjory was unsure whether to be pleased about this or not. 'Well, she absolutely looks like a "pro" with the amount of slap she normally wears,' she replied tetchily.

'Naughty!' giggled Winnie and then fell guiltily silent as the waitress arrived with their chicken and mushroom soups accompanied by 'an assortment of artisan bread rolls'. There was a brief hiatus while they salted their soups and buttered their bread.

'I'm a bit nervous about playing Edith,' Winnie then confessed. 'It's the biggest part I've had so far and there's an awful lot of lines to remember, as well as all that carrying of drinks and walking on and off.'

'You mean "stage business" and "blocking", Winnie. It's so important to use the correct terminology.' Marjory took a large bite from her granary roll and chewed on it thoughtfully before adding, 'I shouldn't worry too much, dear. After all, Edith is only a housemaid, so you won't be required to do very much real acting.'

Laura had finished her lunch and asked for the bill. Just as she was gathering her things to leave, the mention of a familiar name caught her attention.

'I'm sure Geoffrey will be a perfectly serviceable Charles Condomine, but in his younger days Anthony Peardew would have been ideal for the role; tall, dark, handsome and so very charming.' Marjory's voice had taken on an almost wistful tone.

'And he was a writer in real life too,' added Winnie.

Marjory's tongue sought to dislodge a grain from her roll, which had become caught under her dental plate. Having succeeded, she continued, 'It does seem rather odd that he left everything to that rather prickly housekeeper of his, Laura.'

'Mmmn. It's a funny business, all right.' Winnie loved a side order of scurrilous gossip with her lunch. 'I shouldn't wonder if there wasn't a bit of *funny business* going on there,' she added knowingly, delighted at her double entendre.

Marjory drained the last of her gin and tonic and signalled to the waitress to bring her another one.

'Well, I expect she did a little more for him than just the dusting and hoovering.'

Laura had intended to try and sneak past them without being seen, but now she turned and faced them with a brazen smile.

'Fellatio,' she announced. 'Every Friday.'

And without another word, she swept out.

Winnie turned to Marjory with a puzzled expression. 'What's that when it's at home?'

'Italian,' said Marjory, dabbing at her mouth with a napkin. 'I had it in a restaurant once.'

20

Sunshine set the needle onto the spinning liquorice disc and was rewarded with the mellifluous tones of Etta James, hot and rich like smoked paprika.

In the kitchen, Freddy was sitting at the table, and Laura was making sandwiches for lunch.

'She's got great taste.' Freddy tipped his head in the direction of the music.

Laura smiled. 'She's choosing the music for when we scatter Anthony's ashes. She says it's like the film where the dog gets a bone and the clocks stop because Saint Anthony's dead, but he'll be together forever with Therese. But she calls her "The Lady of the Flowers". And your guess is as good as mine.'

She sliced cucumber into translucent slices and drained a tin of salmon.

'She wants to make a speech as well, although I'm not sure we'll make head or tail of it.'

'I'm sure we'll make it out just fine.' Freddy spun a teaspoon that was idling on the table. 'She just has her own way of saying stuff, that's all. She knows the words that we all use, but I suppose she just likes hers better.'

Laura licked a smudge of butter from her finger. She wasn't used to having actual conversations with Freddy. His way of saying stuff was usually a combination of nods, shrugs and grunts. But Sunshine wasn't having any of that. With her solemn eyes and soft, fluty voice she coaxed the words from him like a snake charmer.

'But isn't she just making life harder; setting herself further apart . . .'

Laura's voice trailed off along with her train of thought, stymied by political correctness. Freddy weighed her words carefully and without judgement.

'Further apart from "normal" people, you mean?'

It was Laura's turn to shrug. She didn't really know what she meant. She knew that Sunshine had made few friends at school, and had been mercilessly taunted by the feral teenagers who hung around in the local park drinking cheap cider, vandalising the swings and having sex. Were they normal? And if they were, why should Sunshine want to be like them? Freddy balanced the neck of the teaspoon on the tip of his index finger. Laura went back to the sandwiches and began cutting them viciously into triangles. Now he would think she was a . . . A what? Bigot? Idiot? Maybe she was. The more she saw of Freddy, the more it mattered what he thought of her. Laura's idea of inviting Freddy to take his breaks in the kitchen in order to facilitate a more relaxed relationship between them could not yet be deemed a success, but the time they spent together was the part of the day she looked forward to most.

Freddy placed the teaspoon carefully down in front of him and leaned back in his chair, rocking the two front legs off the floor. She fought the urge to tell him to sit properly at the table.

'I think it's a sort of camouflage' – he rocked back onto four legs – 'the way she speaks. It's like a Jackson

Pollock. There's so many specks and splashes of paint, that if one of them happens to be a mistake, no one can tell. If Sunshine does get a word wrong, we'll never know.' He shook his head, smiling to himself. 'It's genius.'

At that moment, the genius came into the kitchen looking for her lunch. Laura was still thinking about what Freddy had said. A gardener using the art of Jackson Pollock as a linguistic metaphor was a little unexpected, and another intriguing insight into the kind of man he really was. It made Laura both eager and determined to find out more.

'By the way,' said Freddy to Laura, 'the film. It's *Four Weddings and a Funeral*.'

Sunshine grinned and sat down next to her newest friend.

After lunch, they all went through to the study. Sunshine was desperate to show Freddy Anthony's museum of missing things, and Laura was toying with the idea of asking if he had any bright ideas about returning them to their rightful owners. Each time she came into the study it seemed to Laura that the room was filling up; less space, more things. And she felt smaller; shrinking, sinking. The shelves seemed to groan, threatening collapse, and the drawers creak, dovetails about to fly open and burst. She feared she would be buried under an avalanche of lost property. For Sunshine it was a treasure trove. She stroked and held and hugged the things, talking softly to herself – or perhaps to the things themselves – and reading their labels with obvious enchantment. Freddy was appropriately astonished.

'Who'd have thought it?' he whispered, peering at his surroundings. 'So that's why he always carried his bag.'

The frail October sunlight struggled to permeate the trellis of flowers and leaves on the lace panels and the room was dark and stained with shadows. He drew back the lace, shooting a meteorite shower of shimmering dust motes spinning across the room.

'Let's throw a bit of light over things, shall we?'

Sunshine showed him round, like a curator proudly sharing a collection of fine art. She showed him buttons and rings, gloves, teddy bears, a glass eye, items of jewellery, a jigsaw puzzle piece, keys, coins, plastic toys, tweezers, four sets of dentures and a doll's head. And these were the contents of only one drawer. The cream cup and saucer painted with violets was still on the table. Sunshine picked it up and handed it to Freddy.

'It's pretty, isn't it? The lady doesn't want it back to her so Laura's going to keep it for the lovely cup of tea.'

Laura was about to contradict her, but Sunshine's face was set with such absolute certainty that the words died in Laura's mouth.

'That'll be yours, then.'

As Laura took the cup and saucer from him, his fingers brushed against her hand, and he held her gaze for just a moment before turning away and sitting down in Anthony's chair.

'And you're to try and get all the rest of this,' he said, sweeping his arms around the room, 'back to wherever it is that it belongs?' His equable tone gave no quarter to the enormity of the task.

'That's the idea,' Laura replied.

Sunshine was distracted by an object that had fallen out of the drawer she had opened. She picked it up from the floor but immediately dropped it again, howling in pain.

Ladies' glove, navy blue leather, right hand.
Found on the grass verge at the foot of Cow Bridge,
23 December . . .

It was bitter. Too cold for snow. Rose looked up at the black sky pierced with a tracery of stars and a sharp sickle moon. She had been walking briskly for twenty minutes but her feet were numb and her fingers frozen. Too sad for tears. She was almost there now. Thankfully there had been no passing cars; no one to distract or intervene. Too late to think. Here now. This was the place. Over the bridge and then just a shallow, grassy bank. She took off one glove and pulled the photograph from her pocket. She kissed the face of the little girl who smiled back at her. Too dark to see, but she knew she was there. 'Mummy loves you.' Down the grassy slope her gloveless hand clutched at razor frozen grass. At the bottom, shale underfoot. 'Mummy loves you,' she whispered again, as the distant lights pricked the darkness and the rails began to hum. Too hard to live.

'Too hard to live. The lady died.' Sunshine was shaking as she tried to explain.

Freddy pulled her close and squeezed her tight. 'I think that what you need is the lovely cup of tea.'

He made it, under Sunshine's strict supervision. Two cups of tea and a Jammie Dodger later, she tried to tell them a little more.

'She loved her little girl, but the lady was very sad,' was the best that she could do.

Laura was strangely unsettled. 'Sunshine, maybe it would be better if you didn't go into the study any more.'

'Why?'

Laura hesitated. Part of her didn't want Sunshine becoming too involved. She knew it was selfish, but she was desperate to find a way to make Anthony and maybe even her parents proud of her. Posthumously, of course. It was her chance to finally do something right and she didn't want any distractions.

'In case there are other things in here that upset you.'

Sunshine shook her head determinedly. 'I'm okay now.'

Laura looked unconvinced, but Sunshine had a point to make.

'If you never get sadness, how do you know what happy is like?' she asked. 'And by the way, everybody dies.'

'I think she has you in checkmate there,' Freddy murmured.

Laura conceded defeat with a reluctant smile.

'But,' continued Freddy, 'I may have the very thing to cheer you up. I have a plan.'

21

Sunshine stood waiting by the sundial, a solemn figure in a pink duffle coat and silver sequinned baseball boots. The dank October afternoon was already seeping away, the edges of an empty sky tinged with the rhubarb flush of a looming sunset. On Sunshine's signal Freddy started the music and took his place next to Laura to walk down the 'aisle' of flickering tea lights to where Sunshine was waiting to start the ceremony. Freddy was carrying Anthony's ashes in a plain wooden urn, and Laura held a fancy cardboard box full of real rose petal confetti and the photograph of Therese from the garden room. Laura fought the urge to giggle as she walked as slowly as she could to the inevitable accompaniment of Al Bowlly.

Sunshine had planned everything down to the last detail. The gramophone had been conveniently positioned so that Freddy could reach it by leaning in the window, and the confetti and rose-scented candles for the tea lights had been ordered especially. Sunshine had originally wanted to wait until the roses were in bloom again, but Laura couldn't bear the thought of Anthony's ashes languishing on a shelf for the next nine months. She couldn't keep him from Therese any longer. The rose-scented candles and confetti had been a hard-won compromise. Freddy and Laura reached Sunshine just as Mr Bowlly was beginning his final verse and she listened, really listened to the words for perhaps the first time.

It could have been written for Anthony and Therese. Sunshine left a pause just long enough for it to be dramatic before consulting the piece of paper she was clutching.

'Dreary beloved, we are gathered here in the sight of God and in the fate of this complication, to join together this man, Saint Anthony' – she tapped the top of his urn – 'and this woman, The Lady of the Flowers' – gesturing towards the photograph with an upturned palm – 'in holy macaroni which is the honourable estate. Saint Anthony takes The Lady of the Flowers to be the lawful wedding wife, to have and to hold from this day forward, for better for worse, richer or poorer, to love and to perish with death now you start. And it still rhymes,' she added proudly to herself.

She paused again, long enough this time for it to be almost uncomfortable, but no doubt with the intention of underscoring the sanctity of the occasion.

'Earth to earth, ashes to ashes, funky to punky. We know Major Tom's a monkey. We can be heroes just for today.'

She leaned forward and addressed Freddy and Laura in a stage whisper. 'Now you throw the ashes, and you throw the confetti,' and then, as an afterthought, 'Follow me!'

They made an odd little procession filing round the rose garden, Sunshine leading them in and out of the desolate-looking bushes whose summer finery had been reduced to a ragbag of sodden, yellowing leaves stubbornly clinging on. Freddy followed Sunshine, emptying the urn as delicately as he could, with Laura behind him, trying to avoid any backdraught as she scattered confetti on the wispy grey trail of Anthony's remains. The 'scattering of ashes' had always sounded like such an ethereal act to Laura, but in reality, she reflected, it was more akin to emptying a vacuum-cleaner bag. When the urn was finally empty, Sunshine consulted her piece of paper once again.

'He was her north, her south, her east, her west; her working week and Sunday vest.

She was his moon and stars and favourite song; they thought that love would last forever: they weren't wrong.'

Freddy winked at her, smiling broadly. 'And it still rhymes,' he mouthed.

Sunshine wasn't to be distracted. 'I now announce you husband and wife. Those whom God, and Sunshine, have joined together let no man steal their thunder.'

She nodded at Freddy, who scampered off in the direction of the gramophone.

'And now it's time for the bride and groom's first dance.'

As the dying sun stained the ice blue sky crimson and a blackbird's call echoed through the gathering dusk, warning of a prowling tabby, Etta James proclaimed 'At Last'.

As the final note smouldered into the chilly air, Laura looked across at Freddy. He was gazing straight at her and when her eyes met his he smiled. Laura went to gather the tea lights. But Sunshine wasn't quite finished. She rattled her piece of paper and cleared her throat.

'I am the resurrection and the light, saith the Lord: he that believeth in me, though he were dead, yet shall he live. And it's goodnight from me and it's goodnight from him.'

When Laura went up to bed that night the room felt different somehow. Perhaps it was warmer. Or maybe that was just the wine she had shared with Freddy and Sunshine to celebrate Therese and Anthony's reunion. The things on the dressing table were all in order and the little blue clock had stopped at 11.55 as usual. She wound it up so that it could stop at the same time again tomorrow, drew the curtains and turned to get into bed.

There were petals of rose confetti on the bedcovers.

22

Eunice

1987

Bette trotted along just ahead of them, surveying the park for undesirables. Every now and then she would turn to check that they were following her obediently, her velveteen face crumpled into a comical frown. She was named after the film star to whom she bore an unnerving resemblance, but they had taken to calling her Baby Jane after one of her namesake's most memorable characters.

Bomber had been freeze-framed by Douglas's death. He had held the little dog in his arms until long after his final breath had sighed 'the end', and his soft fur had grown cold and strange. Eunice had howled an eruption of pain, but Bomber sat rigid and dry-eyed as an ash cloud of grief settled over him and choked his tears. The Douglas-shaped space in the office hurt every day. They were a man down and a doughnut too many, but Eunice kept going; on automatic pilot at first, but onwards nevertheless. Bomber crashed and burned. He drank away his pain and then he slept away the drink.

In the end only one man could reach him. It was difficult to say who had fallen for Tom Cruise the hardest, Bomber or Eunice, as he swaggered from bike to bar to plane in his Ray-Bans. They had seen *Top Gun* three nights in a row when it had opened at the Odeon the previous year. Three weeks after Douglas died Eunice stormed Bomber's flat with her spare key and kicked his grieving arse out of bed. As he sat at the kitchen table, tears finally released and dripping down his face and into the mug of black coffee Eunice had made, she took his hand.

'God, he loved flying with you, Bomber. But he'd have flown anyway . . . without you. He'd have hated it, but he would've done it.'

The following day, Bomber came into the office sober, and the following week Baby Jane arrived from Battersea Dogs Home; a bossy bundle of black and blonde velvet. Baby Jane didn't like doughnuts. The first time she was offered one, she sniffed at it disdainfully and turned away. It might as well have been a turd tartlet. Baby Jane liked Viennese whirls. For a stray, she had expensive tastes.

As the diminutive pug nosed an empty crisp packet on the grass, Eunice looked up at Bomber and almost recognised him again. His grief was still smudged under his eyes and pinched into his cheeks, but his smile was limbering up and his shoulders unfurling from their disconsolate stoop. She was never going to be a replacement, but she was already a distraction, and if Baby Jane had her way, which she usually did, Eunice had no doubt whatsoever that she would eventually prove to be a superstar in her own right.

Back in the office, Eunice put the kettle on while Bomber went through the post. Baby Jane settled herself onto her cushion and rested her head on her front paws, gathering herself for the arduous task of eating her cake. When Eunice came through with the tea Bomber was waving a slim volume of short stories in the air that had just arrived from a rival publisher.

'*Lost and Found* by Anthony Peardew. Hmm, I've heard of this. It's doing rather well. I wonder why old Bruce has sent it to me.'

Eunice picked up the accompanying compliments slip and read it. 'To gloat,' she answered.

'"Bomber",' she read, '"please accept a copy of this hugely successful collection with my compliments. You had your chance, old chap, and you blew it!"'

Bomber shook his head. 'No idea what he's talking about. If this Peardew fellow had sent it to us first we'd have snapped it up. It's an excess of hairspray. It's addled his brains.'

Eunice picked up the book and flicked through the pages. The author's name and title together, like two flints, sparked a vague memory; a manuscript? Eunice racked her brain for the answer but it was like bobbing for apples; just when she thought she'd got it by the skin of her teeth, it slipped away. Baby Jane sighed theatrically. Her cake was *en retard* and she was weak with hunger. Eunice laughed and ruffled the soft rolls of velvet on her head.

'You're such a diva, young lady! You'll get fat and then no more cakes for you. Just jogging round the park and the occasional stick of celery. If you're lucky.'

Baby Jane stared up at Eunice dolefully, her black button eyes framed by long dark lashes. It worked every time. She got her cake. At last.

Just as she was licking her lips in an optimistic search for remaining flecks of cream, the phone rang. Each pair of rings was followed by an imperious bark. Since her arrival, Baby Jane had quickly assumed a managerial position and she ran a very tight kennel. Bomber answered.

'Ma.'

He listened for a moment. Eunice watched his face and knew immediately that this was not good news. Bomber was on his feet.

'Do you want me to come over? I'll come now if you like. Don't be daft, Ma, of course it's no trouble.'

It would be about Godfrey. The lovely, kind, funny, gentlemanly Godfrey, whose dementia was casting him adrift. A once majestic galleon whose sails had worn thin and tattered, no longer able to steer its own course but left to the mercy of every squall and storm. Last month he had managed to flood the house and set fire to it at the same time. He had started to run a bath and then forgot about it, going downstairs to dry his shirt, which he left on the hotplate of the Aga before setting off for the village to buy a paper. By the time Grace had come in from the greenhouse, the water leaking through the kitchen ceiling had put out the fire started by the shirt. She hadn't known whether to laugh or cry. But she refused to accept that she needed help. He was her husband and she loved him. She had promised 'in sickness and in health'. Till death do us part. She couldn't bear to think of him in a home where the interior design included armchairs with built-in commodes. And yet . . . This time he had run away. Well, wandered off, more like. After an hour of frantically searching the village, Grace had come home to telephone the police. She was met at the gate by the local vicar who, on his way to visit a parishioner, had found Godfrey walking in the middle of the road, with a broom held up against his shoulder like a rifle and Grace's red beret stretched onto his head. He told the Rev. Addlestrop that he was returning to his regiment after a weekend pass.

Bomber dropped the phone back into its cradle with a resigned sigh.

'Do you want me to come with you, or stay here and hold the fort with Baby Jane?'

Before he could answer the buzzer went.

Portia received the news of her father's latest escapade with horrible tranquillity. She refused to join Bomber and go and see her parents, let alone offer any kind of help or support. Bomber tried in vain to crack the surface of her callous composure.

'This is serious, sis. Ma can't be expected to watch over him every minute of the day and night, and he's a danger to himself. And before long, God forbid, he may be to her as well.'

Portia inspected her scarlet fingernails. She'd just had them done and she was quite pleased. She'd even tipped the girl a pound.

'Well? What do you expect me to do about it? He belongs in a home.'

'He *is* in a home,' Eunice hissed. 'His home.'

'Oh, shut up, Eunuch. It's none of your business.'

'Well at least she gives a damn!' snapped Bomber.

Stung by Bomber's painful reprimand and secretly terrified by her father's illness, Portia responded in the only way she knew how to: with insults.

'You heartless bastard! Of course I care about him. I'm just being honest. If he's dangerous, he needs to be locked up. At least I've got the guts to say it. You always were completely spineless; always sucking up to Ma and Pa and never once standing up to them like me!'

Baby Jane could see that things were getting out of hand, and she wasn't having her friends spoken to in that manner. A low growl rumbled her displeasure. Portia sought out the source of the admonishment and found the feisty little pug preparing for battle.

'Is that revolting-looking cushion-pisser still here? I should have thought you'd have had enough when that other little monster finally died.'

Eunice glanced across to where Douglas's ashes sat safe in a box on Bomber's desk and offered a silent apology. She was just wondering how to inflict appropriate and excruciating pain on this execrable woman, when she realised that Baby Jane had already decided. Leaving her cushion with the prowling menace of a lion who has just spotted a dithering gazelle, she fixed Portia with her fiercest stare and turned up the volume until her whole body vibrated. Her lips curled back revealing a small but businesslike set of teeth. Portia flapped her fingers ineffectually at her, but Baby Jane continued her advance, eyes fixed firmly on her prey and growl now punctuated by dramatic snarls.

'Shoo! Shoo! Sit! Down!'

Baby Jane kept coming.

Halfway across the floor, Portia capitulated with an undignified retreat and an unladylike barrage of expletives.

Bomber began gathering his things.

Eunice repeated her offer of help. 'I'll come with you if you want me to.'

He smiled gratefully but shook his head. 'No, no. I'll be fine. You stay here and look after madam,' he said, reaching down to fondle Baby Jane's ears while she gazed up at him adoringly.

'At least we know now that it's true,' he added with a mischievous grin.

'What's that? That Portia's a complete waste of hot air and high heels?'

He shook his head and gently lifted a blonde paw in his hand.

'Nobody puts Baby Jane in a corner!'

Eunice hooted with laughter.

'Get out of here, Patrick Swayze!'

23

'*Lost and Found* by Anthony Peardew. I knew there was a copy somewhere in the house!'

Laura came into the kitchen triumphantly waving a slim volume of short stories. Freddy looked up from the laptop he was hunched over on the kitchen table. He took the book from her and flicked through it.

'Is it any good?'

'It depends what you mean by "good".' Laura sat down in the chair facing him. 'It did very well. Apparently Anthony's publisher at the time was very happy. He was a peculiar little man, I seem to remember. He came to the house once or twice. Used far too much hairspray.'

'Too much!' Freddy expostulated. 'I should think that any is too much. Unless you're Liberace. Or a ball-room dancer.'

'It's called "male grooming",' Laura smiled. 'But I wouldn't exactly call that your specialist subject,' she added, looking at the unruly mop of dark curls that crept over the collar of his shirt and the stubble that shaded the contours of his face.

'No need,' he replied, winking at her. 'I'm naturally handsome.'

He was, Laura silently agreed. Oh God! She hoped it had been silent. But maybe she'd nodded. She could feel a tell-tale flush creeping up her neck. Bugger! Maybe he would just think it was her age. Double bugger! Maybe he *would* just think it was her age. Middle age. Ready for big knickers, hot flushes and winceyette nighties. And she absolutely wasn't. In fact, she was going on a date.

'But did you think it was any good?'

Freddy was speaking.

'Sorry. Miles away. What was that?'

Freddy waved the book at her. *'Lost and Found* – what did you think?'

Laura sighed and spread her hands on the table in front of her.

'I thought it was safe. It was beautifully written, as always, but the content had lost a little of his usual edge. It was a bit too "happy ever after" for me. It was almost as though if he wrote enough happy endings for other people, he'd get one for himself.'

'But it never came?'

Laura smiled sadly. 'Until now.'

Fingers crossed.

'Is that why he stopped writing?'

Laura shook her head. 'No. He wrote several volumes of these short stories – based on the things he found, I now assume. At first they were optimistic tales; congenial and commercial. Bruce the peculiar was delighted with them and, no doubt, the money they brought in. But over time the stories grew darker, the characters more ambivalent; flawed, even. The happy endings gradually gave way to uncomfortable mysteries and unanswered questions. All this was before my time, of course, but when I eventually read them, I thought they were much better and they were certainly more like his earlier work, crediting his readers with both imagination and intelligence. Anthony told me that Bruce had been furious. He just wanted more of the "nice" stories; literary lemonade. But Anthony had given him absinthe. Bruce refused to publish them and that was that.'

'Didn't Anthony look for another publisher?'

'I don't know. By the time I started working for him, he seemed to be writing them more for himself than for anyone else. Eventually he stopped giving me anything to type at all, apart from the odd letter.'

Laura picked up the book from the table and tenderly stroked its cover. She missed her old friend.

'Maybe that's what we should call the website – "Lost and Found"?'

The website had been Freddy's plan. At first Laura had been unsure. For so many years Anthony had resisted the intrusion of technology into his tranquil home, and to throw open the doors to the behemoth Internet and all its goblin relatives so soon after his death somehow felt like a violation. But Freddy convinced her.

'The only thing Anthony asked you not to change was the rose garden. He left the house to you because he knew that you would do the right thing. It's your home now but it came with a covenant on its coat-tails and Anthony trusted you to use whatever method you saw fit to get those things back to the people who are missing them.'

The website would be a huge, virtual 'lost property' department where people could browse the things that

Anthony had found and then re-claim items that belonged to them. They were still working on the details, including the name.

'"Lost and Found". Too boring.' Sunshine had wandered in from the study, looking for biscuits.

'Shall I make the lovely cup of tea?'

Freddy rubbed his hands together in exaggerated delight.

'I thought you'd never ask. I'm as dry as James Bond's Martini.'

Sunshine filled the kettle and set it carefully on the hob.

'How can the drink, which is wet because it's the drink, be dry?'

'That's a good question, kiddo,' said Freddy, thinking *to which I'm buggered if I know the answer.*

Laura saved him. 'How about The Kingdom of Lost Things?'

Sunshine wrinkled her nose in disapproval. 'Saint Anthony kept all the lost things safe. He was the Keeper, and now you are. We should call it The Keeper of Lost Things.'

'Brilliant!' said Freddy.

'Where's the biscuits?' said Sunshine.

Laura arrived back from the hairdresser's salon just as Freddy was leaving for the day.

'You look different,' he said, almost accusingly. 'Have you got a new jumper?'

She could, quite cheerfully, have kicked him. Her jumper was several years old and bore a generous sprinkle of pilling to prove it. But she had just spent the best part of two hours and seventy quid having her hair cut and coloured with what her stylist, Elise, had described as burnished copper lowlights. When she left the salon, tossing her glossy chestnut mane like a frisky show pony, she had felt like a million dollars. Now, for some reason, she felt like she'd wasted her money.

'I've just had my hair done,' she muttered through gritted teeth.

'Oh, right. That must be it then,' he said, rummaging through his rucksack for his car keys. Finding them, he gave her a quick grin and headed for the door.

'I'll be off then. See you tomorrow.'

The door closed behind him and Laura gave the bamboo umbrella stand a petulant kick, toppling its contents onto the floor. As she gathered up the scattered umbrellas and walking sticks, she told herself that her new hair wasn't for Freddy's benefit anyway, so it hardly mattered if he hadn't noticed.

Upstairs, Laura admired the new black dress hanging on the front of the wardrobe. It was elegant and tasteful but with a hint of sexy, exposing just the right ratio of legs to cleavage for a woman of her age, according to the saleswoman who had taken Laura's credit card. Laura thought it was a bit tight and bloody expensive. She would have to eat only a little and be sure not to spill anything down the front of it.

Her date was called Graham. He was Vince's area manager and she had bumped into him in the car park of The Moon is Missing after her lunch there. She had met him many times at dealership Christmas dinners and numerous other social trials while she was married to Vince and he was married to Sandra. But now she wasn't, and neither, since quite recently, was he, and so he had asked her out. And fresh from meeting Felicity for the first time she had thought 'why not?' and said yes.

But now she wasn't so sure. As she wriggled into her dress and checked her hair yet again in the mirror, she was beginning to have doubts. According to Elise, whose salon chair doubled as a confessional for most of her clients, Laura was currently the favourite topic of conversation with the locals. In life, Anthony had attained the status of a minor celebrity on account of him being a published author. In death, therefore, it automatically followed that his affairs should remain squarely, if a little unfairly, in the public domain. His public's assessment of Laura apparently ranged from 'a conniving coffin-chaser' and 'a gold-digging tart' to 'a faithful friend and deserved beneficiary' and 'former traditional Irish dancing national champion'.

'But I think Mrs Morrissey might have got you muddled up with someone else there,' Elise had to admit. 'Well, she is nearly eighty-nine and only eats cabbage on a Thursday.'

Perhaps, thought Laura, she shouldn't be going out at all. People might think she was enjoying herself too soon after Anthony's death. In her new dress, with her new hair, it might look as if she were flaunting her inheritance; dancing on his grave before the earth had a chance to settle. Except, of course, he'd been burned and scattered, so technically there wasn't one. Well, it was too late now. She checked her watch. Graham would be almost there. He had always seemed like a nice man. A gentleman.

'You'll be fine,' she told herself. 'It's only dinner.'

But by the time her taxi came, she wasn't feeling hungry at all.

Graham was indeed a gentleman. He was waiting for her at the restaurant with a champagne cocktail and a slightly nervous smile. He took her coat, kissed her cheek and told her that she looked lovely. As Laura sipped her drink, she began to relax. Well, as much as she could within the bondage of her dress. Perhaps it was going to be fine after all. The food was delicious and Laura ate as much of it as she could manage to squeeze in while Graham told her about his marriage break-up – the spark just fizzled out; they were still friends but no longer lovers; and his new interest in Nordic walking – 'a total body version of walking with the aid of fibreglass poles'. Laura resisted the urge to make a joke about him not looking old enough to need one walking stick, let alone two, but she had to concede that he did look fit. Forty-six next birthday, his torso was happily unencumbered by middle-aged spread, and his shoulders looked broad and hard-muscled beneath his well-pressed shirt.

In the ladies' room, Laura congratulated herself as she reapplied her lipstick. There's certainly nothing wrong with my date, she thought. And he had beautiful table manners. She pressed her lips together and dropped her lipstick back into her bag.

Graham insisted on accompanying Laura home in a taxi, and, relaxed by the wine and his easy company, Laura allowed her head to rest momentarily on his shoulder as she gave the driver directions to Padua. But she wasn't going to invite him in for coffee; the drink or the euphemism. She knew that she shouldn't let the gossip bother her, but she couldn't help it. And the 'tart' epithet was the slap that smarted most. She'd only slept with three men in her entire life, and one of them was Vince, so he didn't count. She wasn't proud of it; in fact she wished there had been more. Perhaps if she'd tried more men out, she might have found the right one for her. But not on a first date. And Graham was a gentleman. He wouldn't expect it.

Ten minutes later, a rather bewildered Graham was on his way home in the taxi. He hadn't even got past the front porch, let alone first base. Laura was in the bathroom gagging and gargling with antiseptic mouthwash. As she spat the stinging liquid into the basin, she glimpsed her still-startled expression in the mirror. Teary mascara was already dribbling black scribbles down her cheeks and her lipstick was smudged into a grotesque clown's mouth. She looked like a tart. She struggled furiously to escape from her dress, wrenching it over her head and viciously screwing it into a crumpled ball. In the kitchen, she flung it into the bin and yanked open the fridge door. The prosecco tasted rank after the mouthwash, but Laura persevered and gulped it down. She took the bottle through to the garden room and lit the fire in the grate, knocking over her glass and breaking it in the process.

'Shit! Bugger! Bollocks! Stupid sodding glass!' she addressed the sharp fragments which sparkled in the firelight. 'Stay there, broken then. See if I care!'

She wandered her way unsteadily back to the kitchen and found another glass. As she worked her way through the rest of the bottle, she stared into the flames wondering what the hell she'd been playing at.

Horribly drunk, and exhausted by sobbing and hiccupping, Laura fell asleep on the sofa, her tear-swollen face buried in her beautiful, newly burnished hair.

24

She slept for roughly ten hours, but when she woke, she looked like she'd been sleeping rough for several weeks. The thudding inside her head was soon echoed by a sharp tapping on the glass of the French windows. With considerable effort, Laura raised herself up just enough to see who it was that was making her already abominable headache even worse. Freddy. By the time Laura had struggled to a sitting position, he was standing over her, stony-faced, holding a mug of steaming black coffee. Laura clutched a blanket tightly around her aching body as Freddy registered the two wine glasses, the empty bottles and Laura's state of dishevelment.

'I see your date went well.' His tone was just a little more clipped than usual.

Laura took the coffee from him and muttered something unintelligible.

'Sunshine said that you were going out with your boyfriend.'

Laura sipped her coffee and shuddered. 'He's not my boyfriend,' she rasped.

Freddy raised his eyebrows at her. 'Well, it looks as though things got pretty *friendly* to me.'

Laura's eyes filled with tears but her belly filled with

anger. 'What the hell's it got to do with you anyway?' she snapped.

Freddy shrugged. 'You're right. It's none of my business.' He turned to go. 'And thanks for the coffee, Fred,' he muttered.

'Oh, bugger off!' Laura replied, just about under her breath.

She took another sip from her mug. Why in God's name had she told Sunshine about her date?

Laura could feel the warning rush of saliva in her mouth. She knew she wouldn't make it to the bathroom, but it would be rude not to try. Halfway across the parquet floor she was sick. Very sick. As she stood cold and miserable with vomit-splashed legs, and still clutching the mug of coffee, she was glad that, at least, she'd missed the Persian rug.

An hour later, having cleared up the mess, been sick twice more, stood under the shower for ten minutes and dragged on some clothes, Laura sat at the kitchen table nursing a cup of tea and staring at a piece of dry toast. Her date had ended in disaster. The memory of Graham's tongue squirming lethargically in her mouth like the death throes of a particularly wet slug brought her out in a cold sweat. Well, that and the aftermath of two bottles of fizz. How could she have been such a fool? The sound of the doorbell pierced her mournful reverie. Sunshine. 'Oh God, no. Please not today,' she thought. There would be endless questions about last night and she just couldn't face it. She hid in the pantry. Sunshine would eventually come round to the back door if her ringing went unanswered, and if Laura stayed where she was, slumped at the table, Sunshine would see her. The ringing continued, patient and persistent, and then the back door opened and Freddy walked in.

'What on earth are you doing?'

Laura frantically shushed him and beckoned him over to the pantry. Even such a slight activity caused her temples to throb. She held onto one of the shelves loaded with ancient jars of pickles to steady herself.

'God, you look rough,' said Freddy helpfully. Again Laura put her finger to her lips.

'What?' He was beginning to lose his patience.

Laura sighed. 'Sunshine's at the front door and I really can't face her today. I know you probably think I'm being pathetic, but I just can't cope with all her questions. Not today.'

Freddy shook his head scornfully. 'I don't think it's pathetic. I think it's just plain mean. You're a grown woman hiding in a cupboard from a young girl who thinks you're great and loves your company, just because you've got a stonking and probably well-deserved hangover. At least have the guts to go and make your excuses to her face!'

Freddy's words stung like nettles on bare flesh, but before Laura could reply the mood at the front door suddenly turned nasty.

Sunshine had no idea who the blonde woman was marching up the path, but she looked pretty cross.

'Hello, I'm Sunshine. I'm the friend to Laura. Who are you?'

The woman narrowed her eyes as she looked Sunshine up and down, trying to decide whether or not she was obliged to answer.

'Is Freddo here?' she demanded.

'Nope,' said Sunshine.

'Are you sure? Because that's his fucking Land Rover on the drive.'

Sunshine watched with interest as the woman grew redder and crosser and began jabbing the doorbell with her immaculately manicured finger.

'That's *Freddy's* fucking Land Rover,' she replied calmly.

'So he *is* here then, the arsing arsehole!' the woman spat.

She jabbed at the doorbell again, and banged on the door with her fist.

'She won't answer,' said Sunshine. 'She's probably hiding.'

Felicity stopped banging for a moment. 'Who is?'

'Laura.'

'What, that funny housekeeping woman? Why in God's name would she be hiding?'

'From me,' Sunshine replied with a sad smile.

'Well, that bloody sodding shit of an arsehole Freddo better not be hiding from me!'

Sunshine decided to try and be helpful. The blonde woman was looking really furious now, and Sunshine was worried that she might break the doorbell.

'Perhaps he's hiding with Laura,' she suggested. 'He really likes her,' she added.

Sunshine's words didn't seem to help as much as she had hoped.

'You mean the bastard's probably humping the help?' The woman crouched down and began yelling through the letter box.

Freddy shoved his way into the pantry beside Laura and pulled the door to behind him. It was Laura's turn to raise her eyebrows.

'It's Felicity,' he hissed. The scorn had disappeared entirely from his voice to be replaced by an edge of desperation.

'And . . . ?'

It was Freddy's turn to sigh. 'We had a date last night, except I couldn't go, but I didn't exactly tell her until it was too late and I guess she's pretty pissed off. . . .' he trailed off lamely.

Despite being cold, feeling sick and with a head that was about to explode, Laura couldn't help but smile. Her next words were delivered with as much relish as crammed the shelves that she was leaning against:

'Well, at least have the guts to go and make your excuses to her face.'

Freddy looked at her, astonished, and then his handsome face broke into a lopsided grin.

'I know you're in there, you bastard!' Felicity's voice shrieked through the letter box.

'You and that tart of a housekeeper! Well, if that dried-up, scruffy old bag lady is the best you can do, you were clearly punching well above your weight with me. You were crap in the sack anyway. She's welcome to you!'

Sunshine stood next to the incandescent Felicity, uncertain how to proceed. She had taken in all the words that had been spoken, or rather yelled, and was hoping to make some kind of sense of them later. Perhaps when Laura had stopped hiding, she would help her. Felicity appeared to have run out of steam.

She gave the front door a parting thump and strode off the way she'd come. Moments later, Sunshine heard a car door slam, an engine rev and tyres squeal as Felicity took her leave, in a foul temper, leaving a good deal of rubber on the tarmac. Just as Sunshine was about to go home, another visitor arrived. This woman was older, smartly dressed and smiling.

'Hello,' she said. 'Does Laura live here?'

Sunshine wondered what this one was going to do.

'Yes. But she's probably hiding.'

The woman didn't seem at all surprised. 'I'm Sarah,' she introduced herself. 'I'm an old friend of Laura's.'

Sunshine offered her a high five. 'I'm Sunshine. I'm the new friend to Laura.'

'Well, I'm sure she's very lucky to have you,' the woman replied.

Sunshine liked this new woman.

'Are you going to yell through the letter box too?' she asked her.

Sarah pondered a moment. 'Well, I thought I might just try the doorbell.'

Sunshine was hungry. It didn't look like she was going to get any lunch at Padua today.

'Good luck,' she wished Sarah, before setting off for home.

Freddy and Laura were still dithering in the pantry, straining their ears to hear if anyone remained at the front door. The doorbell rang again. A single sound, followed by a polite pause. Laura retreated back into the pickles.

'You go,' she pleaded with Freddy. 'Please.'

Freddy relented, fuelled by remorse about the insults Felicity had aimed at Laura.

He opened the door to an attractive, middle-aged brunette with a confident smile and a firm handshake.

'Hello. I'm Sarah. Can I see Laura?'

Freddy stood back to let her in. 'You can, if she comes out from hiding in the pantry.'

At the sound of Sarah's voice, Laura hurried into the hall to meet her. 'You were hiding in there too!' she reminded Freddy.

Sarah looked at them both and winked at Laura.

'*Hiding in the pantry!* Now that's a euphemism if ever I heard one.'

'Not a chance!' Freddy's answer was a knee-jerk, but a kick in the teeth nonetheless for Laura.

Sarah, as usual, saw what was required. She took Laura by the arm.

'Why don't you make me a lovely cup of tea? And by the way, your hair looks gorgeous.'

25

Sarah Trouvay was a first-class barrister with a stellar career, two healthy, rumbustious young boys, and a rugged architect husband. She also had an unexpected talent for yodelling which had earned her extravagant plaudits as Maria in the school production of *The Sound of Music*. She and Laura had met at school and remained close friends ever since. Not close in terms of geography or frequent meetings; they rarely saw or spoke to each other more than two or three times a year. But the bond between them, formed at an early age and tempered over time by triumphs and tragedies, remained as durable as it was dependable. Sarah had witnessed the bright, sparky, dauntless young Laura gradually, relentlessly diluted by a bad marriage and a barrage of self-doubt. But she had never given up hope that one day, the real Laura would re-emerge victorious in glorious, shining Technicolor.

'What on earth are you doing here?' Laura asked as she filled the kettle.

'Well, the six very drunken and virtually unintelligible messages which you left on my voicemail in the early hours of this morning might have had something to do with it.'

'Oh God! I didn't, did I?' Laura hid her face in her hands.

'You most certainly did. And now I want to hear all about it. Every last sordid detail. And I think we'll begin with "Poor Graham". Who the devil is "Poor Graham"?'

Laura told her almost everything. Beginning with the dress, which was still hanging half out of the bin, and ending with the sinking of the second bottle of prosecco in front of the fire. The rest of the night – including the phone calls – had disappeared forever into alcohol-induced oblivion.

'Poor Graham,' Sarah was now able to agree. 'Whatever made you agree to go out with him in the first place?'

Laura looked a little embarrassed. 'Oh, I don't know. Maybe just because he asked. Nobody else has. He always seemed nice enough. Nothing obviously wrong with him.'

Sarah shook her head in disbelief. 'Nothing wrong doesn't make him Mr Right.'

Laura sighed. If only she could stop thinking about Mr Wrong as Mr Right. She hid her face in her hands again.

'Damn that ruddy gardener!' She had said it out loud, before she could stop herself.

'Who?'

Laura smiled ruefully. 'Oh, nothing. I'm just talking to myself.'

'That's the first sign, you know.'

'First sign of what?'

'The menopause!'

Laura threw a biscuit at her. 'I should have known it was never going to work when he started going on about Nordic walking.'

'He was trying to impress you with his pole!' Sarah spluttered with laughter and even Laura couldn't stifle a guilty giggle.

And then she told her about the kiss in the porch. That dreadful, interminable kiss.

Sarah looked at her and shrugged her shoulders in exasperation.

'Well, what in God's name did you expect? You don't fancy him. You never have. It was always going to be like kissing cardboard!'

Laura shook her head emphatically. 'No. It was much, much worse. Cardboard would have been infinitely preferable.' She remembered the slug with disgust. 'And a lot less wet.'

'Honestly, Laura, why didn't you just offer your cheek, or failing that, pull away a bit quicker?'

Laura's cheeks were blotched with laughter and embarrassment.

'I didn't want to be rude. And anyway, his lips locked onto my face like a lunar module docking.'

Sarah was helpless with mirth. Laura felt bad. Poor Graham. He didn't deserve to be ridiculed. She remembered the bewildered look on his face when she finally broke the suction between them and garbled her goodbye before fleeing inside the house and slamming the door behind her. Poor Graham. But that didn't mean that she ever wanted to see him again.

'Poor Graham be damned!' Sarah always had the uncanny ability to know what Laura was thinking. 'Sounds more like "Poor Laura" to me. He's a bad kisser with a dodgy pole. Swill your mouth out and move on!'

Laura couldn't help smiling, but just as her spirits

were beginning to lift, a memory knocked them down like a rogue breaker toppling a tentative paddler.

'Shit!' She slumped forward in her chair and once again buried her head in her hands.

Sarah put down her cup of tea, ready for the next revelation.

'Freddy!' groaned Laura miserably. 'He found me this morning.'

'So?'

'He found me this morning, my face stuck to the sofa with dribble, wearing last night's smudged make-up and not much else, surrounded by empty bottles and two glasses. Two, Sarah! He'll think Graham "came in for coffee"!'

'Well, however compelling the evidence might be, it is purely circumstantial. And anyway, what does it matter what Freddy thinks?'

'He'll think I'm a drunken harlot!'

Sarah smiled and spoke gently and slowly, as though to a small child. 'Well, if it matters that much, tell him what really happened.'

Laura sighed despondently. 'Then he'll think I *am* just a "dried-up, scruffy old bag lady".'

'Right!' Sarah slapped the palms of her hands down on the table. 'Enough of this moaning and wallowing. Upstairs, bag lady, and make yourself look presentable. After you've dragged me away from work to listen to your pathetic and tedious complaining, the least you can do is take me out to lunch. And I don't just mean a sandwich, I mean a proper hot meal. And a pudding!'

Laura clipped the top of Sarah's head playfully as she passed her on the way out of the kitchen, mussing up her perfect cut and blow dry. Almost immediately, Freddy came in the back door.

Sarah stood up and offered him her hand and her brightest smile.

'Hello again. I'm afraid I didn't introduce myself properly. I'm Sarah Trouvay, an old friend of Laura's.'

Freddy shook her hand but refused to meet her gaze, turning instead to the sink to fill the kettle.

'Freddy. I've just come in to make a coffee. Can I get you one?'

'No thanks. We're just going out.'

The silence, deliberate on Sarah's part and embarrassed on Freddy's, was broken only by the rattle of water boiling in the kettle. Looking everywhere but at Sarah, Freddy caught sight of Laura's dress, hanging out of the bin. He fished it out and held it up.

'Hmm. Nice dress.'

'Yes. I bet Laura looked absolutely gorgeous in it.'

Freddy shifted uncomfortably in his muddy boots. 'I wouldn't know.'

At the sound of Laura's footsteps coming down the stairs, Sarah stood up.

'I know it's probably none of my business, but sometimes someone has to say something, even if they're the wrong person to do it. Last night: it wasn't what it seemed.'

She turned to leave the kitchen and over her shoulder added, 'Just *in case* you're interested.'

'None of my business either,' Freddy muttered sulkily as he poured boiling water into his mug.

Liar, liar, pants on fire! thought Sarah.

*

The Moon is Missing was hosting a wake for a ninety-two-year-old former boxing coach and horse dealer called Eddy 'The Neddy' O'Regan. The mourners had clearly been toasting the dear departed enthusiastically for some time already, and the mood was cheerful, rowdy and sentimental. Laura and Sarah managed to squeeze into one of the booths, and over saucisse cassoulet and puréed potato, washed down with a glass of house red for Sarah and a Diet Coke for Laura, they caught up with each other's news. They had spoken briefly after Anthony died, but since then Sarah had been working on an important case that had only just been heard in court.

'Did you win?' Laura asked.

'Of course!' said Sarah, poking with her fork at the rather mushy-looking sausage and bean stew on the plate in front of her. 'But never mind about that. Tell me everything.'

Laura did. She told her about Anthony's will and the letter; the study full of things; hiding from Sunshine; and being the latest and juiciest subject of local gossip. And Felicity.

'I mean, it's lovely in one way; the house is beautiful, but the monumental lost property department that comes with it is another matter entirely. How the hell am I supposed to return all that stuff? It's madness. I have no idea what to do about Sunshine, there's no guarantee that the website will work and most of the locals think I'm a money-grabbing slapper. I'll end up living in a house full of mice and cobwebs and other people's lost property until I'm one hundred and four, and when I do die, it'll be months before anyone notices and by the time they break in and find me, I'll be lique-fying on the sofa.'

'And not for the first time,' Sarah replied with a wink. But then she put down her knife and fork and pushed away her plate.

'Laura. My dear, lovely, funny, clever, absolutely bloody infuriating Laura. You've been left a great big beautiful house, full of treasures with a dishy gardener thrown in. Anthony loved you like a daughter and trusted you with everything that was precious to him, and instead of turning cartwheels you sit here whinge-ing. He believed in you; I've always believed in you. It's not just Sunshine that you're hiding from; it's everything. And it's time to stop hiding and start kick-ing life up the arse. And to hell with what anyone else thinks,' she added, for good measure.

Laura took a sip of her Diet Coke. She wasn't convinced. And she was terrified of disappointing yet another person who loved her.

Sarah looked into her dearest friend's troubled face. She reached over and placed her hand over Laura's. It was time for some long-overdue home truths.

'Laura, you have to let go of the past. You deserve to be happy, but you have to make it happen yourself. It's down to you. You were seventeen when you met Vince, still a child; but you're a grown woman now, so start behaving like one. Don't keep punishing yourself for things you did then, but don't use them as an excuse either. You have a chance now to make a really good life. Grab it by the balls and get on with it.'

Sarah sat back to see what impact her words were having. She was probably the only person in the world who could, and would, talk to Laura like that. She was determined to find the woman whom she knew was still in there and get her out. By force, if necessary.

'You do realise that we all fancied Vince, back then?'

Laura looked at her incredulously.

'Seriously. It wasn't just you. He was handsome, drove a flash car and smoked Sobranies. What more could a girl ask for? We all thought he was sex on legs. It was just bad luck that he chose you.'

Laura smiled. 'You always were an insufferable clever clogs.'

'Yes, but I'm right. Aren't I? Come on, Laura. You're better than this! When did you turn into such a wimp? This is a once-in-a-lifetime, twenty-four-carat-gold, fuck-off fantastic opportunity that most people can only dream about. If you chicken out of this one I'll never forgive you. But more importantly, you'll never forgive yourself!' Sarah raised her glass in a toast. 'And as for it being madness, well that should suit you perfectly. You always were a complete loony-tune!'

Laura smiled. It had been Sarah's nickname for her all those years ago at school, when life had still been exciting and full of possibilities.

'You complete arse . . .' she muttered.

'I beg your pardon?' Even the normally imperturbable Sarah looked a little shocked.

Laura grinned. 'Me, not you.'

'I knew that.' Sarah grinned back at her.

It was slowly dawning on Laura that life was *still* exciting and full of possibilities; possibilities that she had wasted years of her life wishing for instead of chasing. She had some serious catching-up to do.

'What about Sunshine?' she asked. 'Any advice?'

'Talk to her. She has Down's Syndrome, she's not daft. Tell her how you feel. Work something out. And while you're at it, tell her what really happened on your date. If you won't tell Freddy, I'm pretty sure she will.'

Laura shook her head. 'Maybe, but he doesn't care anyway. You heard what he said when you suggested that we'd been up to no good in the pantry. "Not a chance".'

'Oh, Laura! Sometimes you can be really thick.'

Laura resisted the urge to stab her in the back of her hand with a fork.

'Do you remember Nicholas Barker from the boys' school?'

Laura remembered a tall, freckled boy with strong arms and scuffed shoes. 'He was always pulling my hair on the bus or ignoring me completely.'

Sarah grinned. 'He was shy. He did it because he fancied you!'

Laura groaned. 'Oh God. Don't say we're no further forward than we were in the fifth form.'

'You speak for yourself. But in my opinion, you've definitely got some serious ground to make up. Especially if you fancy Freddy as much as he obviously fancies you. And now I want some pudding!'

Sarah called a taxi from the pub to take her back to the station. As they stood waiting in the car park for it to arrive, Laura hugged her friend gratefully.

'Thanks so much for coming. I'm sorry I've been such a pain.'

'No change there,' quipped Sarah. 'But seriously, it's fine. You'd do the same for me.'

'Damn well wouldn't!'

That was Laura; always hiding behind a joke, shrugging away compliments. But Sarah would never forget that it was this Laura, eight years ago, who'd sat wiping away her tears in a side room of a hospital ward, while Sarah's shattered husband paced the car park chain-smoking and sobbing. It was Laura who'd held her hand while she delivered her first child, a precious daughter who died before they had a chance to meet. A daughter who would have been christened Laura-Jane.

Later that afternoon, Laura went and found Sunshine, who was sitting on the bench across the green from the house.

'May I sit down?' she asked.

Sunshine smiled. A warm, welcoming smile which filled Laura with guilt and shame.

'I want to apologise,' she said.

'What for?'

'For not being a good friend back to you.'

Sunshine thought for a moment. 'Do you like me?'

'Yes, I do. Very much.'

'Then why do you hide?' she asked sadly.

Laura sighed. 'Because, Sunshine, this is all new to me; living in this house; the lost things; trying to do what Anthony would have wanted. Sometimes I get cross and muddled and I need to be by myself.'

'So why didn't you just tell me?'

Laura smiled at her. 'Because sometimes I'm just a silly arse.'

'Do you ever get scared?'

'Sometimes, yes.'

Sunshine took her hand and squeezed it in her own. Her soft, chubby fingers were freezing. Laura pulled her up from the bench.

'Let's go and have the lovely cup of tea,' she said.

26

'I think he needs the biscuit,' said Sunshine, tenderly stroking the bundle of fur and bones that ought to have been a lurcher. He watched her with frightened eyes that mirrored the beatings he had endured. Tired of their torture, his tormentors had kicked him out to fend for himself. Freddy had found him the previous evening lying on the grass verge outside Padua. It was raining hard and he was soaking wet and too exhausted to resist when Freddy had picked him up and brought him inside. He had been clipped by a car and had a superficial wound on his rump that Laura had cleaned and dressed while Freddy had held him shaking and wrapped in a towel. He refused to eat anything but drank a little water, and Laura stayed up with him all night, sleeping fitfully in an armchair while the dog lay inches from the fire, wrapped in a blanket and never moving. As the first wraithlike light of the winter dawn seeped through the lace panels of Anthony's study, Laura stirred. Her neck was cricked and complaining after a night spent folded awkwardly into a chair. The fire was reduced to a few struggling embers but the dog hadn't moved.

Please God, she thought as she leaned forward to check for the rise and fall of the blanket that would prove her prayer had been answered. Nothing. No movement. No sound. But before the tears that had filled her eyes could spill, the blanket suddenly twitched. There was a ragged intake of breath and the sonorous snoring that Laura had somehow managed to sleep through resumed.

Sunshine had been ecstatic when she had arrived that morning to find that they had a canine guest. It was the most animated that Laura had ever seen the normally rather solemn and serious girl. Between them they had coaxed him to eat a little cooked chicken and a slice of bread and butter. Sunshine had gently examined his skeletal frame and was determined to feed him everything she could.

'We mustn't feed him too much at once. His stomach will have shrunk and if we overdo it he'll be sick,' Laura warned.

Sunshine pulled a face which admirably communicated her disapproval of vomit.

'Maybe he needs another drink?' she suggested hopefully. Laura could understand her eagerness. She was desperate to do something to make the creature better, fatter, fitter. Happy. But sometimes not doing anything was what was needed, however hard that might be.

'I think he just needs to rest,' she told Sunshine. 'Just tuck the blanket round him and leave him in peace for a bit.'

Sunshine 'tucked him in' very carefully for about ten minutes before Laura finally persuaded her to come and help with the website. Freddy arrived earlier than usual and found them all in the study.

'How's the poor fella doing?'

Laura couldn't bring herself to look up from the screen. 'A bit better, I think.'

Since the episode in the pantry, the awkwardness between Freddy and Laura hung between them like smoke. Laura was desperate to clear the air and tell him what had really happened on her date, but somehow she could never find a way to begin the conversation. He went over to the fire and crouched down by the blanket. A pair of large, sorrowful eyes peered out at him. Freddy offered the back of his hand for the dog to smell but the dog's flinch was instinctive, born from bitter experience.

'Hey, hey, steady, lad. No one's going to hurt you here. I'm the one who found you.'

The dog listened to his gentle voice and poked his nose out warily from beneath the blanket to take a tentative sniff. Sunshine was watching their exchange closely. With an exaggerated sigh she placed both hands on her hips.

'He's supposed to be resting,' she said in a censorious tone.

Freddy held his hands up in surrender and came over to the table where Laura was in front of the laptop.

'So are you going to keep him?'

Sunshine replied before Laura could draw breath. 'That's for double damn sure, cross my heart and learn to fly we're going to keep him! He was lost and you found him. That's what we do,' she said, throwing her hands up in the air to underline and embolden her words. It took a little while for her thinking to catch up with her feelings, but when it did she added defiantly, 'But we're not giving him back.'

She looked to Freddy and Laura in turn for reassurance. Freddy winked at her and smiled.

'Don't worry, Sunshine. I don't think there's anyone to want him back.' But then he added, as though remembering his place, 'Of course, it's Laura's decision.'

Laura looked across at the blanketed bundle still roasting by the fire who was unaware that as soon as he had been carried over her threshold he was safe. From that moment he'd been hers.

'We'll have to give him a name,' she said.

Once again Sunshine was already on the next page.

'He's called Carrot.'

'Is that so?' said Freddy. 'And that's because . . . ?'

'Because he was hit by the car in the dark night because he didn't see it.'

'And?' continued Freddy with an interrogative tip of his head.

'Carrots help you see in the darkness.'

Sunshine delivered her denouement speaking loudly and slowly like an English tourist in a foreign country.

After the lovely cup of tea, which Sunshine permitted Laura to make while she stood guard over Carrot, Freddy went outside to work in the garden and Laura and Sunshine returned their attention to The Keeper of Lost Things. Laura had begun the Herculean task of entering the details of all the lost things onto a database that could be accessed via the website. Sunshine was selecting things from the shelves and drawers. Once Laura had entered the details of a particular object it was marked with a sticky gold star that came in packets of fifty from the post office. They had bought ten packets, but now that they had made a start, Laura had a feeling they might need a good few more. Sunshine placed the objects in a neat line on the table: a pair of tweezers, a miniature playing card (the king of clubs) and a plastic model soldier. The friendship bracelet remained in her hand.

Knotted thread red and black bracelet.
Found in the underpass between Fools Green and
Maitland Road, 21 May . . .

Chloe felt her mouth water just before the first wave of vomit rose. The retching bent her double as she tried not to splash her new shoes. The concrete walls of the underpass reverberated with the sound of her shame and humiliation.

Everyone liked Mr Mitchell. He was the coolest teacher in school. 'The boys want to be him and the girls want to be with him,' her friend Claire had chanted only yesterday when he had passed them in the corridor. Chloe didn't. Not any more. She wanted to be anywhere other than with him. Mr Mitchell ('Call me Mitch – I won't tell if you don't') taught music, and at first she too would have danced to any tune he chose to play. He had the inestimable gift of plausibility. Coupled with a handsome face and slick charm, the adoration of Mr Mitchell was inevitable. Chloe had begged her mother for the private singing lessons she knew Mr Mitchell taught. From his home. Her mother was surprised. Her daughter was a quiet girl; happy to blend in with the chorus rather than take centre stage. She was a 'good' girl. A 'nice' girl. Money for singing lessons would be hard to come by, but perhaps her mother thought that they would be worth it if they gave Chloe a little more confidence. And Mr Mitchell was such a brilliant teacher. He really seemed to care about his pupils, not like some of them at the school who simply put in the hours, took the money and ran.

At first it had been exciting. The eye contact held just a little too long in class; the smile flashed in her direction. She was special to him, she was sure. On the way to that first singing lesson she was giddy with nerves. As she walked to his house she rubbed gloss onto her lips, pink and shiny: 'Passionate Pout'. And then she had rubbed it off again. During the third lesson, he had made her sit next to him at the piano. His hand on her thigh was thrilling, arousing. But wrong. It was like taking a shortcut down a dark alley late at night. You know you shouldn't. You know it's dangerous, but maybe just this once it will be all right. The next time he stood behind her and placed his hands on her chest; gently, caressingly. He said he needed to check that she was breathing correctly. The childish fantasy of romance had been rudely replaced by the sordid reality of his groping hands and hot, ragged breath in her ear. So why had she gone back? Even after that, she had still gone back. How could she not? What would she tell her mother? She wanted it as much as he did. That's what he had told her, and she was shackled by the precarious truth in his words. She had at first, hadn't she?

The physical pain still echoed through her body, amplified by the action replays running through her mind. She had said no. She had screamed no. But perhaps just inside her head and not out loud. The body which had been hers alone was lost forever; taken or given, she still wasn't sure. She wiped her mouth again and as she did the friendship bracelet caught her eye. He had given it to her at the end of the first lesson because, he said, they were going to be very special friends. She ripped it from her wrist and threw it away. Taken. Now she was sure.

Sunshine squeezed the bracelet tight in her hand. Laura didn't see her wince. Her eyes were intent on the screen in front of her, her fingers rattling over the keyboard.

Sunshine raised one warning finger to her lips for the benefit of Carrot and threw the bracelet onto the fire. She went back to the drawers to choose more things.

High on its shelf, the biscuit tin was still waiting for its gold star.

27

'Shall I make the lovely cup of tea when the bored van man comes?' Sunshine enquired helpfully.

Laura nodded distractedly, her mind preoccupied with where they were going to put the enormous Christmas tree that was currently languishing prone and prickly on most of the hall floor. Freddy was insisting that according to his measurements there would be a foot of clear daylight between the top of the tree and the ceiling once they had got it into position, and had gone to fetch the metal stand from the shed in order to prove his point before a full-scale argument broke out. Later that morning they were expecting a man who was coming to sort out broadband.

'We can't give you an exact time,' the customer services woman had told Laura, 'but we can give you a window of between 10.39 a.m. and 3.14 p.m.'

Sunshine had her eye on the clock in the hall, or at least as much of it as she could see beyond the branches. Laura had finally taught Sunshine to tell the time – more or less – and doing so at every opportunity had become her latest obsession. Curious about all the commotion, Carrot had left his comfortable bed by the fire to make tentative investigations.

One brief glance at the forestry lurking in the hallway was enough to send him scurrying back to the study. Freddy returned with the stand, and having decided that perhaps the hall was the best place to accommodate both the prodigious height and girth of the tree, he and Laura were trying to manoeuvre it into position under Sunshine's rather erratic guidance when the doorbell rang and Sunshine skipped off to answer it, leaving Freddy and Laura in an awkward embrace with a giant conifer.

The man waiting on the doorstep had an air of superiority entirely unjustified by rank, appearance, education or ability. He was, in short, a supercilious git. A short, supercilious git. Sunshine didn't know that yet, but she could feel it.

'Are you the bored van man?' she enquired cautiously.

The man ignored her question. 'I'm here to see Laura.'

Sunshine checked her watch.

'You're too early. It's only ten o'clock. Your window doesn't open yet.'

The man looked at her the way the other kids had looked at her at school when they had called her names and pushed and shoved her in the playground.

'What the hell are you drivelling on about? I just want to see Laura.'

He pushed past her into the hall, where Laura and Freddy were still grappling with the tree. Sunshine followed him in, clearly upset.

'It's the bored van man,' she announced, 'and he's not very nice.'

Laura let go of the tree. Caught unawares, Freddy was almost toppled by its weight and let it fall. It missed the intruder by inches, causing him to yell angrily, 'Jesus Christ, Laura! What the bloody hell are you trying to do? Kill me?'

Laura faced him as she had never done before, with steady eyes and a steely composure.

'Now there's a thought.'

The man was clearly not expecting this new version of Laura, and she appeared to be enjoying his discomfort. Freddy was intrigued by this unexpected turn of events but trying hard to feign indifference, and Sunshine was wondering how it was that, if Laura actually knew the bored van man, she had asked him to come to Padua when he was so horrid. And she certainly wasn't going to make him the lovely cup of tea. Laura finally broke up the tense tableau.

'What do you want, Vince?' she sighed. 'You'd better come through to the kitchen.'

As he followed her out of the hall he was unable to resist giving Freddy the once-over, and Freddy returned his gaze with a hard stare. In the kitchen Laura didn't offer him anything other than a brief opportunity to explain his presence.

'Don't I even get a cup of tea?' he asked in a wheedling tone she'd heard him use so frequently in the bedroom when they were first married and it wasn't tea he had wanted. She shuddered at the thought. No doubt Selina from Servicing was horribly familiar with it too by now. She almost felt sorry for her.

'Vince, why are you here? What is it that you want?'

He flashed her a smile, intending seductive but executing sleazy.

'I want us to be friends.'

Laura laughed out loud.

'I do,' he continued, desperation beginning to whet the very edges of his words.

'What about Selina?'

He sat down and buried his head in his hands. It was so hammy that Laura was tempted to offer him the mustard.

'We broke up. I could never love her the way I loved you.'

'Lucky her. She left you, didn't she?'

Vince wasn't ready to give up just yet.

'Look, Laura, I never stopped loving you.'

'What, even while you were servicing Selina?'

Vince stood up and tried to take her hand. 'It was just a physical thing. Just sex. I never stopped thinking about you, missing you, and wanting you back.'

Laura shook her head in weary disbelief.

'So isn't it strange that you never thought to contact me before now? Not a birthday card, a Christmas card, a phone call. Tell me, Vince, why is that? Why now? Nothing to do with this big house that I happen to have inherited, I suppose?'

Vince sat back down, trying to marshal a coherent argument. Laura had always been too clever for him, even when she was just a girl. He *had* loved her then, in his own way, even though he knew that, really, she was out of his league, with her posh education and nice manners. Back then, though, he could still find ways to impress her. Perhaps if their baby had lived, or they had managed to conceive again, things might have been different. He would have liked a son to play football with, or a little girl to take horse-riding, but it wasn't to be, and in the end their fruitless efforts to become parents became another of the things that drove them apart. Over the years, as Laura grew up, she became more of a match for him, and so less of a match in the marital sense. She noticed his faults and he, in turn, exaggerated them to annoy her. It was his only defence. At least Selina hadn't minded his elbows on the table or the toilet seat left up. Well, not at first.

Laura was still waiting calmly for his response. Her composure infuriated him and the mask of civility finally fell from his face, revealing the ugly truth.

'I heard about your date with Graham. You always were a frigid bitch,' he spat at her.

Before he came, he had promised himself that he would not lose his temper. He would show Miss Snooty-Pants that he was as good as her. But as usual, she rattled him, just by being herself. By being better than him.

Laura had finally had enough. She picked up the nearest thing to hand, an open carton of milk, which as luck would have it was on the turn, and hurled the contents at Vince's sneering face. She missed, but hit him squarely on the chest, splashing the rancid liquid all over his designer polo shirt and staining the dark suede of his expensive jacket. Laura was just looking round for further ammunition when the kitchen door opened. It was Freddy.

'Is everything okay?'

She rather reluctantly replaced the bottle of washing-up liquid on the draining board with a resounding thump.

'Yes, everything's fine. Vince is just leaving, aren't you?'

Vince barged past Freddy into the hall where Sunshine was hovering uncertainly. He turned to Laura in order to deliver his final insult with appropriate aplomb.

'I hope you'll be very happy in your big house with your little retard friend and your toyboy.'

Sunshine, no longer the child in the playground, answered him with admirable poise:

'I'm not the retard, I'm dancing drome.'

Freddy continued with rather more menace, 'And nobody talks to my girls like that, so sod off and don't come back.'

Vince had never known when to keep his mouth shut.

'Or else what?'

Seconds after the answer was delivered, Vince was nursing a bloody nose, lying on his back and struggling to extricate himself from the spiny clutches of the Christmas tree. When he finally managed to scramble to his feet, he lunged at the front door claiming grievous bodily harm and threatening to summon the police and his solicitor. As he slammed out of the house, Carrot's head appeared from behind the study door and he barked just once, but very sternly, at Vince's vapour trail. The three of them stared at the dog in astonishment. It was his first bark since coming to Padua.

'Well done, fella!' said Freddy, reaching down to stroke Carrot's ears. 'That certainly saw him off.'

The sound of the doorbell sent Carrot scuttling back to the study. Freddy charged across the hall and flung open the door to find a rather startled-looking young man with a plastic identity card strung around his neck and holding a black tool case.

'I'm Lee,' he said, flashing his card. 'I've come to sort out your broadband.'

Freddy stood aside to let him in and Laura guided him round the still prone Christmas tree and through to the study, which was immediately vacated by a supersonic Carrot. Sunshine trotted along behind them, thinking with all her might and still trying to work out exactly what was happening. Eventually she rolled her eyes and sighed loudly.

'You're the bored van man!' She checked her watch. 'You came in the window.'

Lee smiled, uncertain what to say. He'd been to some strange jobs before and this one was shaping up nicely to be right up there with them.

'Shall I make you the lovely cup of tea?'

The young man's smile broadened. Maybe things were looking up.

'I'd love a cup of coffee, if that's okay?'

Sunshine shook her head. 'I don't do coffee. I only do tea.'

Lee snapped open his tool case. It might be better to just get the job done and get out after all.

'Of course you can have coffee,' Laura intervened hastily. 'How do you take it? Come on, Sunshine – I'll make it and you can watch and then next time you'll know how to make it yourself.'

Sunshine considered for a moment and, remembering Vince's threats, she allowed herself to be persuaded.

'Then when the police get here I'll be able to make them the lovely cup of coffee too.'

28

The very thought of you.

The song broke Laura's sleep, although whether it was part of her dream or real music coming from the garden room downstairs she couldn't be sure. She lay still and listening, snuggled in her duvet cocoon. Silence. Reluctantly she crept out into the cold, rose-scented air, threw on her dressing gown and went over to the window to let the winter morning in.

And saw a ghost.

Laura peered out through the frosted pane, unwilling to trust what she saw: a shadow, perhaps a figure, pellucid as the rimy spiderwebs strung trembling in the icy breeze between the rose bushes. Laura shook her head. It was nothing. Customary common sense was temporarily out of service, and her imagination had cut loose, rampaging through reason with party poppers and a silly hat. That was all it was. Vince's visit had unsettled her. He had stomped dirty footprints all over her nice new life. But he was gone now, she told herself, and unlikely to return. She smiled, remembering with satisfaction the sour milk soaking into his shirt and the horror on his face as he squirmed like an upturned tortoise in the branches of the Christmas tree. But perhaps something else had unsettled her too. Freddy.

He had called her 'his girl'. She had been ridiculously, dangerously flattered. She had replayed the moment over and over in her head, but it was persistently and annoyingly accompanied by a warning voice telling her not to be so stupid. Now she didn't dare think about it at all. Time for the lovely cup of tea.

Downstairs the smell of Christmas tree cut through the air in every room. It was wonderful. The tree itself glittered and sparkled with tinsel and baubles and all manner of decorations that Laura had found in a box in the loft. Anthony had always put up a tree at Christmas, but his had usually been a much more modest affair and most of the decorations had hardly ever been used. Laura slotted two slices of bread into the toaster and poured herself a cup of tea. Noises in the kitchen had finally roused Carrot from his bed by the fire in the study, and he came and sat at Laura's feet waiting for his breakfast of toast and lightly scrambled eggs. In spite of their best efforts to fatten him up, he had barely 'thickened his skin' according to Freddy. But he did look much happier now, and was beginning to view life as a curious adventure rather than a terrifying ordeal. Today, Sunshine was going Christmas shopping with her mum, and Freddy was visiting his sister and her family in Slough. He had told Laura that his pre-Christmas visit was enough to keep his 'good big brother' certificate up to date, provided it was supplemented with generous (preferably cash) presents for his ungrateful niece and his surly nephew. Laura drained her teacup and brushed crumbs of toast from her fingers. Perhaps a day spent in her own company would do her good. Besides, she had Carrot, whose gentle head was resting in her lap. After a quick stroll around the frosty garden, which allowed Carrot to cock his leg up several trees and Laura to check that there were no spectres, wraiths or banshees loitering in the rose garden, she stoked up the fire in the study and Carrot settled himself back into his bed with a contented sigh. She fetched a box from one of the shelves and set out its contents on the table. The laptop bleeped and blinked into life and the vast virtual lost property department, of which she was now the Keeper, opened its doors. Laura picked up the first object in front of her.

Child's umbrella, white with red hearts.
Found at the Alice in Wonderland sculpture, Central
Park, New York, 17 April . . .

Marvin liked to keep busy. It stopped the bad thoughts creeping into his head, like black ants seething over the body of a dead songbird. The drugs from his doctor sometimes helped, but not always. When he had first fallen sick, he used to stuff his ears with cotton wads, hold his nose and keep his eyes and mouth clenched shut. He figured that if all the holes in his head were blocked, the thoughts couldn't get in. But he had to breathe. And no matter how teeny tiny he made the crack between his lips, the bad thoughts always managed to sneak in. But keeping very busy kept them away; and the voices too.

Marvin was the umbrella man. He would take all the broken umbrellas that were thrown in the trash at the New York City Transit Lost Property Unit, and fix them up back in the dark and dingy room that was his only home.

It wasn't raining yet, but it was forecast. Marvin loved the rain. It washed the world clean and made everything shine; made the grass smell like heaven. Clouds the colour of gun smoke rolled in across the blue sky above. It wouldn't be long. Marvin was a giant of a man. He strode along Fifth Avenue, his heavy boots thudding on the sidewalk and his long, grey coat billowing behind him like a cloak. His wild black dreadlocks were frosted with grey and his eyes were never still; flashing whites like a frightened mustang.

'Free umbrellas!'

Central Park was his favourite place to work. He took the entrance on 72nd Street and headed for Conservatory Water. He liked to watch the pond yachts gliding across the water like swans. The boating season had only just begun, and despite the threat of rain a sizeable fleet had already set sail. Marvin's regular pitch was by the Alice in Wonderland sculpture. The children who played there didn't seem to mind him like some of the grown-ups did. Maybe they thought he looked like something out of a story too. There were no children today. Marvin set his bag of umbrellas down by the smallest mushroom on the sculpture, just as the first spots of rain began to polka-dot its smooth, bronze cap.

'Free umbrellas!'

His deep voice boomed like thunder through the rain. People scurried past but looked away when he offered them one of his gifts. He could never figure it out. He was just trying to be a good person. The umbrellas were free. Why did most people scaredy-cat away from him like he was the devil? Still, he stood his ground.

'Free umbrellas!'

A young guy on a skateboard skidded to a halt in front of him. Sopping wet in just a T-shirt, jeans and baseball boots, he was still grinning like the Cheshire Cat peeping over Alice's shoulder. He took the umbrella that Marvin was offering and high-fived his gratitude.

'Thanks, dude!'

He sped away, his board splashing through the puddles, holding a huge pink umbrella aloft. The rain slowed to a drizzle and the

172

people in the park slowed to a stroll. Marvin didn't see her at first. A little girl in a red raincoat. She was missing one of her front teeth and had freckles across her nose.

'Hello,' she said. 'I'm Alice, like the statue.' She pointed to her namesake. Marvin hunkered down so he could see her better and offered her his hand.

'I'm Marvin. Pleased to meet you.'

She was British. Marvin recognised the accent from the TV. He always thought that Britain would be a good place for him, with his crooked teeth and fondness for rain.

'There you are, Alice! What have I told you about talking to strangers?'

The woman who had joined them was looking at him as though he might bite.

'He's not a stranger. He's Marvin.'

Marvin smiled his best smile and offered the woman the best from his bag. 'Free umbrella?'

The woman ignored him. She snatched Alice's hand and tried to drag her away. Trash. That's how she was treating him; like he was trash. Marvin's face grew hot. The hairs on the back of his neck prickled and his ears began to ring. He was not trash.

'Take it!' he roared, thrusting the umbrella at her.

'Don't touch me, you moron,' she hissed as she turned on her heel, towing a tearful Alice behind her. As soon as her mother's grip slackened, Alice pulled free and ran back towards the sculpture.

'Marvin!' she yelled, desperately wanting to make things right. Their eyes met and before her mother could retrieve her Alice blew him a kiss. And he caught it. Before he went home he left a white umbrella with red hearts leaning against the White Rabbit. Just in case she came back.

*

Laura yawned and stretched back into her chair. She checked her watch. Three hours in front of the screen was more than enough for today. She needed some air.

'Come on, Carrot,' she said. 'Time for a walk.'

Outside the sky was marbled grey. 'Looks like rain,' she said to the reluctant dog. 'I think we might need an umbrella.'

29

The dining room looked like something out of a fairy tale. The table was laid with a snow white linen tablecloth and napkins. Silver cutlery framed each place setting and cut-crystal glasses winked and sparkled under the light from the chandelier. It was her first Christmas as mistress of Padua and Laura wanted to do the house justice. If she did, perhaps it would banish the unwelcome thoughts that crept into her head like black ants through a crack in the wall of a pantry. She just couldn't shake the feeling that the previous mistress still hadn't quite gone. She pulled the silver and white crackers from their cardboard box and set one on top of each precisely folded napkin.

That morning, even in the dark, she knew that something in the bedroom had changed. It was the same feeling that had told her, as a child on Christmas morning, that the stocking at the foot of her bed, empty when she had fallen asleep, was now full. She could sense, somehow, the alteration. As she padded over to the window in bare feet, she trod on things which were not the carpet: soft, hard, sharp, smooth. Daylight confirmed that the drawers of the dressing table had been pulled out and their contents strewn across the floor.

Laura picked up one of the wine glasses and polished away an imaginary smudge. Sunshine and her mum and dad were coming for Christmas dinner. Her brother had been invited, but he 'wasn't bovvered'. Freddy was coming too. She hadn't known whether to ask him or not, but a stern pep talk from Sarah had convinced her. He said 'yes', and since then Laura had wasted an inordinate amount of time trying to work out why. Her hypotheses were numerous and varied: she'd caught him by surprise; he was lonely; he wanted a roast turkey dinner but couldn't cook; he had nowhere else to go; he felt sorry for her. The one explanation she was most reluctant but also most excited to entertain was the simplest and most nerve-racking. He was coming because he wanted to.

Perhaps she had done it in her sleep, like sleep walking. Sleep trashing. It wasn't a burglary because nothing was missing. Yesterday she had found Sunshine in the garden room dancing to the Al Bowlly song that had begun to haunt her, night and day.

'Did you put the music on?'

Sunshine shook her head. 'It was already on and when I heard it I came in for the dance.'

Laura had never known Sunshine to tell a lie.

'They're done!' Sunshine burst into the dining room, looking at her watch. She had been making mince pies and now the kitchen was dusty with flour and icing sugar. Laura followed Sunshine as she trotted purposefully back to the kitchen and hopped from foot to foot excitedly while Laura took the pies from the oven.

'They smell lovely,' she said, and Sunshine blushed proudly.

'Just in time,' said Freddy as he came in through the back door accompanied by a blast of freezing cold air. 'Time for the lovely cup of tea and an even lovelier mince pie.'

As they sat round the table, drinking tea and fanning mouthfuls of mince pies, which were still a little too hot, Freddy gazed thoughtfully at Laura.

'What's up?' he asked.

'Nothing.' It was a reflex rather than an answer.

Freddy raised his eyebrows. Sunshine shoved the rest of her mince pie in and then spoke with her mouth full.

'That's a lie.'

Freddy laughed out loud. 'Well, no points for tact there, but ten out of ten for honesty.'

They both looked at Laura expectantly. She told them. About the dressing table; the music; even about the shadow figure in the rose garden. Sunshine was unimpressed.

'It's just the lady,' she said, as though it ought to have been obvious.

'And what lady might that be?' Freddy asked, keeping his eyes firmly fixed on Laura.

'Saint Anthony's wedding wife. The Lady of the Flowers.' She reached for another mince pie and dropped it under the table for Carrot. Freddy winked at her and mouthed, 'I saw that.' Sunshine almost smiled.

'But why would she still be here, now that Anthony's gone?' Laura surprised herself by taking the idea seriously enough to ask.

'Yes. Why would she still be here making a mess and disturbing the peace? And after we gave her such a lovely wedding, too?' Laura had no idea if Freddy was being serious or not.

Sunshine shrugged. 'She's upset.'

Despite her scepticism, Laura's stomach tipped like a tombola machine.

Christmas Day dawned bright and sunny, and as Laura ambled round the garden with Carrot, her spirits lifted. Christmas Eve had passed uneventfully, and she had even been to Midnight Mass at the local church. She'd had a few words with God and maybe that had helped. Laura and God didn't get together too often, but he was still on her Christmas card list.

Sunshine and her mum and dad arrived at twelve on the dot.

'Sunshine's been ready since eight,' her mum told Laura as she took their coats. 'She'd have been here for breakfast if we'd let her.'

Laura introduced them to Freddy. 'This is Stella and this is Stan.'

'We call ourselves "The SS",' Stella chuckled. 'It's very kind of you to invite us.'

Stan grinned and thrust a poinsettia and a bottle of pink cava at Laura.

'There's nothing like a drop of pink fizz at Christmas,' said Stella, smoothing down the front of her best dress and checking her hair in the hall mirror. As Sunshine proudly gave them a guided tour of the house, Stella and Stan oohed and aahed appreciatively. Back in the kitchen Freddy was whisking gravy, basting roast potatoes, stabbing boiling brussels sprouts and drinking vodka martinis. And occasionally sneaking an appreciative glance at Laura. A couple of times, their eyes met, and he refused to look away. Laura was beginning to feel rather warm. He had insisted on helping, to show his appreciation for the invitation. He raised his glass to Laura.

'If they're The SS, then I'm 007.'

Christmas dinner was every bit as glorious as it ought to be. In the fairy-tale setting of silver and white and sparkle, they ate too much, drank too much, pulled crackers and told terrible jokes. Carrot camped out under the table taking tit-bits from whichever hand offered them. Laura discovered that Stella was in a book club and did flamenco, and Stan was in the darts team at his local pub. They were currently second in the league, and with three more matches in hand, they were hoping to take the championship. But Stan's real passion was music. Much to Freddy's delight, they shared a broad and eclectic taste, from David Bowie to Art Pepper to The Proclaimers to Etta James. It was easy to see where Sunshine's love of music and dancing came from.

While Laura, Sunshine and Stella cleared the table and then set about tackling the bombsite that had once been the kitchen, Freddy and Stan slumped back in their chairs like a pair of deflated soufflés.

'That was the best Christmas dinner I've had in years.' Stan rubbed his belly affectionately. 'Only don't tell the missus,' he added, winking at Freddy.

Carrot had ventured out from under the table and was sleeping contentedly at Freddy's side. Freddy poured Stan a glass of whisky.

'So is it as great as it sounds being a train driver? Every schoolboy's dream?'

Stan swirled the amber-coloured liquid in his glass and sniffed it approvingly.

'For the most part,' he replied. 'Some days I feel like I'm the luckiest man alive. But I nearly packed it in before I really got started.'

He sipped his whisky, reaching back for once to the memories he had struggled so hard to forget.

'I'd only been driving solo for a couple of weeks. It was my last run of the day; cold and dark outside and I was looking forward to my dinner. I didn't even see her until she hit the cab. After that, there wasn't much left of her to see.'

He took another sip of his whisky, bigger this time.

'It was in the local paper. She was ill, they said; bad nerves. Stood waiting in the cold. Waiting for my train. Terrible shame it was. She had a nipper; a girl. Dear little thing. They put her picture in the paper.'

Freddy shook his head and whistled through his teeth. 'Jesus, Stan, I'm sorry.'

Stan drained his glass and thumped it down on the table.

'It's the whisky,' he said. 'It makes me maudlin. It was a long time ago. Thank God, Stella drummed some sense into me and persuaded me to carry on driving.' They sat in silence for a moment and then Stan added, 'Not a word to Sunshine, though. I never told her.'

'Of course.'

Carrot's ears flicked at the sound of footsteps in the hall. Sunshine came in carrying a tray, followed by Laura and Stella. She set the tray down on the table.

'Now it's time for the lovely cup of tea and the even lovelier mince pies,' she said, pointing at the plate,

piled high. 'And then we're going to play "Conveni-
ences".'

Halfway through the first round, Sunshine remembered something that she had been meaning to tell her
parents.

'Freddy's crap in the sack.'

Freddy nearly choked on his whisky, but Stella
responded with admirable composure.

'What on earth makes you think that?'

'Felicity told me. She's Freddy's girlfriend.'

'Not any more,' growled Freddy.

Stan was shaking with laughter and Freddy was
clearly mortified, but Sunshine was undeterred.

'What does it mean – crap in the sack?'

'It means not very good at kissing.' It was the first
thing that came into Laura's head.

'Perhaps you should do more practice, then,' said
Sunshine kindly, patting Freddy's hand.

When Sunshine and 'The SS' went home, the house
fell silent. Laura was left alone with Carrot. And Freddy.
But where was he? He'd disappeared while she had
been seeing Sunshine and 'The SS' out and waving
them off. She felt like a giddy teenager, uncertain if she
was excited or afraid. It was the wine, she told herself.
Freddy came out of the garden room and took her by
the hand.

'Come.'

The garden room was lit with dozens of candles and
there was a bottle of champagne chilling in an ice
bucket, flanked by two glasses.

'Will you dance with me?' Freddy asked.

As he placed the needle on the record, Laura spoke

silently to God for the second time in as many days. *Please, please let it not be Al Bowlly.*

In Freddy's arms she wished that Ella Fitzgerald would improvise a few more verses for 'Someone to Watch Over Me'. Freddy looked up and Laura followed his gaze to the bunch of mistletoe that he had attached to the chandelier above their heads.

'Practice makes perfect,' he whispered.

As they kissed, the photograph of Therese shattered silently into a starburst of splintered glass.

30

Eunice

1989

The photographs on the sideboard were supposed to help Godfrey remember who people were, but they didn't always work. As Bomber, Eunice and Baby Jane came into the sunny sitting room, Godfrey reached for his wallet.

'I'll have a tenner on My Bill in the 2.45 at Kempton Park.'

Grace patted him affectionately on the hand. 'Godfrey, darling, it's Bomber – your son.'

Godfrey peered at Bomber over the top of his spectacles and shook his head.

'Rubbish! Don't you think that I'd know my own son? Can't remember this chap's name, but he's definitely my bookie.'

Eunice could see the tears welling up in Bomber's eyes as he remembered the countless times he had placed bets for his father under the strict instruction, 'Don't tell your mother.' She took Godfrey gently by the arm.

'It's a beautiful place you have here, and it's a lovely day. I wonder if you'd be kind enough to show me round the gardens?'

Godfrey smiled at her, delighted.

'It will be my pleasure, young lady. I expect my dog could do with a walk too,' he said, looking at Baby Jane with a slightly puzzled air. 'Although, I must confess, I'd almost forgotten I had him.'

Godfrey put on the hat that Grace passed to him.

'Come along, Bomber,' he said to Baby Jane, 'time to stretch our legs.'

However offended Baby Jane might have been about being mistaken for a boy dog with her master's name, she hid it well. Better than Bomber managed to hide his sadness at being mistaken for his father's bookie. Grace put her hand to his face.

'Chin up, darling. I know it's tough. Yesterday morning he sat bolt upright in bed and accused me of being Marianne Faithfull.'

Bomber smiled in spite of himself. 'Come on, Ma. We'd best follow them before they get into mischief.'

Outside, the vapour trail of a plane was scrawled across the blue sky like the knobbled spine of a prehistoric animal. Folly's End House sadly had no folly, but it did have very beautiful and extensive gardens for its residents to enjoy. Grace and Godfrey had moved in just over three months ago, when it became clear that Godfrey's reason had set sail for faraway climes, and Grace could no longer cope with him alone. He occasionally took a brief shore leave in reality, but for the most part the old Godfrey had jumped ship. Folly's End was the perfect harbour. They had their own rooms, but help was on hand when they needed it.

Godfrey strolled arm in arm with Eunice in the sunshine, greeting everyone they met with a smile.

Baby Jane ran ahead. When she stopped for a wee, Godfrey shook his head and tutted.

'I do wish that dog would learn to cock his leg. Next thing we know, he'll be wearing lilac and singing show tunes.'

They stopped at a wooden bench by an ornamental fish pond and sat down. Baby Jane stood right at the edge of the pond, fascinated by the flashes and swirls of silver and gold as the koi carp gathered in hope of food.

'Don't even think about it,' Eunice warned. 'It's not sushi.'

As Grace and Bomber caught up with them, Godfrey was telling Eunice all about the other residents.

'We've got Mick Jagger, Peter Ustinov, Harold Wilson, Angela Rippon, Elvis Presley, Googie Withers and Mrs Johnson who used to run the laundrette in Stanley Street. And you'll never guess who I woke up in bed with the other morning.'

Eunice shook her head, agog. Godfrey paused for a moment and then shook his head sadly.

'No, and neither will I. I had it a moment ago, and now it's gone.'

'You told me it was Marianne Faithfull,' said Grace, trying to be helpful. Godfrey laughed out loud.

'Now that, I think I would remember,' he said, winking at Bomber. 'By the by, have you placed my bet yet?'

Before Bomber could answer, Eunice directed his attention to a distant figure wearing enormous sunglasses and vertiginous heels, teetering in their direction.

'Oh God!' moaned Bomber. 'What on earth does she want?'

It took Portia some while to reach them across the lawn, and Eunice watched her precarious progress with quiet amusement. Baby Jane had jumped, unbidden, into Godfrey's lap and was warming up her growl. Godfrey watched Portia's approach with only mild curiosity and no sign of recognition whatsoever.

'Hello, Mummy! Hello, Daddy!' Portia crowed without enthusiasm. Godfrey looked behind himself to see who she was talking to.

'Portia,' began Bomber gently, 'he doesn't always remember . . .' Before he could finish she had squashed herself next to Godfrey on the bench and tried to take his hand. Baby Jane growled a warning and Portia leapt to her feet.

'Oh, for pity's sake. Not that vicious dog again!'

Godfrey clutched Baby Jane protectively. 'Don't you speak about my dog like that, young woman. Who are you anyway? Go away at once, and leave us in peace!'

Portia was livid. She had driven twenty miles from London with a banging hangover and got lost three times on the way. And she was missing Charlotte's 'designer bags and belts' brunch.

'Don't be so bloody ridiculous, Daddy. You know damn well that I'm your daughter. Just because I'm not here every five minutes sucking up to you like your precious bloody son and his pathetic, lovelorn sidekick. You know bloody well who I am!' she fumed.

Godfrey was unmoved.

'Young woman,' he said, looking at her scarlet face, 'you have clearly been out in the sun without a hat for far too long and have taken leave of your senses. No daughter of mine would use such language or behave in such an abhorrent manner. And this man is my bookie.'

'And what about her?' Portia sneered, pointing at Eunice.

Godfrey smiled. 'This is Marianne Faithfull.'

Grace managed to persuade Portia to go inside with her for a drink. Bomber, Eunice, Godfrey and Baby Jane continued on their stroll around the gardens. Under one of the apple trees, a small table was laid for tea and an elegant elderly lady sat drinking from a cup and saucer with a younger woman who was eating a lemon curd tart.

'They're my favourite,' she announced, as they said 'hello' in passing. 'Would you like one?' She offered them the glass cake stand. Bomber and Eunice declined, but Godfrey helped himself. Baby Jane personified dejection. The elderly lady smiled and said to her companion, 'Eliza, I think you have forgotten someone.' Baby Jane got two.

Back in the main house, they found Grace alone.

'Where's Portia?' Bomber asked.

'Taken herself back to London in high dudgeon, I shouldn't wonder,' said Grace. 'I tried to reason with her, but . . .' She shrugged sadly.

'I don't understand how she can behave so appallingly,' said Bomber.

Grace glanced over to where Godfrey was chatting to Eunice, to make sure that he was out of earshot.

'I think I can.' Grace took Bomber's arm and led him over to the sofa.

'I remember when she was very young.' She sighed sadly, summoning the memory of her small daughter with a gap-toothed smile and uneven pigtails. 'She always was her daddy's little girl.'

Bomber took her hand and squeezed it.

'And now she's losing him,' Grace continued, 'and perhaps for the first time in her adult life, she's faced with something that her money can't fix. Her heart is breaking and she can do nothing about it.'

'Except hurt those who love her,' replied Bomber crossly.

Grace patted his knee. 'She simply doesn't know how to cope. She left here in floods of tears, having called her darling daddy a wicked old trout.'

Bomber gave his mother a hug. 'Never mind, Ma, you've always got your "precious bloody son".'

Just as they were leaving, Godfrey beckoned Eunice over to his side.

'A word in your ear,' he winked conspiratorially at her and lowered his voice. 'Pretty damn sure that woman *was* my daughter. But there have to be some consolations for having this ruddy awful disease.'

31

According to Sunshine, Laura had had Freddy on a 'sleepover'. But Laura had not *had* Freddy on a 'sleepover'. She had slept with him, in the same bed, but she had not *slept* with him. Laura smiled to herself at how peculiarly British it was, using the same words for different meanings but still not actually saying what you mean. Sex. She had not had sex with Freddy. Yet. There. In the space of a few sentences she had gone from innuendo to intercourse!

On Christmas night, she and Freddy had danced and drunk champagne and talked. And talked and talked. She had told him all about school and tray cloths and Vince. She told him about the baby she had lost, and he had held her close, and she told him about the short stories that she had written for *Feathers, Lace and Fantasy Fiction* and he laughed until he cried. He had told her about his ex-fiancée, Heather – a recruitment consultant who wanted marriage and children, and he didn't. At least, not with her. He had also told her why he'd sold his small IT consultancy (much to Heather's consternation and the final wheel to fall off their relationship) to become a gardener. He'd got sick of watching the world through a window instead of living outside in it. Laura finally told him about Graham and their disastrous date, and after some hesitation and another glass of champagne, she even told him about the kiss.

He grinned. 'Well at least you haven't rushed upstairs yet to swill your mouth out, so I'll take that as a good sign. And I hope you kept that dress!'

He was quiet for a moment. 'I was too embarrassed to kiss a girl until I was seventeen because of this,' he said, lightly touching the scar that ran onto his mouth. 'I was born with a cleft lip, and the surgeon's needlework wasn't the neatest . . .'

Laura leaned forward and kissed him softly on the mouth.

'Well, it certainly doesn't seem to hamper your technique now.'

Freddy told her all about Felicity, a blind date set up by a woman whose garden he'd been working on for several years. She swore they'd get on 'like a house on fire'. They didn't, but Felicity was one of the woman's closest friends, so Freddy carried on seeing her whilst trying to work out a dignified escape route.

'One night, I couldn't face any more of her bragging and braying and calling me bloody Freddo, so I just stood her up. Not very dignified, I know, but damned effective as it turned out. I lost my client, but it was worth it.'

Finally, when Freddy and Laura had run out of words, they took comfort in each other's arms, sleeping furled around one another like petals in a bud.

They slept in the guest bedroom next to Therese's old room. The day Laura woke to find the drawers emptied onto the floor, she had moved her things into the room next door. She wasn't afraid, exactly. Or perhaps she was, a little. She had a horrible feeling that there was, if not a spectre, then an uninvited guest at her feast. A soup spoon was missing; one of the table legs was too short; one of the champagne cocktails was flat; one of the second violins was sharp. A sliver of disharmony jangled Padua and Laura had no idea what she should do to restore peace. Carrot would never go into Therese's bedroom, but he was perfectly happy to abandon his place by the fire on Christmas night to nestle at their feet on the bed where Freddy and Laura slept.

When Sunshine found out about the 'sleepover' she wanted to know all the details. Whose pyjamas did Freddy wear; how did he clean his teeth without his toothbrush; did he snore? And did they kiss? Freddy told her that he had borrowed one of Laura's nighties, cleaned his teeth with soap and a flannel, and no, he didn't snore, but Laura did – enough to rattle the windows. And yes. They had kissed. Sunshine wanted to know if Freddy was any better at kissing now and he told her that he'd been having lessons. Laura had never seen Sunshine laugh so hard, but how much of it she believed was difficult to guess. How much of it she would repeat when she got home wasn't.

It was New Year's Eve and still very early. The guest room also had a view of the rose garden, but this morning it was barely visible through the driving rain. Freddy would be here later. They were going out this evening to join the celebrations at the local pub. But in the meantime, Laura was drawn inexorably to the study. Armed with enough toast for both of them and a pot of tea, Laura went into the study followed by Carrot and lit the fire. She took a small box down from its shelf and laid the contents on the table. Outside, it was raining harder than ever, and the sound of running water played counterpoint to the spit and crackle of the fire. For the first time Laura held in her hand an object she could not name, and even after reading its label, she was no wiser as to its purpose or origin.

Wooden house, painted door and windows, no. 32.
Found in a skip outside no.32 Marley Street, 23 October . . .

Edna peered at the young man's identity card. He said he was from the Water Board, come to check all the plumbing and the pipes. It was just a courtesy call. They were doing it for all their customers over seventy before the winter set in, he said. Edna was seventy-eight and she needed her reading glasses to see what was on the card. Her son, David, was always telling her to be extra careful about opening the door to strangers. 'Always keep the chain on until you know who they are,' he warned. The trouble was that with the chain on she could only open the door a crack, and then she was too far away from it to read the card. Even with her reading glasses on. The young man smiled patiently. He looked right. He was wearing a smart pair of overalls with a badge on the right-hand chest pocket, and was carrying a black plastic tool box. The identity card had a photo that looked like him, and she thought that she could just about make out the words 'Thames' and 'Water'. She let him in. She didn't want him thinking that she was a foolish, helpless old woman.

'Would you like a cup of tea?' she asked.

He smiled gratefully. 'You're a diamond and no mistake. I'm proper parched. The last brew I had was at seven o'clock this morning. Milk and two sugars and I'm a happy man.'

She directed him to the downstairs lavatory and then upstairs to the bathroom and airing cupboard on the landing which housed the water tank. In the kitchen, she put the kettle on and as she waited for it to boil, she looked out at the long strip of back garden. Edna had lived in her east London terrace for nearly sixty years. She and Ted had moved in when they got married. They had brought up their kids here, and by the time David and his sister Diane had grown up and left home, it was bought and paid for. Of course, they could never have afforded it now. Edna was the only one left from the old days. One by one, the houses had been bought up, tarted up and their prices hiked up as high as a tom's skirt, as her Ted would have said. These days, the street was full of young professionals with flash cars, fondue sets and more money than they knew what to waste it on. Not like the old days, when kids played in the street and you knew all your neighbours and their business.

The young man found his way back into the kitchen just as Edna was pouring the tea.

'Just how I like it,' he said, gulping it down. He seemed to be in a hurry. 'Everything's shipshape upstairs.'

He took a quick look under the sink in the kitchen and then rinsed his mug under the tap. Edna was impressed. He was a good boy like her David. His mum had obviously brought him up well.

Early that afternoon, the doorbell rang again. Two visitors in one day was almost unheard of. The crack revealed a small, smartly dressed black woman who appeared to be somewhere in her sixties. She was wearing a navy blue suit with a blouse so white it dazzled. Perched on her concrete-set coiffure of brandy snap curls sat a navy blue hat with a wisp of spotted net that just covered the top half of her face. Before either of them could speak, the woman appeared to buckle at the knees and clutched at the door frame to prevent herself from falling. Moments later, she was *sitting in Edna's kitchen, fanning her face with her hand and apologising profusely in a rich Jamaican accent.*

'I'm so sorry, my dear. It's just one of my funny turns. The doctor says it's to do with my sugars.' She lurched forward in her chair and almost fell off it before recovering herself.

'I feel so bad imposing myself on you like this.'

Edna flapped away her apologies.

'What you need is a hot, sweet cup of tea,' she said, filling the kettle once again. To be honest, she was glad of the company. The woman introduced herself as Sister Ruby. She was knocking on doors offering her skills as a spiritual healer, reader and advisor. She told Edna that she could read palms, cards and crystals, and was a practitioner of Obeah, Jadoo and Juju. Edna had no idea about Obadiah, Jedi or Judy, but she had always been fascinated by fortune tellers and the like, and was deeply superstitious. Hers was a house where new shoes were never put on the table, umbrellas were never opened indoors and nobody crossed on the stairs. Her Irish grandmother had read tea leaves for all the neighbours, and one of her aunts made her living as Madame Petulengra, giving crystal ball readings on Brighton Pier. When Sister Ruby, revived by her tea, offered to read Edna's palm, she was only too willing. Sister Ruby took Edna's hand, palm upwards, in her own, and passed her other hand over it several times. She then spent a full minute studying the crinkled topography of Edna's palm.

'You have two children,' she said, at last. 'A boy and a girl.'

Edna nodded.

'Your husband passed . . . eight years ago. He had a pain, here.' Sister Ruby clutched at her chest with her free hand. Ted had died of a heart attack on the way home from the pub. Family flowers only, but donations, if desired, to the British Heart Foundation. Sister Ruby tipped Edna's hand this way and that, as though she were trying to decipher a particularly complex message.

'You are worried about your home,' she finally announced.

'You want to stay, but someone wants you to leave. It's a man. Is it your son? No.' She peered closely at Edna's hand and then leaned back and closed her eyes as though trying to picture the man in question. Suddenly she sat bolt upright and slapped her hands flat on the table.

'He is a businessman! He wants to buy your house!'

Over a second cup of tea and a newly opened packet of Bourbons, Edna told Sister Ruby all about Julius Winsgrave, property developer, entrepreneur and sleazy, greedy gobshite (except she didn't use the word 'gobshite' what with Ruby being a Sister and all). He had been trying to get her to sell for years, having bought most of the other houses in the street and made a killing on them. In the end, his bully-boy tactics had forced David to consult his solicitor and take out an injunction against Julius to prevent any further harassment. But Edna always felt the threat of him circling above like a vulture, waiting for her to die.

Sister Ruby listened carefully. 'He sounds like a bad and dangerous man.'

She reached down and picked up her capacious, well-used handbag and began rifling through its contents.

'I have something here that can definitely help you.'

She placed on the table a small, flat piece of wood in the shape of the front of a house. It was crudely painted with four windows and a blue front door. The same colour as Edna's.

'What number is your house, please?' Sister Ruby asked.

'Thirty-two.'

Sister Ruby took a pen from her bag and drew a large '32' on the front door of the house.

'Now,' she said, 'this is the most powerful Juju and it will protect you as long as you do exactly as I say.'

She held the house tightly in both hands and closed her eyes. Her lips worked furiously in silent incantation for several minutes before she finally placed the house in the centre of the kitchen table.

'Here it must stay,' she said decisively. 'This is the centre of your home and from here it will protect you. But you must know that now this house,' she said, pointing to the wooden model, 'has become your house. All the while you keep it safe, so too will your house be safe. But if you allow harm to come to it, the same and more will come to the bricks and mortar around you; whether it be fire, water, breaking, whatever. Nothing can undo the magic and nothing can undo the curse.'

Edna looked at the little wooden house and wondered if it could really protect her from Julius Winsgrave. Well, it certainly couldn't do any harm to try it. Sister Ruby took her cup and saucer to the sink, and despite Edna's protests, washed them thoroughly before setting them on the draining board to dry. As Edna turned her back to put the biscuits in their tin, Sister Ruby shook a wet hand over the wooden house and three drops of water splashed onto its painted facade.

'There now,' she said, picking up her bag. 'I've taken up quite enough of your time.'

Edna was searching for her purse, but Sister Ruby refused to take any payment for her services.

'It was a pleasure chatting with you,' she said, as she made her way towards the front door.

As the make-up came off, the face in the mirror grew younger. Under the fat curls of the wig was black hair, ironed straight. In jeans, boots and a leopard-print coat, Sister Ruby disappeared into Simone La Salle. She checked her designer watch and grabbed her designer bag. At the restaurant, Julius was already waiting; drumming his fingers impatiently on the immaculate linen tablecloth.

'*Champagne, please,*' *she told the passing waiter in confident Estuary English.*

Julius raised his eyebrows. 'Do you deserve it?'

Simone smiled. 'What do you think?' she said. 'It went like clockwork. My boy went this morning and sorted the stopcock. As luck would have it, the bathroom was directly above the kitchen.' She checked her watch again. 'The kitchen ceiling should be down by now.'

Julius smiled. 'Mother and son make a good team.'

He pushed a fat brown envelope across the table. Simone checked the contents and then slid it into her bag. The waiter brought the champagne and filled both their glasses. Julius made the toast.

'*It's been a pleasure doing business with you.*'

After seeing Sister Ruby out, Edna went for a little lie-down on the sofa. Two visitors in one day were lovely but a little tiring. When she woke about an hour later it was raining. In the kitchen. The wooden house on the table was soaked. The paint had run and the windows had all but washed away, but the number 32 was still plainly visible. Edna looked up and saw a dark patch creeping horribly across the ceiling. The last thing she heard was the groan of lathe and plaster surrendering.

'Okay! Okay! I surrender.' Laura stroked the warm head that had been gently butting her knee for the last five minutes. Carrot was hungry and he needed a wee. It was long past lunchtime. Laura surveyed the sea of objects dotted with gold stars in front of her on the table and then checked her watch. It was nearly three o'clock.

'Poor Carrot,' she said. 'I bet you've been keeping your legs crossed.'

It was still pouring with rain, but fortunately Carrot had been given (amongst a great many other things) a waterproof coat for Christmas. He trotted out into the garden whilst Laura made their lunch. He was soon back, padding a pattern of wet paw prints across the floor tiles. After lunch, Laura went upstairs to decide on her outfit for that evening. She embarrassed herself with how long it took to choose appropriate under-wear. Appropriately inappropriate. Searching for a favourite pair of earrings, she wondered if she might have left them in Therese's bedroom and went to look. She turned the cold brass doorknob. The door was locked. From the inside.

32

Freddy poked Carrot with his toe from underneath the bedcovers.

'Get up, you lazy hound, and go and make us a cup of tea.'

Carrot snuggled deeper into his duvet nest and groaned contentedly. Freddy looked at Laura pleadingly and she promptly hid her head under the pillow.

'I suppose it's down to me then,' he said, hopping out of bed and searching for something to put on for the sake of warmth rather than modesty. Laura's dressing gown was hardly fit for purpose but conveniently to hand. Freddy threw open the curtains onto a new year and a blue sky and sunshine day. Laura stretched out, naked under the warm covers, and wondered if she had time to nip to the bathroom and make herself look a little more presentable, a little less middle-aged. But then, what was the point? Freddy had already seen her. Laura raked through her hair with her fingers and checked in the small mirror on the bedside table to see if she had any of last night's mascara smudged underneath her eyes. At least she had nice teeth.

It was a full two hours later before they were up, dressed and eating beans on toast when Sunshine arrived. They had promised her that if it was a nice day, they would all take Carrot for a walk on the nearby common. Laura and Freddy strolled arm in arm as Sunshine ran ahead with Carrot, throwing a ball-on-a-rope (another Christmas present) for him to retrieve.

'I get the distinct impression that young Carrot is only going along with this for Sunshine's amusement rather than his own,' said Freddy.

Laura watched as Carrot dutifully returned the ball to Sunshine only to have her fling it away in a random direction and command that he 'fetch!'

'I suspect that he'll only play along for so long before he finds something more interesting to do.'

Sure enough, after the very next throw, Carrot watched as the ball descended into a gorse bush and then wandered off to look for rabbits. Poor Freddy was designated by Sunshine as Carrot's second and was soon elbow deep in gorse spines.

'Leave it,' said Laura, as Freddy risked multiple puncture wounds. 'We'll get him another one.'

'No!' wailed Sunshine. 'It was the Christmas present to him. He'll be really upsetted and he'll hate me because I can't throw straight in a line because I'm a ming-mong.'

Sunshine was close to tears.

'You most certainly are not a ming-mong!' said Freddy, finally surfacing from the depths of the gorse bush, triumphantly waving the ball-on-a-rope. 'Who on earth called you that?'

'That's what Nicola Crow used to call me at school when I dropped the ball in rounders.'

'Well, Nicola Crow was an ignoramus and you, young lady, are dancing drome. And don't you forget it.'

He handed her the toy, smoothing away the pain from her face. But a smile was still too much to hope for. Tired of rabbits and having missed all the drama, Carrot wandered back and sniffed at his toy. Then he licked Sunshine's hand. The price of a smile.

As they walked on, Laura now holding Carrot's toy for safekeeping and Freddy inspecting his wounds, Sunshine pounced on a small, shiny object trodden into the grass.

'Look,' she said, digging it out of the mud with her fingers.

'What is it?' Freddy took it from her and rubbed the dirt away. It was a brass key ring in the shape of a baby elephant.

'We should take it home,' said Sunshine. 'We should write it a label and put it on the webside.'

'Don't you think that we've got more than enough lost things already?' said Laura, picturing the study crammed with things still waiting on shelves or in boxes for their gold stars. But Freddy agreed with Sunshine.

'Listen, I've been thinking about how we get people interested in the website. Putting all the stuff on there is only half the job. Getting the right people to look at it is the other. Now, Anthony's is a great story, and I'm sure we'll be able to get the local press, maybe even radio and television interested, but if we have some really recent things that have been lost and found as well as all the old stuff, I think it could really help.'

And what really helped Laura was that Freddy had said 'we'. She was no longer facing Anthony's daunting legacy alone; she had help. Help that she had been too proud or too afraid to ask for.

Back at Padua Sunshine went straight to the study to find a label for the key ring. They had all been invited to tea by Sunshine's mum and dad, but she was determined to have the label written and the key ring on a shelf or in a box before they left. Laura went upstairs to get changed and Freddy rubbed the worst of the mud from Carrot's feet and legs with an old towel in the kitchen. On the way past, Laura tried the door handle of Therese's room. It was still locked. Back in the kitchen, she wrote a label for the key ring under Sunshine's watchful eye.

'Sunshine?'

'Umm?' She was concentrating hard to make out what Laura was writing.

'You know the other day when you said that The Lady of the Flowers was upset?'

'Yep.'

Laura put the pen down and blew on the wet ink. As soon as she put the label down, Sunshine picked it up and blew on it some more. Just to be sure.

'Well, do you think that she's upset with me?'

Sunshine adopted her 'how can you be so stupid?' expression and stance, which involved rolling her eyes, huffing and jamming her hands onto her hips.

'She's not upsetted with just you' – the 'of course' was understood – 'she's upsetted with everyone.'

That was not an answer that Laura was expecting. If she believed what Sunshine was saying (and the jury were still having a latte break on that one), then she was relieved not to be the sole target of Therese's anger, but was still absolutely none the wiser as to what she could do to appease her.

202

'But why is she angry?'

Sunshine shrugged. She had lost interest in Therese for the moment and was looking forward to her tea. She studied her watch. She could do all of the 'o'clocks' and most of the 'half pasts', and anything in between became a 'nearly'.

'It's nearly four o'clock,' she said, 'and tea's at four o'clock on the spot.' She went and stood by the door. 'This morning I made fairy cakes, scones, the even lovelier mince pies and prawn folly fonts. For our tea.'

Freddy grinned. 'Which explains why you didn't get here until nearly half past eleven.' He winked at Laura and mouthed, 'Luckily for me.'

'And Dad made sausage rollovers,' said Sunshine, pulling on her coat.

33

Eunice

1991

'These sausage rolls are not a patch on Mrs Doyle's,' said Bomber, bravely soldiering on through his second. Since Mrs Doyle's retirement to a seafront flat in Margate, the bakery had been taken over by a franchise, and the handmade cakes and patisseries had been replaced with ready-made, mass-produced imitations. Eunice passed him a paper napkin as flakes of pastry fluttered down his front and into his lap.

'I'm sure Baby Jane will happily help with any leftovers,' she said, glancing across at the little pug's eager face. Baby Jane was out of luck. Despite its inferior quality, Bomber finished his lunch and did his best to redistribute the flakes of pastry he was wearing in the general direction of the wastepaper bin. Eunice had bought him two sausage rolls as a special treat, for once forsaking her concern for his health and waistline. They were going to see Grace and Godfrey later and visits to Folly's End had become increasingly difficult over the past year. She wished that there was something, anything, she could do to lessen Bomber's pain as he watched the man he once knew as his father recede inexorably towards some far distant, inaccessible horizon. Godfrey's physical health was a bitter irony cruelly yoked, as it was, to his mental fragility, leaving him like an overgrown, frightened and angry child. 'Body like a buffalo, mind like a moth' was how Grace described him. His plight was a dreadful punishment to those who loved him. To Godfrey, his friends and family were now strangers to be feared and, if possible, avoided. Any attempts at physical affection – a touch, a kiss, a hug – were met with a fist or a kick. Grace and Bomber both had the bruises to prove it. Grace was stoical as ever, but now, almost two years after they had moved to Folly's End, she no longer shared a room with her husband. These days it was only safe to love him from a distance. Portia kept her distance entirely. Her visits had stopped when the violence began.

Bomber shook his head in disbelief as he slipped a heavy manuscript from a brown envelope that had arrived with that morning's post.

'I'm sure she only does it to wind me up.'

It was his sister's latest manuscript.

'Does she send them to anyone else?' Eunice peered over his shoulder and helped herself to the synopsis sheets.

'I'm sure she does. I'm beyond embarrassment now. She definitely sent the last one to Bruce. He said he was almost tempted to publish it just to see the look on my face.'

Eunice was already engrossed in the pages she was holding, shaking with silent mirth. Bomber leaned back in his chair and tucked his hands behind his head.

'Well, come on then. Put me out of my misery.'

Eunice wagged her finger at him, grinning. 'It's funny you should say that, but I was just thinking that maybe we could get Kathy Bates to kidnap Portia, tie her to a bed in a remote woodland cabin, break both her legs thoroughly with a lump hammer, and then give her some top tips on how to write a novel.'

When they had first seen the film *Misery*, they had amused themselves over dinner afterwards by compiling a list of writers who might benefit from a term at the Kathy Bates school of creative writing. Eunice couldn't believe that they had forgotten Portia.

'Might be simpler if she just broke all her fingers, and then she wouldn't be able to write at all.'

Eunice shook her head at Bomber in mock disapproval.

'But then we would be deprived of such literary gems as this,' she said, waving the synopsis in the air. She cleared her throat and paused for dramatic effect. Baby Jane yapped at her to get on with it.

'Janine Ear is a young orphan being raised by her cruel, wealthy aunt, Mrs Weed. She is a strange child who sees ghosts, and her aunt tells everyone that she is "on drugs" and sends her to a private rehab clinic called High Wood. The owner of High Wood, Mr Bratwurst, spends all the fees on heroin, and only feeds the girls bread and lard. Janine makes friends with a kind and sensible girl called Ellen Scalding, who dies when she chokes on a crust of dry bread because there is no nominated first aider on duty and Janine doesn't know how to do the Heimlich manoeuvre.'

Eunice paused to check that Bomber wasn't in need of such assistance himself. He was convulsed with silent laughter and Baby Jane was sitting at his feet looking vaguely puzzled. Eunice waited for him to compose himself a little before continuing.

'Mr Bratwurst is sent to prison for failing to meet the requirements of the health and safety legislation, and Janine accepts the position of au pair at a stately home called Pricklefields in Pontefract, where her charge is a lively little French girl named Belle, and her employer is a dark, brooding man with hidden troubles called Mr Manchester, who shouts a lot but is kind to the servants. Janine falls in love with him. One evening, he wakes up to find that his hair is on fire and she saves his life. He proposes. The wedding day is a disaster.'

'It's not the only thing,' spluttered Bomber.

Eunice went on.

'Just as they are about to exchange their vows, a man called Mr Mason turns up claiming that Mr Manchester is already married to his sister, Bunty. Mr Manchester drags them back to Pricklefields where they witness Bunty, out of her brains on crack cocaine, crawling round the attic on all fours, snarling and growling and trying to bite their ankles, chased by her carer brandishing a syringe of ketamine. Janine packs her bag. Just as she is about to die from hypothermia wandering round on the moors, a kind, born-again Christian vicar and his two sisters find her and take her home. As luck would have it, they turn out to be her cousins, and even luckier than that, a long-lost uncle has died and left her all his money. Janine kindly shares her inheritance, but refuses to marry the vicar and join him as a missionary in Lewisham, because she now realises that Mr Manchester will always be the love of her life. She returns to Pricklefields to find that it has been burned to the ground. An old lady passing by tells her that the "junkie bitch Bunty" started the fire and died dancing on the roof while it burned. Mr Manchester bravely rescued all the servants and the kitten, but was blinded by a falling beam and lost one of his ears. Now he is single again, Janine decides to give their relationship another chance, but explains to Mr Manchester that they will have to take things slowly, as she still has "trust issues". Six weeks later they marry and when their first son is born, Mr Manchester miraculously regains the sight in one eye.'

'It's comedy genius!' announced Eunice, grinning as she handed the pages back to Bomber. 'Are you sure you're not tempted to publish?'

Bomber threw a rubber which just missed her head as she ducked.

Eunice sat down at her desk and cupped her chin in her hands, lost in thought.

'Why do you think she does it?' she asked Bomber. 'I mean, she can't just do it to wind you up. It's too much effort. And anyway, knowing Portia, the joke would have worn thin by now. There has to be more to it than that. And if she wanted to, she could self-publish. She could certainly afford it.'

Bomber shook his head sadly. 'I think that she genuinely wants to be good at something. Unfortunately, she's just picked the wrong thing. For all her money and so-called friends, I expect that hers is a pretty empty life sometimes.'

'I think, perhaps, that it's all about you.' Eunice stood up again and strolled over to the window. She could order her thoughts better when she was moving.

'I think she wants her big brother's approval – praise, love, validation, whatever you want to call it – and she's trying to earn it through writing. She's painted herself into a corner in every other way: she's rude, selfish, shallow and sometimes downright cruel, and she'd never admit that she cares a flying fortress what you think of her, but she does. Deep down, your little sister just wants you to be proud of her, and she's chosen to write, not because she has any talent or because it gives her any joy. It's a means to an end. You are a publisher and she wants to write a book that you think good enough to publish. That's why she always "borrows" her plotlines from the classic greats.'

'But I do love her. I can't approve of the way she behaves – the way she treats Ma and Pa and the way she talks to you. But she's my sister. I'll always love her.'

Eunice came and stood behind him, and placed her hands gently on his shoulders.

'I know that. But I don't think Portia does. Poor Portia.' And for once, she meant it.

34

Laura sat on the bed, her fists clenched so tightly that her fingernails bit crescents into the flesh of her palms. She didn't know whether to be frightened or furious. Al Bowlly's voice drifted up from the garden room below, and his seductive tones were like fingernails scraping relentlessly down a blackboard.

'Well, I'm sick at the very thought of you!' she exploded and launched the book from her bedside table violently across the room. It hit one of the glass candlesticks on the dressing table, which fell to the floor and smashed.

'Bugger!'

Laura made a silent apology to Anthony. She got up and went downstairs to fetch a dustpan and brush, and to check what she knew already to be absolutely, unarguably, indubitably true. The Al Bowlly record was still in its faded paper cover, in the middle of the table in the study. She had put it there herself only yesterday, sick of hearing the tune which now haunted her, quite literally, day and night. She had hoped, rather foolishly now it seemed, that if she physically removed the record from the vicinity of the gramophone player it would stop. But Therese didn't have to play by those rules; physical rules. Her death had seemingly dispensed with such prosaic constraints, and she was free to make mischief in many more imaginative ways. And who or what else could it be? Anthony had been unfailingly kind to her while he was alive, so it was unlikely that he would take up such petty persecutions now he was dead. After all, Laura had done or was trying to do everything that he had asked of her. She picked up the record and looked at the smiling face of the man on the cover, with his slick black hair and his sultry dark eyes.

'You have no idea,' she told him, shaking her head. She put the record in a drawer and leaned back against it with all her weight as though to emphasise its closing. As if that would make any difference. She had told Freddy about the door to Therese's room and asked him to see if he could get it open. He had tried the handle and declared the door to be locked, but then said that he didn't think they should do anything about it.

'She'll unlock it when she's ready,' he had said, as though he were talking about a naughty child being left to exhaust a tantrum. Both Freddy and Sunshine seemed to accept Therese with an equanimity that Laura found infuriating. The troublesome presence of someone who was definitely dead and scattered in the garden should surely cause some consternation? Particularly as she should, by now, and thanks to their efforts, be existing somewhere in a state of postnuptial – although admittedly post-mortem – bliss. It was damned ungrateful. Laura smiled to herself ruefully. But who else could it be except Therese? Where reason fails, chimera flourishes. Just as she was finishing sweeping up the shards of broken glass, she heard Freddy and Carrot coming in from their walk.

Downstairs in the kitchen over tea and toast, she told Freddy about the music.

'Oh, that,' he said, feeding bits of buttered toast to Carrot. 'I've heard it too, but I never take much notice. I never know whether it's Sunshine or not.'

'I took the record away, but it made no difference, so now I've put it in a drawer in the study.'

'Why?' said Freddy, stirring sugar into his tea.

'Why did I take it away, or why did I put it in the drawer?'

'Both.'

'Because it's driving me mad. I took it away so that she couldn't play it any more.'

'Who? Sunshine?'

'No.' Laura paused for a moment, reluctant to say it out loud. 'Therese.'

'Ah. Our resident ghost. So, you took it away, which didn't work, and you thought that shutting it in a drawer might?'

'Not really. But it made me feel better. I keep wondering what else she might do. Why is she being such a bloody prima donna? She's got Anthony now, so what's the problem with me having the house? It's what he wanted.'

Freddy sipped his tea, frowning as he mulled over her question. 'Remember what Sunshine said. She said that Therese wasn't cross with you, she was cross with everyone. Her ire is indiscriminate. So it isn't about the house. Did anything like this ever happen while Anthony was still alive?'

'Not as far as I know. There's always been that scent of roses in the house, and a vague sense that Therese was still about, but I never saw or heard anything definite. And Anthony didn't mention anything.'

'So it's only since Anthony died that madam's started playing up?'

'Yes. But that's what's so wrong about it. I always assumed that she'd been waiting for him somewhere in the ether or wherever for all these years, practising her foxtrot or painting her nails . . .'

Freddy wagged his finger at her, gently admonishing the catty tone that had crept into her voice.

'I know, I know. I'm being horrid,' Laura laughed at herself. 'But honestly, what more does she want? She should be happy now she's got him back. Instead she's hanging around here misbehaving, like a disgruntled diva; deceased.'

Freddy put his hand over hers and squeezed it. 'I know it's unsettling. She's certainly a bit of a live wire—'

'Especially for someone who's supposed to be dead,' interrupted Laura.

Freddy grinned. 'I think you two might have got on rather well. From what Anthony told me about her, I reckon you're more alike than you realise.'

'He talked to you about Therese?'

'Sometimes, yes. Especially towards the end.' He drained his mug and refilled it from the teapot. 'But maybe we're missing something here. We're assuming that, just because Anthony's dead and we scattered him in the same place where he scattered Therese, they must be together. But are the ashes really what matters? Aren't they just "remains"; what's left behind when the person is gone? Anthony and Therese are both dead, but maybe they're not together and that's the problem. If you and I both went to London separately and didn't arrange a place to meet, what would be the likelihood of us ever finding one another? And let's face it, wherever it is that they've gone has to be a whole hell of a lot bigger than London, bearing in mind all the dead people who will have pitched up there since . . . well, since people started dying.'

Freddy leaned back in his chair, looking rather pleased with himself and his explanation. Laura sighed and slumped back in her own chair despondently.

'So what you're saying is that Therese is actually worse off now than before he died, because at least then she knew where he was? Well that's just marvellous. We could be stuck with her for years. Forever. Bugger!'

Freddy came and stood behind her and placed his hands gently on her shoulders. 'Poor Therese. I think you should put the record back in the garden room.'

He kissed the top of her head and went out to work in the garden. Suddenly Laura felt guilty. It was probably all nonsense, but just supposing it wasn't? She had Freddy now, but what if, after all this time, Therese still didn't have Anthony?

Poor Therese.

Laura got up and went to the study. She fetched the record from the drawer and took it back to the garden room, where she placed it on the table next to the gramophone player. Picking up the photograph of Therese, she gazed at the woman, now blurred and distant behind splintered glass. She saw, perhaps for the first time, the person behind the paper picture.

Freddy might think that they were alike, but Laura could see the differences. She had already lived fifteen years longer than Therese, but she had no doubt that Therese had lived her short life harder, brighter, faster than Laura ever had. What a waste.

Laura gently ran her fingertips over the face behind the cruel mosaic. What was it that Sarah had said? 'It's time to stop hiding and start kicking life up the arse.'

'I'll get you fixed,' she promised Therese.

Then she took up the record again and placed it on the turntable. 'Play nicely,' she said out loud to the room. 'I'm trying to be on your side.'

35

Eunice

1994

Eunice would never forget the scent of sun-warmed roses wafting in through the open window as she sat with Bomber and Grace watching Godfrey die. He was almost gone now. Just a worn-out body remained, barely ticking over, breaths too shallow to lift even a butterfly's wings. The fear and anger and confusion that had racked his last years had finally relinquished their tyranny over Godfrey and left him in peace. Grace and Bomber were able, at last, to hold his hands, and Baby Jane snuggled in close to him with her head gently resting on his chest. They had long since stopped trying to make conversation to fill the uncomfortable space between dying and death itself. Every now and then, a nurse would knock softly on the door, bringing tea and unspoken sympathy to a closing scene she had witnessed countless times before.

Eunice got up and went over to the window. Outside, the afternoon was passing by without them. People were strolling in the gardens or snoozing in the shade, and a group of children were chasing one another across the lawns, squealing with delight. Somewhere, high in one of the trees, a thrush was scatting against the metro-nome tick of a sprinkler. Now would be a good time, she thought. To slip away on the coat-tails of a perfect English summer's afternoon. It seemed that Grace was in accord. She leaned back in her chair and exhaled a long sigh of resignation. Keeping hold of Godfrey's hand she struggled to her feet, grudging joints stiff from too long sitting. She kissed Godfrey on the mouth and stroked his hair with a frail but steady hand.

'It's time, my love. It's time to let go.'

Godfrey stirred, but just barely. Translucent eyelids fluttered and his weary chest rose for one final ragged breath. And then he was gone. Nobody moved except Baby Jane. The little dog stood and with infinite care, she sniffed every inch of Godfrey's face. Finally satisfied that her friend was gone, she jumped down from the bed, shook herself thoroughly and sat down at Bomber's feet, looking up at him beseechingly with an expression that clearly said, 'And now I really need a wee.'

An hour later they were sitting in what was called the 'relatives' room' drinking yet more tea. The relatives' room was the place where the Folly's End staff gently shepherded people once they were ready to leave the newly deceased. Its walls were the colour of faded prim-roses and the light was soft through muslin curtains, hung as a veil from prying eyes. With sofas plush and deep, fresh flowers and boxes of tissues, it was a room designed to cushion the sharp edges of raw grief.

After a few initial tears, Grace had rallied and was ready to talk. In truth, she had lost the man she married long ago, and now, with his death, at least she could begin to mourn. Bomber was pale but composed, dabbing at the tears that occasionally leaked silently down his face. Before they had left Godfrey's room he had kissed his father's cheek for the final time. He had then removed Godfrey's wedding ring from his finger for the first time since Grace had placed it there a life-time ago. The gold was scratched and worn, the circle a little misshapen; a testament to a long and robust marriage where love was rarely voiced, but manifest every day. Bomber had handed the ring to his mother who slipped it onto her middle finger without a word. Then he had telephoned Portia.

Grace came and sat next to Bomber and took his hand.

'Now, son, while we wait for your sister, I have some-thing to say. You probably won't want me to talk about this, but I'm your mother and I have to say my piece.'

Eunice had no idea what was coming, but offered to leave them in private.

'No, no, my dear. I'm sure Bomber won't mind you hearing this, and I'd rather like you to back me up on this one if you don't mind.'

Eunice sat back down, intrigued. Baby Jane, who was sitting on the sofa next to Bomber, crawled onto his lap, as though to lend moral support.

'Right-ho. Here goes.' Grace squeezed her son's hand and gave it a little shake.

'Darling, I've always known since you were a little boy that you were never going to be the sort of chap who got married and provided me with any grandchil-dren. I think that, secretly, your father knew that too, but of course we never spoke about it. Now, I want you to know that I don't give a jot about any of that. I've always been proud to have you as my son, and as long as you're happy and leading a decent life, well, that's all that matters.'

Bomber's cheeks were growing very pink, although whether it was his tears or Grace's words that were to blame Eunice couldn't tell. She was deeply moved by Grace's sentiments, but fighting a fit of the giggles at her peculiarly British way of trying to say something without *actually* saying it.

'Last week, Jocelyn took me to the cinema. It was supposed to be a little treat, to take my mind off your father for a bit.' There was the tiniest catch in Grace's voice, but she swallowed hard and carried on.

'We didn't pay too much attention to what was on; just bought the tickets and some mint imperials and went and sat down.'

Baby Jane wriggled in Bomber's lap to get comfortable. This was taking a little longer than she had expected.

'The film was *Philadelphia* with that nice Tom Hanks, Paul Newman's wife and that Spanish fellow.'

She thought carefully about her next words and finally settled upon: 'It wasn't very cheerful.'

She paused, hoping perhaps that she had said enough, but the puzzled expression on Bomber's face forced her to continue. She sighed.

'I just want you to promise me that you'll be careful. If you find a "special friend" or' – the thought clearly just occurring to her – 'you have one already, just promise me that you won't get Hives.'

Eunice bit down hard on her lip, but Bomber couldn't hold back a smile.

'It's HIV, Ma.'

But Grace wasn't listening. She just wanted to hear him promise.

'I couldn't bear to lose you as well.'

Bomber promised. 'Cross my heart and hope to die.'

36

'It wasn't me, I promise,' said Sunshine.

They had come into the study to put some more things onto the website, and had found Anthony's treasured fountain pen lying in a pool of black ink in the middle of the table. It was a handsome Conway Stewart and Sunshine had admired it many times, lovingly stroking its shiny scarlet and black surface before reluctantly returning it to its drawer.

Laura saw the worried look on Sunshine's serious face and gave her a reassuring hug.

'I know it wasn't, sweetheart.'

She asked Sunshine to rinse the pen carefully under the tap and then put it back where it belonged while she cleaned up the mess on the table. When Laura returned to the study after washing her ink-stained hands, Sunshine was busy choosing more things from the shelves.

'It was The Lady of the Flowers, wasn't it?' she asked Laura.

'Oh, I don't know about that,' Laura bluffed. 'Perhaps I left it there and forgot about it, and somehow it leaked.'

She knew how unlikely it sounded, and the expression on Sunshine's face confirmed that she was completely unconvinced. Laura had been thinking about what Freddy had said, and the more she thought about it, the more concerned she became. If all these things were Therese's doing, and a physical demonstration of her pain at still being apart from Anthony, then surely the longer it went on, the worse it would get? She remembered Robert Quinlan's description of Therese as having 'a wild streak, and a fiery temper when roused'. Good God, at this rate she'd soon be setting fires and smashing up the place, and Laura was already a little tired of clearing up after a grumpy ghost.

'We should try and help her,' said Sunshine.

Laura sighed, slightly shamed by Sunshine's generosity of spirit. 'I agree. But how on earth do we do that?'

Sunshine shrugged her shoulders, her face crumpling into a perplexed frown. 'Why don't we ask her?' she eventually suggested.

Laura didn't want to be unkind, but it was hardly a practical suggestion. She wasn't about to hold a séance or buy a Ouija board on eBay. They spent the rest of the morning adding things to the website while Carrot snored contentedly in front of the fire.

After lunch, Sunshine and Freddy took Carrot for a walk, but Laura stayed behind. She was thoroughly unsettled. Normally the task of entering data onto the website was a therapeutic distraction, but not today. She could only think about Therese. Like a creature whose fur has been brushed against the nap, her skin prickled and her thoughts skimmed and zigzagged like a water boatman across the surface of a pond. She needed to do something about Therese. There had to be what Jerry Springer and his fellow reality TV ringmasters called 'an intervention'. If only she knew what the hell it ought to be.

Outside, gauzy sunlight seeped through clear patches in a grey marbled sky. Laura took her jacket from the hall and went out into the garden for some air. In the shed, she found Freddy's 'secret' packet of cigarettes and helped herself to one. She was only a high days and holidays smoker, really, but today she thought it might help. She wondered if Therese had smoked.

As Laura strolled aimlessly round the rose garden, puffing like a guilty schoolgirl, Sunshine's words slipped back into her head.

'Why don't we ask her?' It might not be very practical, but nothing about this whole situation was exactly run-of-the mill and there was no point in Laura trying to deal with it as though it were. So maybe Sunshine was right. If it was Therese doing all these things – and some days Laura clung on to that 'if' like a passenger on the *Titanic* to a life jacket – then leaving her to her own devices would only mean more and more trouble.

'Why don't we ask her?' Laura was embarrassed even to be considering it. But what else could she do? Put up or shut up until . . . Laura didn't want to think about the possible endings to that sentence. She took a final puff on her cigarette and then, glancing round furtively to make sure that she couldn't be seen or heard, she let her words escape out loud into the chill of the afternoon air.

'Therese,' she began, just to clarify to whom she was talking – and just in case any other ghosts happened to be listening, she joked to herself – 'you and I need to have a serious chat. Anthony was my friend, and I know how desperately he longed to be with you again. I want to help, and if I possibly can I will, but wrecking the house, locking me out of my bedroom, and keeping me awake all night with your music isn't exactly appealing to my better nature. Clearly ghostbusting isn't my area of expertise, so if you know how I can help, then you'll have to try and find a way of sharing that with me.'

Laura paused, not expecting an answer, but feeling somehow that she should leave a gap for one anyway.

'I don't have the patience for puzzles and riddles, and I'm hopeless at Cluedo,' she continued, 'so you'll have to try and make it as clear and simple as you can. Preferably without breaking or setting fire to anything . . . or anyone,' she added, under her breath.

Once again, she waited. Nothing. Except for the cooing and canoodling of two amorous pigeons on the shed roof, practising for spring. She shivered. It was getting colder.

'I meant what I said, Therese. I'll do whatever I can.'

She marched back down the garden, feeling a little foolish and in need of a cup of tea and a consoling choc-olate biscuit. Back in the kitchen, she put the kettle on and opened the biscuit tin. Inside was Anthony's pen.

37

'Well, if that's her idea of "clear and simple", I dread to think what her "cryptic" would be like.'

Laura was walking hand in hand with Freddy and they were mulling over the mystery of Anthony's pen. Carrot was trotting along in front of them, sniffing and marking his territory at alternate lamp posts. They had been to The Moon is Missing for a few drinks. Freddy had thought it might take Laura's mind off Therese for a bit, but the entire cast of *Blithe Spirit* was reliving the triumph of their first night in the bar. Marjory Wadscallop was still in full Madame Arcati hair and make-up and wasted no time in pointing out to Winnie the arrival of Laura and Freddy *together*. It had hardly been the quiet drink that Freddy had been hoping for.

'Are you sure that Sunshine put the pen back in the drawer?'

'Well, I didn't actually see her do it, but I'm sure she would have. Why? You don't think she's playing games, do you?'

Freddy smiled and shook his head.

'No, I don't. I really don't. Sunshine's probably the most honest out of all of us, including you,' he said to Carrot as he clipped the lead to his collar, ready to cross the road.

Back at Padua Laura poured them both another drink and Freddy livened up the fire that was barely smouldering in the garden room.

'Now,' said Freddy, snuggling up to Laura on the sofa, 'let's see if the wine has aroused our deductive juices.'

Laura giggled. 'That sounds positively smutty.'

Freddy raised his eyes in feigned surprise and took a swig from his glass.

'Right. Let's look at the clue again – a pen in a biscuit tin.'

'Not just any pen – Anthony's best, beloved Conway Stewart fountain pen; red and black marbled shaft with an 18-carat gold nib,' Laura added.

'Thank you, Miss Marple, but does that really help our investigation?'

'Well, it was the pen that Anthony used to write his stories.'

They sat in contemplative silence, listening to the spit and crackle of the fire. Carrot groaned blissfully as he stretched his spindly legs nearer to the hearth. Freddy nudged him with his toe.

'Watch it, mister. If you get any closer, you'll roast your toes.'

Carrot ignored him and wriggled infinitesimally nearer.

'Have you read all of Anthony's stories? Maybe the clue is in one of them.'

Laura shook her head. 'I told her I wasn't any good at clues. I specifically asked her to make it clear and simple.'

Freddy drained his glass and set it down on the floor. 'Well, maybe it *is* clear and simple to her.'

Laura resisted the temptation to point out that of course it was, because Therese already knew the answer.

'I read everything he asked me to type, obviously, and certainly all of the short stories. But that was years ago now. I can't possibly remember all of them.'

'What about that book you showed me? The collection of short stories?'

'That was only the first of several that were published. I suppose he must have kept copies of the others somewhere, but I don't remember seeing them.'

Freddy grinned. 'I bet they're in the attic.'

'Why?'

Freddy pulled the face that Sunshine always pulled when she thought that they were being particularly obtuse.

'Because that's where everyone always puts the stuff they don't know what else to do with,' he said triumphantly. 'Although if I'd had a book published, I'd have it on my bookshelf in pride of place.'

Laura thought about it for a moment.

'But he wasn't proud of all the short stories that were published. Remember, I told you? His publisher wanted insipid, simple, happy ever afters and they fell out over it in the end.'

Freddy nodded. 'I do remember. Bruce wanted lemonade and Anthony gave him absinthe.'

Laura smiled. 'You would remember that. Anything to do with alcohol . . .' she teased. 'But I suppose it's worth a try. I haven't really had a proper look in the attic, and even if the books aren't there, there might be something else.'

'Tomorrow,' said Freddy, standing up and dragging her to her feet. 'We'll look tomorrow.'

He kissed her firmly on the lips.

'Now what was that you said about being smutty . . . ?'

Laura woke with a jolt that broke her fall. Was she dreaming about falling or falling out of the dream? She could never tell. It was still dark and the silence was barely rippled by the hushed duet of Freddy and Carrot's breathing. The back of Freddy's warm hand rested on the outside of her thigh, and as her eyes grew accustomed to the dark, she could just about make out the rise and fall of his chest. She wondered what Anthony would think. She hoped he would approve; be pleased for her. After all, he had told her to be happy and she was. Mostly. She still worried about returning the lost things. The website was coming along nicely, thanks to Freddy, and though her fear of failing Anthony was deeply rooted in the fertile tract of her self-doubt, now courage grew alongside. Finally, she had found the guts to try. Therese was a constant shadow, but the general sweep of her life, the day-to-day at Padua was definitely happy. Oh, and of course she worried about Freddy. But surely that was an occupational hazard in a new relationship, particularly at her age? She worried that he hadn't yet seen the full horror of her treacherous stretch marks and her crow's feet in the unforgiving glare of the midday sun. She worried that he might not yet have noticed the insidious creep of cellulite crumpling her once pert bottom and threatening her thighs. And she was sorry, too, that Freddy had not seen her bottom at the peak of its pertness. Instead, it had been wasted on Vince. If only she had met Freddy when she was young. Younger, even. If only she had married Freddy. She smiled to herself at her foolishness and then stopped, mindful of the crow's feet, and vowed to wear enormous sunglasses and a wide-brimmed hat should she ever be foolish enough to venture outside in the sunlight again. And she wasn't even going to think about the menopause. The clue was in the name, wasn't it? But not so much a pause as a bloody great full stop as far as being remotely attractive to men was concerned. She was even breaking out in a sweat *not* thinking about it. She turned her pillow over and buried her face in the cool, fresh cotton. 'Get a grip, Laura!' she told herself. She reached for Freddy's hand and took it in her own. Instinctively he squeezed it, and Laura lay there in the darkness, blinking away the tears until eventually she drifted back to sleep.

Things always look better in the morning. It wasn't the sunlight that poked fun at Laura's imperfections, but the darkness with its looming doubts that mocked her in the sleepless spells that broke the night. After breakfast, she went out into the garden, hatless, and squinted into the morning sun. Freddy had gone into town and she was going up into the attic. She fetched the step-ladder from the shed and carted it upstairs with some difficulty. Carrot had decided to help by running up and down the stairs, barking excitedly in an attempt to ward off the invasion of the clanking, rattling metal legs that were clearly an instrument of the devil. As Laura propped the fully extended ladder against the wall, she could already hear Freddy scolding her for not waiting.

'We'll do it when I get back,' he had said.

But she was too impatient to wait. Besides, Sunshine would be here soon, and she was perfectly capable of calling an ambulance. As she pushed open the hatch into the attic, the musty smell of warm dirt and dust wafted out to greet her. She flicked on the light switch and, at once, her hand was sticky with cobwebs. Where to start? There were a few bits of old furniture, a large rug rolled into a sausage and a variety of boxes. She lifted the lids on those closest to her. They contained general household flotsam and jetsam: an unused tea service, a canteen of silver-plated cutlery and various pieces of useless but decorative china. One contained books, but as far as she could see, none had been written by Anthony. Laura made her way cautiously across the joists, stooping awkwardly under the pitch of the rafters. A child's push-along horse on wheels stood lonely in a corner next to a large brown cardboard suitcase and a box from a dress-maker in London. Laura stroked the soft teddy-bear fur of the horse's nose.

'Well, you're not staying up here,' she promised him.

The suitcase was thick with dust, but not locked, and a quick peek inside told Laura that it was probably her best hope of finding something useful or interesting. She clipped its rust-freckled fasteners shut and dragged it over to the hatch. How on earth was she going to get it down? It was heavy, and she doubted if she could manage its weight and the ladder at the same time. The answer, of course, was to wait for Freddy, but if she did that, she might just as well have waited for him before going up there. Perhaps she could just let it slide down the ladder on its own. It looked pretty robust, and from what she had seen, it didn't appear to contain anything breakable. The 'slide down the ladder' turned out to be more of a sheer drop. As Laura let it go, it crashed onto the landing with an almighty thump and an explosion of dust. Laura went back for the horse, which was light enough for her to carry down the ladder. Having given him a softer landing than the suitcase, she went back up and fetched the box from the London dress-maker.

By the time Freddy returned, the ladder was back in the shed, Sunshine was in the garden brushing the dust out of the horse, and Laura had the suitcase open on the table in the study and was going through the contents. There were several old photograph albums, with thick pages the colour of dark chocolate inter-leaved with crispy embossed tissue papers; a couple of typed manuscripts, and some letters and assorted paper-work. The albums contained the first years of Anthony's life, long before Therese. A curly-haired toddler sat, legs splayed, on a tartan rug in a summer garden. A sturdy little boy rode astride a push-along horse on a neatly clipped lawn. A gangling youth with a shy grin wore oversized shin pads and wielded a cricket bat. It was all there: a parade of seaside holidays, country picnics, birthdays, christenings, weddings and Christmases. At first they were three; but then only two. The tall, dark man, so often in uniform, disappeared from their pictures as he did from their lives. Laura carefully unhooked one of the photographs from the brown paper corners that fixed it into the album. The man stood straight-backed and proud; so very handsome in his dress uniform. His arm was wrapped fondly round the shoulder of the woman, soignée in a Schiaparelli evening gown. And between them was a little boy wearing his pyjamas. A picture-perfect happy family.

The very thought of you.

Laura could hear the music playing in her head, or perhaps it was in the garden room. She wasn't always sure these days that she could tell the difference. This was the photograph; the evening that Robert Quinlan had described when he had come to read the will. This was the last time that Anthony had seen his father. The last dance, the last kiss, the last photograph. She would put it in a silver frame beside the photograph of Therese in the garden room.

'Found anything interesting yet?'

Freddy had brought her a cup of coffee and a sandwich. He rummaged around in the suitcase beneath the papers and took out a small, velvet-covered box.

'Ah-ha! What's this? Hidden treasure?'

He flipped open the lid to reveal a white-gold ring set with an exquisite star sapphire and sparkling diamonds. He set it down in front of Laura who took it out of the box and held it up to the light. The star across the cabochon of cornflower blue was clearly visible.

'It was hers. Her engagement ring.'

'How do you know?' Freddy took it from her to inspect it more closely. 'It could have been Anthony's mother's.'

'No. It was hers, I'm sure. Therese wasn't a humdrum diamond solitaire type of woman,' she said, smiling ruefully at the thought of her own half-carat set in 9-carat gold. 'She was, by all accounts, extraordinary, like this ring.'

Freddy slipped it back into the velvet box and handed it to Laura.

'Well, it's yours now.'

Laura shook her head.

'It will never be mine.'

Freddy went outside to help Sunshine. He had promised to give the horse's wooden hooves a fresh coat of varnish. Laura continued emptying the contents of the suitcase onto the table. She found a bill of sale for fifty rose bushes: 'Albertine' x 4, 'Grand Prix' x 6, 'Marcia Stanhope', 'Mrs Henry Morse', 'Etoile de Hollande', 'Lady Gay' – the list went on – and a pamphlet on how to plant and care for them. The manuscripts were collections of Anthony's short stories that Laura had typed. As she flicked through the pages, she recognised them. Attached to the front was a harsh rejection letter from Bruce, the publisher.

'. . . entirely inappropriate for our readership . . . unnecessarily complex and self-indulgently ambiguous . . . dark and depressing subject matter . . .'

Someone had scribbled across the insulting comments with a red pen, and written 'Arse!' over Bruce's extravagant signature. It was Anthony's handwriting. 'Quite right too,' Laura agreed. She would re-read the manuscripts thoroughly later, but somehow she didn't think they would contain the answer she was looking for.

There was a rattle of metal wheels across the hall floor and Sunshine entered the study pushing the horse, followed by Freddy and a curious Carrot.

'He looks like a different horse!' Laura exclaimed, and Sunshine grinned proudly.

'He's called Sue.'

Laura looked at Freddy to see if he could provide an explanation, but he simply shrugged his shoulders.

'Sue' it was, then. Sunshine was eager to examine the contents of the suitcase and was spellbound by the ring. As she slipped it onto her middle finger, turning it this way and that to 'catch the sparkles', Laura had an idea.

'Perhaps it's the ring Therese wants us to find. Maybe that's what it's all about.'

Freddy was uncertain. 'Hmm, but what's the connection with the pen?'

Laura ignored the flaw in her argument; instead, warming to her theory, she said, 'It was her engagement ring. Don't you see? It's all about their connection, the bond between them. That's what an engagement is.'

Freddy was still doubtful. 'But so is a wedding, and that didn't work when we gave them one.'

The face that Sunshine was pulling clearly showed that not only was she totally unconvinced, but she thought that they were both being particularly obtuse once again.

'The pen was for the clue. That means writing,' she said.

She picked up the photograph of Anthony and his parents.

'That's why she plays the music,' she said, handing Freddy the picture. It was his turn to look to Laura for an explanation.

'It's Anthony and his parents. Robert Quinlan told us about it. His parents were going out one evening while his father was home on leave, and he came down to say goodnight and found them dancing to the Al Bowlly song. It was the last time he saw his father before he was killed.'

'And then when Saint Anthony met The Lady of the Flowers,' Sunshine was eager to tell the rest of the story, 'he told her all about it and so she danced with him in the Convent Gardens to stop him being sad.' She twisted the ring, which was still on her finger, and added, 'And now we have to find a way to stop her being sad.'

'Well, I think the ring's worth a try,' said Laura, holding out her hand to Sunshine, who reluctantly took it off and gave it to her. 'We'll put it in the garden room next to her photograph. Now, where shall we put this splendid steed?' she added in an attempt to distract Sunshine. But Sunshine had seen the box from the dress-maker and carefully removed the lid. Her gasp of astonishment drew both Laura and Freddy to her side. Laura lifted from the box a stunning dress made of cornflower blue silk chiffon. It had clearly never been worn. Sunshine stroked the delicate fabric lovingly.

'It was her wedding dress,' she said, almost in a whisper. 'It was The Lady of the Flowers' wedding dress.'

Freddy was still holding the photograph. 'What I don't understand is why all these things were shoved into a suitcase and hidden away in the attic? It seems to me these were some of the things that must have been most precious to him: the ring, the photo, the dress, the beginnings of the rose garden. Even the manuscripts. He stood by them, refusing to change them, and so he must have been proud of them.'

Sunshine traced circles in the dust on the lid of the suitcase.

'They made him hurt too much,' she said simply.

Carrot poked his head round the door of the study and whined. It was time for his tea.

'Come on,' said Laura, 'let's put the ring and the dress in the garden room and find a home for this horse.'

'Sue,' said Sunshine, following behind Laura and Freddy. 'And it's not the ring, it's the letter.' But Laura and Freddy had already gone.

38

Eunice

1997

'I'm damn sure the ruddy man's just doing it to be bloody awkward!'

Bruce flounced across the office and flung himself into a chair like the tragic heroine of a silent black and white film. Eunice quite expected him to raise the back of his hand to his forehead to better illustrate his anguish and frustration. He had arrived, uninvited, and begun his rant before he had even reached the top of the stairs.

'Steady the Buffs, old chap,' said Bomber, fighting to keep his amusement from contaminating his platitudes. 'You'll do yourself an unpleasantness.'

Baby Jane, perched majestically on a new faux fur cushion, gazed at Bruce and concluded that his presence was unworthy of any acknowledgement.

'Would you like a cup of tea?' Eunice asked him, through gritted teeth.

'Only if it's accompanied by a large whisky,' Bruce retorted rudely.

Eunice went to put the kettle on anyway.

'Now what's brought all this on?' Bomber was genuinely interested to find out who had managed to infuriate Bruce so thoroughly. Bruce's hair, in the style of Barbara Cartland but the colour and consistency of cobwebs, quivered his indignation.

'Damn that Anthony Peardew! Damn and blast the man to hell.'

Bomber shook his head. 'I say – that's a bit harsh, isn't it? Unless, of course, he's passed the port to the right or ravished your only daughter.'

When first confronted by a man as camp as Bruce, Eunice had assumed that he was gay. But Bruce was married to a large German woman with Zeppelin breasts and the suggestion of a moustache who bred fancy mice and entered them into mouse shows. Astonishingly, Bruce and Brunhilde had managed to produce offspring: two boys and a girl. It was one of life's great mysteries, but not one upon which Eunice was inclined to dwell.

'He's gone completely round the bend,' expostulated Bruce, 'deliberately writing the kind of subversive codswallop he knows I won't publish, full of dark deeds and weird endings, or no proper endings at all. I suppose he thinks it's clever or fashionable or some sort of catharsis for his personal grief. But I'm not having any of it. I know what normal, decent people like, and that's good, straightforward stories with a happy ending where the baddies get their comeuppance, the guy gets the girl and the sex isn't too *outré*.'

Eunice plonked a cup of tea down in front of him, deliberately sploshing some of the dishwater-coloured liquid from the cup into the saucer.

'So you don't think that any of your readers might like to be challenged at all? Flex their intellectual muscles, so to speak? Form their own opinions or extrapolate their own conclusions for once?'

Bruce lifted the cup to his lips and then, seeing its contents close up, changed his mind and set it down again with an irritated clatter.

'My dear, the readers like what we tell them they will like. It's as simple as that.'

'Then why can't you tell them to like Anthony Peardew's new stories?'

Bomber kept the 'touché' under his breath. Just. 'Anthony Peardew. Wasn't he the chap whose collection of stories did rather well for you?'

Bruce raised his eyebrows so high in exasperation that they disappeared into his cobweb coiffure.

'For God's sake, Bomber! Do try and keep up. That's what I've been saying. The first lot did really well; happy stories, happy endings, happy bank balances all round. But not any more. He's gone from *The Sound of Music* to *The Midwich Cuckoos*. But I've drawn the line. I've told him: it's either "Doe a deer" or out on your ear!'

Bruce had once worked from offices in the same building as Bomber, and still visited for a free cup of tea and a gossip if he was passing. However, failure to enlist Bomber in his condemnation of the villainous Anthony Peardew, and scant sympathy from Eunice meant that, on this occasion, Bruce's visit was a short one.

'I wish we'd managed to sign poor Anthony before Bruce did,' sighed Bomber. 'I liked his first collection but his new stories sound intriguing. I wonder if I should try a spot of poaching . . .'

Eunice took a small parcel from the drawer in her desk and handed it to Bomber. It was wrapped in thick, charcoal grey paper and tied with a bright pink ribbon.

'I know it's not your birthday until next week' – Bomber's face lit up like a small boy's; he loved surprises – 'but I thought that after a visit from Bruce the Bogeyman, you could do with cheering up.'

It was a copy of *The Birdcage*. They had been to see it on Bomber's birthday the previous year, and he had laughed so hard that he had almost choked on his popcorn.

'I wish Ma could have seen it,' he had said. 'It's a damn sight more cheerful than *Philadelphia*.' Grace had been dead for eighteen months now. She had survived Godfrey by just over a year, and then died suddenly but peacefully in her sleep at Folly's End. She had been buried next to Godfrey in the grounds of the church where they had been members of the congregation and stalwarts of the flower-arranging team and the summer fête and harvest supper committees for almost half a century. As Bomber and Eunice had stood side by side in the sun-and-shade-dappled churchyard on the day of Grace's funeral, their thoughts had turned to their own leaving ceremonies.

'I'm for burning not burial,' declared Bomber. 'Less room for error,' he added. 'And then I want you to mix my ashes with Douglas's and Baby Jane's – providing, of course, that I outlive her – and scatter us somewhere fabulous.'

Eunice watched as the funeral party wandered slowly back to their cars.

'What makes you so sure that you'll die before me?'

Bomber took her arm as they too began to make their way out of the churchyard.

'Because you're a good few years younger than me, and you've led a purer life.'

Eunice snorted her contention, but Bomber continued, 'And because you're my faithful assistant and you must do as I command.'

Eunice laughed. '"Somewhere fabulous" isn't a very specific command.'

'When I think of somewhere specific, I'll let you know.'

Just before they reached the lychgate, Bomber had stopped and squeezed her arm.

'And one more thing.' He had held her in his gaze with eyes that shone with unspilled tears. 'Promise me that if I ever end up like Pa, mad as a box of frogs and stuck away in a home, that you'll find a way to . . . you know what. Get. Me. Out.'

Eunice had forced a smile, though at that moment someone walked across her grave.

'Cross my heart and hope to die,' she had told him.

Now Bomber showed his present to Baby Jane, but once she had ascertained that it was inedible and didn't squeak or bounce, she lost what little interest she had mustered.

'So, what do you want to do for your birthday?' Eunice asked, twirling the pink ribbon around her fingers.

'Well,' said Bomber, 'how about combining my birthday with our usual annual outing?'

Eunice grinned. 'Brighton it is!'

39

'It's not the ring, and now Therese is sulking.'

Laura kicked one of Carrot's many tennis balls across the lawn in frustration. Freddy stopped digging and leaned on his spade, ready to commiserate as required. Laura had come out into the garden, where Freddy was digging compost into the rose garden, with little purpose other than to vent her frustration. Freddy grinned at her.

'Never mind. We'll sort it out eventually.'

Laura was in no mood for platitudes. Therese and Sunshine were both sulking; no doubt for very different, but for the moment, equally unfathomable reasons; she was running behind with the data input for the website, and Carrot had got completely over-excited when the new postwoman had called to deliver a parcel and had weed on the Chinese rug in the hall. She took another petulant swing at a tennis ball, missed and nearly fell over. Freddy resumed his digging in order to disguise his laughter. Laura had had high hopes that the sapphire ring might be the perfect panacea. She had replaced the broken glass in Therese's photograph, placed the picture of Anthony and his parents beside it, and the ring in its box in front of her. She had even tried to play the Al Bowlly song for her.

'How do you know that Therese is sulking?'

Freddy had recovered himself sufficiently by now to try to be helpful.

'Because the bedroom door's still locked and because of that damn record!'

Freddy frowned. 'But I can't remember hearing it for days now.'

Laura raised her eyebrows in exasperation. 'For God's sake, Freddy! Do try and keep up. That's what I've been saying.'

Freddy ditched the spade and came and gave her a hug.

'Well, not very clearly, I'm afraid. I'm not very good at clues. You'll have to make it "clear and simple",' he said, bracketing the phrase in the air with his fingers.

'Touché.' Laura grinned in spite of herself.

'Right,' said Freddy. 'How does Therese *not* playing dear old Al signify that she's sulking?'

'Because now, instead of playing it morning, noon and night, she won't allow it to be played at all.'

Freddy looked sceptical. 'I'm not sure I understand.'

Laura sighed. 'I've tried to play it over and over, but it simply won't. At first, I did it to be nice. I set up the photographs and the ring, and then, as a finishing touch, I thought I'd play the music; their song. But it won't play. She won't let it.'

Freddy chose his next words very carefully.

'Well, it is an old record and an old player. Maybe the needle needs changing or the record has been scratched . . .'

One look at Laura's face was enough to derail his argument.

'Okay, okay. You've checked. Of course you have. They're both fine.'

Laura picked up yet another tennis ball and threw it at him. But this time with a laugh.

'Oh God, I'm sorry. I'm such a grumpy cow, but I'm doing my best to help her and now she's just being bloody awkward. Come on, I'll make you a cup of tea. There might even be a chocolate biscuit if Sunshine hasn't finished them.'

Freddy took her hand. 'I shan't raise my hopes.'

In the kitchen, Sunshine had just put the kettle on.

'Perfect timing!' said Freddy. 'We just came in for the lovely cup of tea.'

Sunshine set out two more cups and saucers in ominous silence as Freddy washed his hands at the sink.

'Are there any chocolate biscuits left?' he asked her with a wink.

An unsmiling Sunshine placed the biscuit tin in front of him without a word, and then turned away to watch the kettle boil. Freddy and Laura exchanged puzzled glances and then began discussing the progress of the website. They had decided that in order to create more interest, people who claimed back their lost possessions could post their stories on the website if they wanted to. Freddy had come up with an online form people had to complete, giving very specific details of where and when they lost whatever it was that they were claiming. The website simply displayed a photograph of each item, the month and year, and the general location where it had been found. The specific details on Anthony's labels were withheld in order for them to be sure that the people who came forward were the legitimate owners. Laura still had hundreds more items to photograph and post on the website, but enough had been completed to justify the site going live. It was, in any case, always going to be a work in progress, if they continued to gather things that other people had lost. There was going to be an item in the local newspaper that week, and Laura had already given an interview to the local radio station. There were now only days to go before the website went live.

'What if no one comes forward to claim anything?' worried Laura, chewing nervously on her fingernail. Freddy playfully slapped her hand away from her mouth.

'Of course they will!' he said. 'Won't they, Sunshine?'

Sunshine shrugged her shoulders dramatically, her bottom lip pouting like a ship's prow. She poured the tea and plonked the cups and saucers down in front of them hard. Freddy raised his hands in surrender.

'Okay, okay. I give up. What's up, kid?'

Sunshine put her hands on her hips and treated them both to her sternest look.

'No one ever listens to me,' she said quietly.

They were now. Her words dropped into the air and hung there, expectantly, waiting for a response. Neither Freddy nor Laura knew what to say. Each felt a prickle of guilt that Sunshine might actually have a point. With her diminutive stature and ingenuous features, it was easy to slip into the habit of treating her like a child and weighting her opinions and ideas accordingly. But Sunshine was a young woman – albeit 'dancing drome' – and perhaps it was about time that they started treating her as such.

'We're sorry,' said Laura.

Freddy nodded, for once without a trace of a smile on his face.

'We're sorry if you've tried to talk to us and we haven't listened.'

'Yes,' said Freddy, 'and if we do it again, just bash us.'

Sunshine thought about it for a moment and then clipped him round the ear, just for good measure. Then, serious again, she addressed them both.

'It's not the ring. It's the letter.'

'Which letter?' said Freddy.

'Saint Anthony's dead letter,' she replied. 'Come on,' she added.

They followed her from the kitchen into the garden room, where she picked up the Al Bowlly record and placed it on the turntable.

'It's the letter,' she said again, and with that she set the needle down onto the disc and the music began to play.

40

Eunice

2005

'The thought of you publishing that . . .' Eunice consulted her inner omnibus of obscenities and, finding nothing suitably disparaging, expostulated her final word like a poisonous blow dart: 'thing!'

The hardback floozy of a book, with its trashy red and gold cover, languished half undressed in its brown paper wrappings alongside a bottle of champagne that Bruce had sent with it, according to the card, 'as some consolation for not having the wit to publish it yourself'.

Bomber shook his head in bewildered disbelief. 'I haven't even read it. Have you?'

Portia's latest book had topped the bestseller lists for the past three weeks, and as its publisher, Bruce's swaggering peacockery knew no restraint. His self-importance was index-linked to his bank balance which, thanks to Portia, now warranted a platinum credit card and first name terms with the branch manager.

'Of course I've read it!' Eunice exclaimed. 'I had to in order to slander it from an informed perspective. I've also read all the reviews. You do realise that your sister's book is being hailed as 'a searing satire on the saccharine clichés of contemporary commercial fiction'? One critic called it 'a razor-sharp deconstruction of the sexual balance of power in modern relationships, pushing the boundaries of popular literature to exhilarating extremes and giving the finger to those luminaries of the literary establishment who habitually kowtow to the conventions of Man Booker and its staid stablemates.'

Despite her fury, Eunice couldn't keep a straight face, and Bomber was in stitches. He eventually composed himself sufficiently to ask, 'But what's it about?'

Eunice sighed. 'Do you really want to know? It's so much worse than anything else she's ever done.'

'I think I can cope.'

'Well, as you are already painfully aware, it goes by the intriguing title of *Harriet Hotter and the Gobstopper Phone*.'

Eunice paused for effect.

'Harriet, orphaned at an early age and raised by a dreadful aunt and a clinically obese and very sweaty uncle, vows to leave their home as soon as she can and make her own way in the world. After her A levels she gets a job in a pizza and kebab shop, Pizzbab, near King's Cross, where she is constantly mocked for her posh voice and her bifocal spectacles. One day, an old man with a very long beard and a funny hat comes into the shop to buy a kebab and chips, and tells her that she is "very special". He hands her a business card and tells her to call him. Fast forward six months and Harriet is earning a small fortune from phone sex. Her customers love her because she has a posh voice, "as though her cheeks were stuffed with gobstoppers" – and so the ingenious title is explained. Our heroine, not satisfied with mere financial reward, seeks self-fulfilment and enhanced job satisfaction. In partnership with the beardy old man, aka Chester Fumblefore, she sets up a training school for aspiring phone sex workers called Snogwarts, so called because Harriet teaches her students to speak to every customer as though he were a handsome prince, even though most of them are more likely to be warty toads. Among her first pupils are Persephone Danger and Donna Sleazy who become her best friends and training assistants. Between them, they set up a vast call centre where their pupils can earn an honest living while they are training. Harriet invents a game called Quids In to increase productivity and raise morale in the workplace. The winner, who receives a cash bonus and a month's supply of gobstoppers, is the worker who satisfies the most customers in one hour whilst cunningly introducing the words "brothel", "todger" (twice) and "golden snatch" into each phone sex liaison.'

Bomber laughed out loud.

'It's not funny, Bomber!' exploded Eunice. 'It's an absolute bloody disgrace. How can anybody give such utter drivel shelf room? Millions of people are paying hard-earned money for this excrement! It's not even well-written excrement. It's execrable excrement. And if it's not enough that Portia's being interviewed on every poxy chat show that's aired, there's a horribly tenacious rumour doing the rounds about her being invited to speak at the Hay festival this year.'

Bomber clapped his hands in glee. 'Now *that* I should gladly pay good money to see.'

Eunice shot him a warning look and he shrugged his shoulders in reply.

'How could I resist? I'm just thankful that Ma and Pa aren't around to witness the whole ruddy circus. Especially with Ma having been the chairwoman of the local WI.'

Bomber chuckled to himself at the thought of it, but then donned a more appropriately serious expression for his next question.

'Now, I'm almost afraid to ask, but I probably need to know. Is it terribly . . . explicit?'

Eunice let out a hoot of derision.

'Explicit?! Remember that time when Bruce was here ranting on about that Peardew chap and lecturing us on the key components of a bestseller?'

Bomber nodded.

'And he told us, and I quote, that the sex should never be too *outré*?'

Bomber nodded again, more slowly this time.

'Well, unless his definition of *outré* is informed by a far more adventurous carnal relationship with Brunhilde than we ever gave them credit for, I think he's changed his mind.'

Bomber placed his hands on the small wooden box that stood next to Douglas's on his desk and warned, 'Cover your ears and don't listen to this, Baby Jane.'

Eunice smiled a little sadly and continued.

'One of Harriet's customers has sex with a bread-making machine, another lusts after women with beards, hairy backs and ingrowing toenails, and yet another has his testicles bathed in surgical spirit and then stroked with the mane of a My Little Pony. And that's only chapter two.'

Bomber picked up the book from its wrappings and opened the front cover to be greeted by a glossy photograph of his sister wearing a self-satisfied smile and a silk negligee. He snapped it shut again with a resounding thump.

'Well at least she didn't simply steal someone else's plot wholesale this time. She did make some of it up herself.'

'Let's hope so,' said Eunice.

The next day all thoughts of Portia were purged by the glittering aquamarine waves and warm, salty wind of Brighton seafront. It was the 'annual outing', and this was the first without Douglas or Baby Jane. They had been coming every year since Eunice's twenty-first birthday trip with Bomber, and the day followed a familiar pattern that had been fine-tuned over the years to provide enjoyment and entertainment to all members of their small party. First they walked along the promenade. In the past, when Douglas and then Baby Jane had accompanied them, the dogs had gloried in the compliments and cosseting of passers-by that they inevitably attracted. Then there was the visit to the pier and an hour frittered away on the flashing, clanging, jangling slot machines. Then lunch of fish and chips and a bottle of pink fizz, and finally the Royal Pavilion. But as they strolled towards the pier, worry was washing away Eunice's happiness. Bomber had asked her twice in the space of ten minutes if they'd been there before. The first time, she'd hoped he was joking, but the second time she looked at his face and her world tipped sharply on its axis when she saw an expression of innocence and genuine enquiry. It was horribly, gut-wrenchingly familiar. Godfrey. He was following his father's painful footsteps to a destination Eunice couldn't bear to think about. So far, it was barely noticeable; a hairline crack in his solid, dependable sanity. But Eunice knew that in time he would be as vulnerable as a name written in the sand at the mercy of an incoming tide. As yet, Bomber seemed unaware of his gentle unravellings. Like a man with petit mals, he passed through them blithely oblivious. But Eunice lived them all, second by second, and her heart was already breaking.

The coloured lights and bells and buzzers of the pier's amusement arcade welcomed them in to waste their money. Eunice left Bomber standing by a two-penny slot machine, watching lanes of tightly packed coins shunting back and forth to see which would tip over the edge, while she went to fetch some change. When she returned, she found him, like a lost child, coin in hand staring at the coin slot on the machine but completely unable to fathom the connection between the two. Gently, she took the coin from him and dropped it into the slot, and his face lit up as he watched a pile of coins tip and fall, rattling into the metal tray beneath.

The rest of the day passed happily and uneventfully. For the first time, as they were without a canine companion, they were able to sample the exotic delights of the Pavilion interior together, where they 'oohed' and 'aahed' their amazement at the chandeliers and clucked their disgust at the spit-roaster in the kitchen, which was originally driven by an unfortunate dog. As they sat on a bench in the gardens, basking in the coral light of the late- afternoon sun, Bomber took Eunice's hand and let out a sigh of blissful contentment Eunice remembered to treasure.

'This place is utterly fabulous.'

41

The navy blue leather glove belonged to a dead woman. Not the most promising of starts for The Keeper of Lost Things. The day after the website launched a retired reporter had emailed. For many years she had worked for the local newspaper and she remembered it well. It was the first proper news item she had covered.

It made the front page. The poor woman was only in her thirties. She threw herself in front of a train. The train driver was in a terrible state, poor bloke. He was new to his job too. He'd only been driving solo for a couple of weeks. Her name was Rose. She was ill; what they called 'bad nerves' back then. I remember she had a little girl; such a pretty little thing. Rose had a picture of her in her coat pocket. They printed it in the paper with the story. I wasn't very comfortable with that, but I was overruled by the editor. I went to her funeral. It was a gruesome business altogether; not much of a body left to bury. But the photo was still in the pocket of her coat and she was wearing only one glove. It's such a small detail, but it seemed so poignant. And it was so cold that night. That must be why I've remembered it for all these years.

It was the glove Sunshine had dropped in horror when it had fallen out of the drawer. She had said at the time 'the lady died' and 'she loved her little girl'. Laura was dumbfounded. It seemed that Sunshine was right and once again they had been guilty of underestimating her. She had a very special gift and they would do well to listen to her a bit more carefully. Sunshine had read the email impassively. Her only comment had been, 'Perhaps her little girl will want it back.'

Sunshine was out with Carrot. She went out most days now to gather more lost things for the website, carrying a small notebook and pencil so that she could jot down the details for the labels before she forgot. Freddy was out laying a new lawn for one of his customers, so Laura was alone. Except for Therese.

'I know, I know!' she said out loud. 'I'm going to look for it today, I promise.'

Since Sunshine's revelation that Anthony's letter was the clue they needed, Laura had been trying to remember where she had put it. At first she thought that she might have left it in the dressing table in Therese's room, but the door remained locked, so she hadn't been able to check. In any case, it hardly seemed likely that Therese would be preventing her from finding the very thing that she wanted her to find. Even she couldn't be *that* awkward. Laura went into the study. She would just check the emails first. The website was proving popular, with hundreds of hits already. There were two emails. One was from an elderly lady who said that she was eighty-nine years of age and a silver surfer of two years thanks to her local retirement centre. She had heard about the website on the radio and decided to take a look. She thought that a jigsaw puzzle piece found years ago in Copper Street might be hers. Or rather, her sister's. They hadn't got on, and one day when her sister had been particularly vicious she had taken a piece from the puzzle her sister was working on. She went for a walk to get out of the house, and threw the piece into the gutter. 'Childish, I expect,' she said, 'but she could be the very devil. And she was livid when she found that it was missing.' The old lady didn't want it back. Her sister was long dead anyway. But it was nice, she said, to have something to practise her emails on.

The second was from a young woman claiming a lime green hair bobble. Her mum had bought the bobbles for her to cheer her up, the day before she started a new school she was feeling nervous about. She'd lost one in the park on the way home from a day out with her mum, and it would be nice to have it back as a memento.

Laura replied to both emails and then set about searching for Anthony's letter. By the time Sunshine returned with Carrot, Laura was poring over the letter at the kitchen table. She had found it tucked away in the writing desk in the garden room. As soon as she had found it, she had helpfully remembered that, of course, that was where she had placed it for safekeeping. Sunshine made the lovely cup of tea for them and then sat down next to Laura.

'What does it say?' she asked.

'What does what say?' said Freddy, bursting through the back door, his boots covered in mud. Laura and Sunshine both looked at his feet and commanded in unison, 'Off!'

Freddy laughed as he struggled out of his boots and left them outside on the doormat.

'Talk about henpecked!' he exclaimed. 'Now, what's all this?'

'It's Saint Anthony's dead letter and now we're going to find the clue,' Sunshine exclaimed with far more confidence than Laura felt. She began to read out loud, but resurgent grief choked his generous words in her throat before she could even finish the first line. Sunshine took the letter gently from her and began again, reading slowly and deliberately, helped by Freddy with some of the more difficult words. When she reached the final paragraph, where Anthony asked Laura to befriend her, her face lit up with a smile.

'But I asked you first!' she said.

Laura took her hand. 'And I'm very glad you did,' she replied.

Freddy slapped his palms on the table.

'Enough with the mushy stuff, you girls,' he said, rocking his chair backwards on two legs. 'What's the clue?'

Sunshine looked at him with dutiful amusement which quickly withered into undisguised scorn when she realised that he wasn't joking.

'You cannot be serious,' she said, looking to Laura for support.

'Well, it could be anything . . .' Laura ventured uncertainly.

Freddy was studying the letter again.

'Well, come on, John McEnroe,' he said to Sunshine. 'Enlighten us.'

Sunshine sighed and like a schoolteacher sorely disappointed with her class she shook her head slowly before announcing, 'It's so obvious.'

And when she explained, they realised that, of course, it was.

42

Eunice

2011

Today was a good day. But the term was only relative. No day now was truly good. The best that Eunice could hope for were a few bewildered smiles, an occasional recollection of who she was and, most of all, no tears from the man she had spent most of her adult life in love with. She strolled arm in arm with Bomber around the bleak patchwork of bare earth and concrete paving slabs that the officer-in-charge of the Happy Haven care home grandiosely termed 'the rose garden'. The only trace of the roses were a few bent, brown sticks poking out of the earth like the detritus of a bush fire. Eunice could easily have wept. And this was a good day.

Bomber had wanted to go to Folly's End. Before he was too often lost in random bouts of oblivion, but knew that to be his inevitable fate, he had made his wishes clear. He had always intended to give Eunice his power of attorney when the time came, and thus salvage whatever scraps of dignity and security that could be wrung from a future as bleak as the one he faced. He could trust Eunice with his life, however worthless it might become. She would always do the right thing. But Portia got there first. Armed with ridiculous but omnipotent wealth and next-of-kin affiliation if not affection, she tricked Bomber into seeing a 'specialist', who, no doubt with her financial encouragement, legally declared him to be 'no longer capable of making rational decisions' and turned his future welfare over to his sister.

The following week Bomber was installed at Happy Haven.

Eunice had fought his corner as hard as she could; she had argued ferociously for Folly's End, but Portia was unmoved. Folly's End was 'too far away' for her to conveniently visit, and in any case, she claimed with astonishing callousness, it was only a matter of time before Bomber wouldn't have a clue where he was anyway. But for now, he did. And it was killing him.

Surprisingly, Portia did visit him. But they were strained, uncomfortable encounters. She veered wildly between bossing him about and cowering fearfully away from him. His reaction to both approaches was the same: painful bewilderment. Having deprived him of the one thing he wanted, she showered him with expensive, often pointless gifts. He had no idea what the espresso machine was, let alone how to work it. He poured the designer aftershave down the toilet and used the fancy camera as a doorstop. In the end, Portia spent most of the time during her visits drinking tea with Sylvia, the sycophantic officer-in-charge, who was a devoted fan of the Harriet Hotter books, of which there was now, regrettably, a trilogy.

Eunice did her best to make Bomber's room a little piece of home. She brought things from his flat, and put photographs of Douglas and Baby Jane on every shelf and table. But it wasn't enough. He was drifting away. Giving up.

Eunice and Bomber were not alone in the garden. Eulalia was feeding a magpie with bits of toast she'd saved from her breakfast. She was an ancient, wizened husk of a woman with skin the colour of stewed prunes, wild eyes and an alarming cackle. Her twisted hands clutched knobbled walking sticks that she used to anchor and propel herself in a jerky, shuffling gait. Most of the other residents avoided her, but Bomber always greeted her with a friendly wave. Round and round they walked, mindlessly, like prisoners in an exercise yard. Eunice, because she couldn't bear to think, and Bomber just because, most of the time, he couldn't. Eulalia threw her last piece of toast at the black and white bird who snatched it from the ground and gobbled it down, never taking his bright, elderberry eyes off Eulalia. She shook her stick at him and squawked, 'Off with you, now! Away, before they put you in a pot for dinner! They would, you know,' she said, turning to Eunice and screwing one of her eyes into a grotesque wink. 'They feeds us all kinds of shit in here.'

Judging by the smell from the kitchen, which was wafting into the garden through an open window, Eunice had to concede that she might have a point.

'Him nuts, that one,' said Eulalia, waggling a hooked claw at Bomber, whilst somehow still managing to keep hold of the walking stick. 'Mad as an ant with his arse on fire.' She planted her sticks onto the concrete and began her painful, awkward shuffle back to the house.

'But him a lovely man inside,' she said to Eunice as she passed. 'Lovely, but dying.'

Back in Bomber's room, Eunice threw back the curtains to let in what little light the pale winter sun could spare. It was a nice room on the second floor; clean and spacious with rather grand French windows and a pretty balcony. Which Bomber wasn't allowed to use.

Eunice had opened them the first time that she had visited Bomber. It was a sultry summer day and the room was hot and stuffy. The key had been left in the lock, but an officious care assistant who had come in to check on Bomber banged the windows shut and locked the key in the medicine cabinet on the wall in Bomber's room. 'Health and safety,' she had spat at Eunice. After that day, Eunice never saw the key again.

'Let's watch a film, shall we?'

Bomber smiled. For him, now, his own life story was like an unbound manuscript, badly edited. Some of the pages were in the wrong order, some torn, some rewritten or missing altogether. The original version was lost to him forever. But he still found pleasure in the familiar stories told in the old films that they had watched so many times together. There were more days, now, when he didn't know his own name or what he'd just eaten for breakfast. But he could still quote, word for word, from *The Great Escape*, *Brief Encounter*, *Top Gun* and scores of other films.

'What about this one?' said Eunice, holding up a copy of *The Birdcage*.

He looked up and smiled and, for a precious, fleeting moment, the mists cleared.

'My birthday present,' he said, and Eunice knew that her Bomber was still in there.

43

'H e's still in there,' said Sunshine in a worried voice. Carrot had taken up a sentinel post in the shed, having caught a whiff of a resident rodent, and Sunshine was growing increasingly anxious that Carrot's lunch might have mouse on the menu. Laura was in the study retrieving an item someone had contacted the website about and was coming to collect that afternoon.

'Don't worry, Sunshine. I'm sure the mouse will have the good sense not to show a single whisker while Carrot's in there.'

Sunshine was unconvinced.

'But he might. And then Carrot would kill him and be a murderinger.'

Laura smiled. She knew Sunshine well enough by now to know that she wouldn't give up until something was done. Two minutes later, Laura was back, towing a recalcitrant Carrot on his lead. In the kitchen she gave him a sausage from the fridge and unclipped his lead. Before Sunshine could raise an objection Laura pacified her.

'Mickey or Minnie will be quite safe now. I've shut the shed door, and now he's had a sausage, Carrot won't be hungry anyway.'

'He's always hungry,' muttered Sunshine, as she watched Carrot slope out of the room with mischief still clearly on his mind. 'When's the lady coming?' she asked.

Laura checked her watch.

'Any time now. She's called Alice and I thought you might like to make the lovely cup of tea when she gets here.'

As if on cue, the bell rang and Sunshine was at the front door before Laura was out of the starting blocks.

'Good afternoon, Lady Alice,' Sunshine greeted the rather taken-aback teenager at the door. 'I'm Sunshine. Please do come in.'

'What a great name.'

The girl who followed Sunshine into the hall was tall and slim, with long fair hair and a splatter of freckles across her nose. Laura held out her hand.

'Hi, I'm Laura. Lovely to meet you.'

Sunshine deftly commandeered Alice and took her through to the garden while Laura was left to make the tea. When she came out with the tray of tea things, she found Alice and Sunshine swapping musical heroes.

'We both love David Bowie,' Sunshine announced proudly to Laura as she began to pour the tea.

'I'm sure he'll be delighted,' said Laura, smiling. 'How do you take it?' she asked Alice.

'Builder's for me, please.'

Sunshine looked worried.

'I don't know if we've got any of that, have we?' she asked Laura.

'Don't worry, Sunshine,' said Alice, quick to spot her discomfort, 'it's just me being silly. I meant nice and strong with milk and two sugars.'

Alice had come to collect an umbrella; a child's umbrella, white with red hearts.

'I didn't actually lose it,' she explained, 'and I can't be absolutely certain that it was meant for me . . .'

Sunshine picked up the umbrella that was already on the table and handed it to her.

'It was,' she said simply. Although, judging by the look of undisguised adoration on Sunshine's face, Laura reckoned she would have given Alice the family silver without a second thought and thrown in the deeds to Padua for good measure.

Alice took the umbrella from her and stroked its folded ruffles.

'It was my first time in America,' she told them. 'Mum took me to New York. It was more of a working holiday for her. She was an editor of a fashion magazine and she'd bagged an interview with a hotshot new designer who was tipped to be the next big thing on the New York fashion scene. He was, as it turned out. But all I remember about him then was that he looked at me like I'd escaped from a leper colony or something. Apparently he didn't "do" children.'

'What's a leopard colony?' Sunshine asked.

Alice looked over to Laura, but then decided to wing it anyway.

'It's a place where, in olden times, they used to put people who had a terrible illness that made their fingers and toes drop off.'

Laura would have bet money that Sunshine spent the next five minutes surreptitiously counting Alice's digits. Thank goodness she was wearing sandals.

'There wasn't much time for sightseeing,' Alice

continued, 'but she promised to take me to see the sculpture of Alice in Wonderland in Central Park. I remember being utterly thrilled. I thought that the statue was named after me.'

She slipped off her sandals and wriggled her toes in the cool grass. Sunshine studiously followed suit.

'It was raining that afternoon and Mum was already running late for her next appointment, so she wasn't in the best of tempers, but I was beyond excited. I ran off ahead of her and when I got to the sculpture, there was this huge, strange-looking black guy with dreadlocks and big boots giving away umbrellas. He bent down and shook hands with me and I can still remember his face. It was a mixture of kind and sad, and he was called Marvin.'

Alice drained her cup and helped herself to another from the pot with confident teenage ease.

'My favourite story at the time was "The Selfish Giant" by Oscar Wilde, and to me Marvin looked like a giant. But he wasn't selfish. He was giving things away. Free umbrellas. Anyway, when Mum caught up with me she dragged me away. But it wasn't just that. She was rude to him. Really horrible. He tried to give her an umbrella and she was an absolute bitch.'

Sunshine's eyebrows hiccupped in astonishment at the casual use of an expletive, but her expression was one of admiration.

'I only met him for a moment, but I've never been able to forget the look on his face as she dragged me away.' She sighed heavily, but then smiled as another memory eclipsed the last. 'I blew him a kiss,' she said, 'and he caught it.'

The date on the umbrella's label matched the exact day of Alice's visit to Central Park and the umbrella was found on the sculpture. Laura was delighted.

'I think it must have been meant for you.'

'I really hope so,' said Alice.

For the rest of the day Carrot lay guarding the door of the shed, and Sunshine talked about her new friend Alice. Alice was at university studying English Litter Tour and Drama. Alice liked David Bowie, Marc Bolan and Jon Bon Hovis. And 'the lovely cup of tea' had been summarily supplanted by the builder's variety.

That evening over a late supper of spaghetti bolognese, Laura told Freddy all about their visitor.

'It's working, then,' said Freddy. 'The website. It's doing what Anthony wanted you to do.'

Laura shook her head. 'No. Not really. Not yet, anyway. Remember what the letter said? "If you can make just one person happy, mend one broken heart by restoring to them what they have lost . . ." And I haven't done that yet. Of course Alice was pleased to find the umbrella, but we can't be absolutely sure that it was meant for her. And the girl with the hair bobble; her heart wasn't exactly broken when she lost it.'

'Well, at least it's a start,' said Freddy, pushing back his chair and getting up to take Carrot for a final stroll around the garden before bed. 'We'll get there in the end.'

But it wasn't just about the lost things. There was the clue; the one that was so obvious once Sunshine had pointed it out. The thing that had started all this. Anthony had called it 'the last remaining thread' that had bound him to Therese, and when he lost it on the day she died that final thread was broken. If her communion medal really was the key to reuniting Therese with Anthony, how on earth were they supposed to find it? Freddy had suggested that they post it on the website as a lost item needing to be found, but as they had no idea what it looked like or where Anthony had lost it, there was very little useful information that they could share.

Laura cleared the plates from the table. It had been a long day and she was tired. The satisfaction that she had felt after Alice's visit had gradually dissipated, only to be replaced by a familiar feeling of unease.

And in the garden room the music began again.

44

Eunice

2013

In the residents' lounge at Happy Haven the music began again. Mantovani's 'Charmaine'. Quietly at first and then louder and louder. Too loud. Edie turned the volume up as high as it would go. Soon she would be gliding round the ballroom to the strings' *glissandos* in a froth of net and sparkles. Her feet would spin and sweep in her best gold dancing sandals and the glittering lights would swirl around her like a snowstorm of rainbows.

As Eunice and Bomber passed through the lounge on the way to Bomber's room, they saw a ragged bundle of nightclothes barely inhabited by a thin, whiskery old woman with a greasy straggle of grey hair and tartan slippers. She was stumbling round the room with her eyes closed and her arms lovingly wrapped around some invisible partner. Suddenly there was an explosion of sticks and expletives from one of the armchairs.

'Not again! Jesus fucking Christ and Jehovah! Not again! Not again! Not again!'

Eulalia had burst out of her chair cursing and thrashing.

'Not a-fucking-gain, you stupid, crazy, dirty bitch! Me just want a bit of peace!' she roared, flinging one of her sticks at the dancer, who had stopped in her tracks. The stick missed Edie by a mile, but she let out an anguished yowl as tears began to course down her cheeks and urine down her legs and into her slippers. Eulalia had struggled to her feet and was pointing with one of her claws.

'Now she piss herself! Piss her pants. Piss the floor,' she cackled furiously through spittle-flecked lips. Eunice tried to move Bomber on, but he was frozen to the spot. Some of the other residents had begun shouting or crying, and others stared into the distance, oblivious. Or pretending to be. It took two members of staff to restrain Eulalia as Sylvia led poor Edie away. She was trembling and snivelling and dripping piss from the hem of her nightgown as she shuffled out miserably, clinging to Sylvia's arm and wondering where on earth the ballroom had gone.

Back in the safety of Bomber's room, Eunice made him a cup of tea. As she drank her own, she took in the new additions to Bomber's growing collection of swag. He had begun stealing things; random items that he didn't need. A vase, a tea cosy, cutlery, rolls of plastic bin bags, umbrellas. He never stole from the rooms of other residents, just from the communal areas. It was a symptom of his disease apparently. Petty theft. But he was losing things too. Thick and fast now he was losing words like a tree loses leaves in the autumn. A bed might be 'a soft sleep square' and a pencil 'a stick with grey middle writing coming out'. Instead of words, he spoke in clues; or, more often, not at all. Eunice suggested that they watch a film. It was all that was left of them now. Eunice and Bomber, who for so long had been colleagues and best friends. Bomber's occasional boyfriends had come and gone, but Eunice was his constant. They were husband and wife without sex or certificate and these were the last paltry scraps of their once rich relationship: walking and watching films.

Bomber chose the film. *One Flew Over the Cuckoo's Nest.*

'Are you sure?' Eunice asked. She had been hoping for something a little more jolly, for her own sake and for his, after what they had just witnessed. Bomber was adamant. As they watched the patients at the state mental hospital walking in the chain-link-fenced exercise yard, Bomber pointed at the screen and winked at her.

'That's us,' he said.

Eunice looked into his eyes and was shocked to see the clarity reflected back at her. This was the Bomber of old speaking; sharp, funny, bright and back for a rare visit. But for how long? Even the briefest visit was precious, but heartbreaking. Heartbreaking because he must know that he would have to go back. And to what?

It was a film that they had watched many times before, but this time it was very different.

As the Chief placed the pillow over Mac's pitifully vacant face and tenderly suffocated him, Bomber gripped Eunice's hand and spoke his final three words.

'Get. Me. Out.'

He was calling in her promise. Eunice stared at the

screen and held on tight to Bomber's hand as the giant Chief wrenched the marble water cooler from the tub-room floor, hurled it through the massive windows and then loped off towards the breaking dawn and freedom. As the credits rolled, Eunice couldn't move. Bomber took her other hand in his. His eyes were full of tears but he was smiling as he nodded and mouthed silently at her, 'Please.'

Before Eunice could say anything one of the nurses burst in without knocking.

'Time for your medication,' she bustled, rattling the keys to the medicine cabinet on the wall. She unlocked it and was just reaching for the tablets when there was a terrified scream from the corridor outside followed by Eulalia's unmistakable cackle.

'That damn woman!' cursed the nurse, rushing to the door to investigate and leaving the cabinet unlocked.

It was time for Eunice to go. She must leave, but until she did she still had Bomber, and so she couldn't bear to go. But every minute was just a marker between now and then, not time to be cherished. Because the decision had been made. Eunice knew that there would only be one chance; one moment when all the love she had ever felt for this man would crystallise into the inconceivable strength that she would need. It was time. The imprint of the key was embedded into the flesh of her palm where she had gripped it so tightly. Eunice unlocked the windows and opened them, leaving them just ajar. She wanted so desperately to hug him one last time; to hold his warmth and feel him breathing against her. But she knew that if she did her strength would desert her, so instead she placed the key in his hand and kissed his cheek.

'I'm not going without you, Bomber,' she whispered. 'I wouldn't leave you this way. You're coming with me. Let's go.'

And then she left.

45

ELDERLY MALE IN DEATH FALL AT CARE HOME

Police are investigating the death of an elderly male resident of the Happy Haven care home in Blackheath, who fell from a second-floor balcony early on Saturday evening. The man, who has not yet been named, was suffering from Alzheimer's and is believed to have been a retired publisher. A post-mortem is due to be carried out later this week and police enquiries into what they are calling 'an unexplained death' are ongoing.

London Evening Standard

46

'There's a dead person in the study,' Sunshine announced in a conversational tone. She had come to find Laura, who was in the garden cutting roses for the house, to tell her this piece of news and to chivvy her along into making lunch. Carrot was lolling lazily on his back in the sun, with his legs in the air, but as Sunshine approached he jumped up to greet her.

It had been a year now since the website had launched and it kept both Laura and Sunshine busy. Sunshine had learned how to take photographs, and post them and the details of objects onto the website, and Freddy had even shown her how to run a Keeper of Lost Things Instagram account. Laura dealt with the emails. They were still working their way through Anthony's collection, as well as adding the new things that Sunshine gathered on her walks with Carrot. Laura and Freddy had also got into the habit of picking up things they found wherever they went, and now people had begun to send them lost items as well. At this rate the shelves in the study would always be groaning.

'A dead person? Are you sure?'

Sunshine gave her one of her looks. Laura went inside to investigate. In the study, Sunshine showed her a sky blue Huntley & Palmers biscuit tin. Its label read:

Huntley & Palmers biscuit tin
containing cremation remains?
Found, sixth carriage from the front, 14.42
train from London Bridge to Brighton.
Deceased unknown. God bless and rest in peace.

Lupin and Bootle funeral directors (Est. 1927) was on the corner
of a busy street opposite a fancy bakery. As she stood outside,
Eunice smiled to herself, remembering Mrs Doyle's and thinking
that this was an appropriate place for Bomber to end up. He had
been dead for six weeks now, and Eunice still hadn't had any
details about his funeral. The coroner had eventually returned a
verdict of accidental death, but the staff at Happy Haven had
been severely criticised for their cavalier approach to health and
safety procedures and had only narrowly escaped prosecution.
Portia had wanted Sylvia's head in a bedpan. She had been
mourning extravagantly all over the press and the media, but
Eunice couldn't help wondering whether it was fuelled by genuine
grief or the associated publicity it was bound to generate for her
forthcoming book tour. Portia was too famous to talk to Eunice
directly now. She had assistants for that kind of trivial task.
Which was why Eunice found herself staring through an
immaculate plate-glass window at a scale model of a horse-drawn
hearse and a tasteful display of arum lilies. The only information
she had been able to extract from the lowliest assistant twice
removed was the name of the funeral directors who were dealing
with all enquiries. She could have telephoned, but the temptation
to be in the same building as Bomber was too great.

The woman behind the reception desk looked up at the sound of
the bell and gave Eunice a smile of genuine welcome. Pauline was a
large lady, dressed in Marks & Spencer's finest, with an air of
capability and kindness. She put Eunice in mind of a Brown Owl.

Unfortunately, the news she had to deliver was the cruellest and most shocking that Eunice could possibly hear.

'It was very small. Family only at the crematorium. The sister organised it; the one who writes those mucky books.'

It was clear from the repugnance with which Pauline imbued the word 'sister' that she and Portia had not exactly bonded. Eunice felt her head go into a tailspin and the floor rise up to meet her. Not long afterwards she was sitting on a comfy sofa drinking hot sweet tea with a nip of brandy and Pauline was patting her hand.

'It was the shock, love,' she said. 'Your face went as white as a ghost.'

Fortified by tea, brandy and biscuits, Eunice was made party to the whole dreadful story by a very forthcoming Pauline. Portia had wanted it done and dusted as quickly and quietly as possible.

'She was off on her book tour, you see, and she didn't want her schedule disrupted.' Pauline took a sip of her own tea and shook her head vigorously in disapproval. 'But she's having a proper showy-offy shebang when she gets back; a memorial service and then a burial of the ashes. She's inviting "everyone who is anyone, darling" and the music will be provided by choirs of angels with his Holiness the Pope presiding by the way she was talking. It'll knock Princess Diana's do into a cocked hat, apparently.'

Eunice listened in horror.

'But that wasn't what he wanted at all,' she whispered tearfully. 'He told me what he wanted. He was the love of my life.'

And now, right at the last, she was going to fail him.

Pauline was good at listening and mopping up tears. It was her job. But deep inside her sensible suit and her easy-iron blouse beat the brave heart of a maverick. Back in the day, her blonde bob had been a pink Mohican and her nose still bore the tiny scar of a safety-pin piercing. She handed Eunice another tissue.

'All the boys are out at a big funeral this afternoon. I wouldn't normally do this, but . . . Follow me!'

She led Eunice through from the reception area down a corridor past the staff kitchen, the chapel of rest and various other rooms to the place where the cremation remains were stored awaiting collection. From one of the shelves she took down an impressive wooden urn and checked the label.

'Here he is,' she said gently. She checked her watch. 'I'm going to leave you alone with him for a bit to pay your respects. The boys won't be back for another hour, so you won't be disturbed.'

Less than an hour later, Eunice was sitting on a train with Bomber's ashes in a Huntley & Palmers biscuit tin on the seat beside her. She had had to think and act fast after Pauline had left her. She found a plastic carrier bag and a biscuit tin in the little kitchen where Pauline had made tea. She emptied the biscuits into the bag and then tipped Bomber into the biscuit tin. She refilled the urn with the biscuits but it was too light. Frantically searching for additional ballast, she found a box of decorative gravel samples in one of the other rooms. She threw in a couple of large handfuls and then screwed the lid back on as tightly as she could and returned the urn to its shelf. As she made her way out through the reception area clutching the biscuit tin, Pauline didn't look up from her desk, but raised her thumbs to Eunice in a good luck gesture. She hadn't seen a thing.

As the guard blew his whistle, Eunice patted the tin affectionately and smiled.

'Brighton it is.'

Laura was astonished. She picked up the tin and gave it a gentle shake. It was certainly heavy.

'Don't shake it!' said Sunshine. 'You'll wake him up.' And then she giggled at her own joke.

Laura was wondering what else might be lurking in the dark corners of the study.

'No wonder this place is haunted,' she said to Sunshine.

After lunch Laura helped her to post the details on the website, but this was one thing she was fairly certain no one would come forward to claim.

That evening Freddy, Laura, Sunshine, Carrot, Stella and Stan had a celebratory dinner in the garden of The Moon is Missing, to mark the birthday of the website. Sunshine was full of stories about all the things that were currently posted, but most especially about the biscuit tin.

'It's certainly a queer thing to lose,' said Stella, tucking into her crumb-dusted, sautéed crayfish tails with hand-cut chips. 'And why on earth would you put your loved one in a biscuit tin?'

'Perhaps that's just it, love,' said Stan. 'Perhaps the bloke in the tin wasn't particularly loved and someone was just trying to get rid of him.'

'Perhaps it's not human remains at all. Maybe it just the sweepings-out of somebody's fireplace. That's exactly what it looks like,' said Freddy, taking a long swig of his ice-cold beer.

Sunshine was about to remonstrate with him when he winked at her and she realised he was only joking.

'It is a dead person and he was the love of her life and she *will* come and get him,' she replied defiantly.

'Okay,' he replied. 'Let's have a bet. What do you want to bet me that someone will come and get the biscuit tin?'

Sunshine screwed up her face in concentration and fed Carrot a couple of chips while she was thinking about it. Suddenly a huge smile lit up her face and she leaned back in her chair and folded her arms across her chest with a sigh of victorious satisfaction.

'You have to marry Laura.'

Laura spilled her wine in shock.

'Steady on, old girl,' said Stan. 'Blimey, Sunshine, you certainly know how to frighten the horses.'

Laura could feel her face reddening. Stella and Stan were chuckling merrily and Sunshine was grinning from ear to ear. Laura wished that the ground would open up and swallow her, and so swallowed her wine too quickly and ordered another large glass. Freddy said nothing. He looked as though he was somewhere between annoyed and disappointed, but then when he saw Laura's face, he leapt to his feet and thrust his hand out to Sunshine.

'It's a bet!'

It was hot that night and the air was heavy with the warm velvet scent of roses as Freddy and Laura wandered round the garden, while Carrot searched the shrubbery for intruders. Laura was still fretting about the bet that Freddy had made. He had been very quiet on the way home from the pub. Although they had been together for a little over a year, and Freddy virtually lived at Padua now, they had never made any real plans for the future. She counted herself very lucky to have a second chance at both life and love, but she was still afraid that any attempt, however light-hearted, to tether their relationship might cause love to bolt. And she did love him. Not in the silly, girlish way that she had been infatuated with Vince. This had, for her, grown stealthily into an abiding love, sparked first by passion and then sustained by friendship and trust. But alongside her love for Freddy grew the fear of losing him; the two emotions cruelly shackled together, each feeding the other. Laura had to say something.

'That bet with Sunshine, it's just a joke. I don't expect you to . . .' She was so uncomfortable that she didn't know how to continue. It suddenly dawned on her that marrying Freddy might be exactly what she wanted and that was why she was so upset. Her foolish hopes of a Happy Ever After had been turned into a joke, and she felt like a laughing stock.

Freddy took her hand and swung her round to face him. 'A bet's a bet, and I'm a man of my word!'

Laura pulled her hand away. In that moment, all the doubts about their relationship, all the fears of failure and all the frustrations at her own imperfection converged to create a perfect storm.

'Don't worry,' she snapped, 'you don't have to wait until you've worked out a dignified escape route! I'm fully aware that I'm the one who's hitting above my weight in this relationship!'

'Punching,' replied Freddy quietly. 'It's "punching above your weight".'

He was trying to find a way of breaking into the emotional vortex that Laura was whipping up, but she wouldn't listen.

'I'm not a charity case! Poor old Laura! Couldn't keep her husband out of someone else's knickers and the only date she's had in years was an unmitigated disaster, so what did you think, Freddy? Take her out and make her feel like she's worth something and then let her down gently when someone better comes along?'

Like a songbird caught in a trapper's net, the harder she fought, the more entangled she became, but she couldn't help herself. She knew how unreasonable she was being, how hurtful, but she couldn't stop. The insults and accusations flew while Freddy stood silently waiting for her to burn herself out and when she turned to go back into the house he called after her.

'Laura! For God's sake, woman! You know how much I love you. I was going to ask you, anyway. To marry me.' He shook his head sadly. 'I had it all planned. But then Sunshine well and truly stole my thunder.'

Laura stopped, but couldn't face him – nor could she silence the desperate and completely untruthful coup de grâce with which she finally broke her own heart.

'I would have said "no".'

As she walked on to the house, silent tears ran down her face, but somewhere in the darkness of the rose garden there was the sound of someone else weeping.

47

Eunice

2013

Portia gave the biscuits a magnificent send-off. She had wanted St Paul's Cathedral or Westminster Abbey, but finding that even her obscene wealth couldn't buy them, she had settled for the ballroom of a swanky Mayfair hotel. Eunice sat at the back in her designated seat, which was bedecked, as were all the others, with an extravagant black silk chiffon bow, and took in the splendid surroundings. The room was truly stunning, with a sprung wooden floor, floor-to-ceiling antique mirrors and, judging by the acoustics breathing Mozart's 'Lacrimosa' into the rarefied air, a state-of-the-art sound system. Either that or Portia had the entire London Philharmonic Orchestra and London Symphony Chorus hidden behind a screen somewhere. The mirrors reflected the monstrous arrangements of exotic lilies and orchids that loomed from shelves and pedestals like albino triffids.

Eunice had come with Gavin, a long-term friend of Bomber's since their school days together, who now made a living cutting, colouring and cosseting the hair of both genuine and manufactured celebrities.

His client list was one of the reasons that Portia had invited him.

'Bloody hell!' hissed Gavin, under his breath. Well, almost. 'Talk about rent-a-mob. Most of these people didn't know Bomber from Bardot.'

He smiled superciliously at the photographer who was prowling up and down the aisle between the rows of seats snapping any of the 'mourners' whom the public might recognise. Portia had sold the rights for the occasion to a glossy magazine that any intelligent woman would only ever admit to reading at the hairdresser. The seats were mostly filled with Portia's own friends, associates and hangers-on, with the occasional celebrity punctuating the populace like a sparse sequin on an otherwise dull dress. Bomber's friends were gathered at the back around Eunice and Gavin, like theatre-goers in the cheap seats.

At the front of the room, on a table festooned in yet more flowers, stood the urn. It was flanked on one side by an enormous framed photograph of Bomber ('He'd never have chosen that one,' whispered Gavin. 'His hair's a complete mess') and on the other by a photograph of Bomber and Portia as children, with Portia on the crossbar of Bomber's bike.

'She had to get her face in the frame, didn't she!' fumed Gavin. 'She can't even let him be the star at his own bloody memorial! But at least I managed to persuade her to invite some of Bomber's real friends and include something in this whole damn fiasco that Bomber might actually have liked.'

Eunice was impressed. 'How on earth did you manage that?'

Gavin grinned. 'Blackmail. I threatened to go to the press if she didn't. "Selfish Sister Scorns Brother's Dying Wishes" wasn't the kind of headline her publisher would want to see and she knows it. Speaking of which, where is Bruce the Bouffant?' He scanned the rows of heads in front of him, searching for the offending barnet.

'Oh, I expect he'll come with Portia,' Eunice replied. 'What exactly are you doing?'

Gavin looked very pleased with himself.

'It's a surprise, but I'll give you a clue. You remember the wedding at the beginning of *Love Actually* where members of the band are hidden in the congregation?'

Before he could go any further the music changed and Portia and her entourage swept down the aisle to 'O Fortuna' from *Carmina Burana*. She was wearing a white Armani trouser suit and a hat with a brim the size of a tractor wheel swathed in black spotted net.

'Jesus Christ!' spluttered Gavin. 'You'd think she was marrying Mick Jagger!'

He clutched Eunice's arm, barely able to contain his hysteria. Eunice's eyes filled with tears. But they were tears of laughter. She only wished that Bomber were here to share the fun. In fact, she wished she knew where Bomber was at all. She hadn't told Gavin about it yet. She was waiting for the right moment. The service itself was strangely entertaining. A children's choir from a local school – private and very exclusive – sang 'Over the Rainbow', Bruce read a eulogy on Portia's behalf as though he were delivering a soliloquy from *Hamlet*, and an actress from an minor soap opera read a poem by W. H. Auden. Prayers were said by a retired bishop whose daughter was apparently an old friend of Portia's. They were short and rather difficult to decipher on account of the whisky that he'd had with his breakfast. Or perhaps for his breakfast.

And then it was Gavin's turn.

He rose from his chair and stood in the aisle. Using the microphone he had concealed under his seat, he addressed the gathering with a theatrical flourish.

'Ladies and gentlemen, this one's for Bomber!'

He sat back down and a frisson of anticipation shivered through the assembly. Gavin looked at Eunice and winked.

'Show time!' he whispered.

There was a single, thrilling chord and then from somewhere at the back of the room, a man's voice singing softly, accompanied only by a piano. The voice came from a staggeringly handsome man wearing an immaculate dinner suit and a subtle sweep of eyeliner, who was indeed his own special creation. The opening bars of 'I Am What I Am' from *La Cage aux Folles* floated up into the hushed air and Gavin rubbed his hands together in delight.

As the singer made his way down the centre of the room and the tempo of the song picked up, he too picked up six showgirls seated strategically at the aisle end of their rows. Each one stood in turn and shed respectable coats to reveal risqué costumes, lavish jewels and astonishing tail feathers. Eunice was amazed that they had been able to sit on them. By the time the gorgeous creature and his extraordinary entourage had reached the front of the room, the song was reaching its climax. He turned in front of the urn to face his audience and belted out the final lines while his chorus line high-kicked in unison behind him. With the final, defiant note, all but one person in the room erupted into a spontaneous standing ovation. Portia simply passed out.

Gavin basked unashamedly in his triumph all the way to the country churchyard in Kent where the biscuits were to be buried next to Grace and Godfrey. Portia had provided a cavalcade of black stretch limousines to transport everyone, but Eunice and Gavin chose to travel independently, listening to show tunes and eating salt and vinegar crisps in Gavin's Audi convertible. Eunice felt slightly guilty about Godfrey and Grace being forced to share their grave with an urn of assorted biscuits under false pretences, but she was hopeful that, given the circumstances, they would understand that it had been unavoidable. As they pulled into the very churchyard where Eunice had promised to carry out Bomber's final wishes, Eunice confessed everything to Gavin.

'Holy Mary mother of God and Danny La Rue in a shoe box!' he exclaimed. 'My poor darling girl, what on earth are you going to do now?'

Eunice checked her hat in the rear-view mirror and reached for the door handle.

'I have absolutely no bloody idea whatsoever.'

48

Shirley switched on the computer and checked the voicemail messages. It was Monday morning, and Mondays were always busy because of all the strays that were brought in over the weekend. She had worked at Battersea Dogs & Cats Home for fifteen years now and had seen a lot of changes. But one thing never changed; the strays kept coming. The post had already arrived and Shirley began sorting through the pile of envelopes. One envelope was addressed in fountain pen. The writing was in a sweeping, extravagant hand and Shirley was curious. Inside was a handwritten letter.

> *To whom it may concern,*
>
> *Please find enclosed a donation in memory of my beloved brother who has recently died. He was very fond of dogs and adopted two from your establishment. The only condition that I attach to said donation is that you erect a plaque in his memory in some public place in your grounds. It should read:*
>
> *'In loving memory of Bomber,*
>
> *a precious son, an adored brother, a loyal friend and a devoted dog lover.*
>
> *Rest in peace with Douglas and Baby Jane.'*

> *I shall send my representative in due course to ensure*
> *that these instructions have been carried out in a*
> *satisfactory manner.*
> *Yours faithfully,*
> *Portia Brockley*

Shirley shook her head in disbelief. Damn cheek! It was true that all donations were gratefully received, but a plaque like that would cost a pretty penny. She turned her attention to the cheque that was attached, rather quaintly, by a paperclip to the letter and nearly fainted. There were so many noughts that it looked as though the '2' at the beginning of the figure had been blowing bubbles.

49

Laura felt as though she were poised on the brink of a precipice and didn't know whether she was going to fall or fly. She had made sure that she was going to be alone today. Sunshine was having a rare day out with her mum and she hadn't seen Freddy since her shameful outburst in the rose garden. She had tried ringing him, but his phone went straight to voicemail where she had left a grovelling and heartfelt apology, but it seemed it was too late. She had heard nothing in reply and Freddy had not been back to Padua since that night. She couldn't think what else to do. Sunshine kept telling her that Freddy would come back, but Laura knew now that he wouldn't. She had slept fitfully and woke stranded in a no-man's-land somewhere between excitement and foreboding. The house felt oppressive. Even Carrot was restless, pacing up and down, his nails clicking on the tiles. As Laura prepared for her visitor, she had a feeling that the storm was about to break. Padua had been very quiet for the past few days. The door to Therese's bedroom remained locked from the inside and there had been no music. But it was not the kind of quiet that came with peace and contentment. It was a bitter silence brought on by desolation and defeat. Laura had failed Therese and in so doing she had failed Anthony. His final wishes remained unfulfilled.

Someone was coming to collect the ashes in the biscuit tin. They had been claimed. Laura hadn't told Sunshine and it wasn't just because of the bet. She wanted to do this alone. She couldn't explain why, even to herself, but it was important. The doorbell rang at precisely two o'clock, the agreed hour of their appointment, and Laura opened the door to a small, slim woman in her sixties, stylishly dressed and wearing a cobalt blue trilby.

'I'm Eunice,' she said.

As Laura took the hand she was offered, she felt the tension that had gripped her melt away.

'Would you like tea, or perhaps something stronger?' asked Laura. For some unfathomable reason it felt as though they had something to celebrate.

'Do you know, I'd actually love a stiff drink. I never dared to hope that I would ever get him back, and now I'm about to, frankly I feel a tad wobbly.'

They settled on gin and limes in Anthony's honour, and took them through to the garden, collecting the biscuit tin from the study on the way. As Eunice sat nursing her drink in one hand and the biscuit tin in the other, her eyes filled with tears.

'Oh my dear, I'm so sorry. I'm just being a complete silly arse. But you have no idea how much this means to me. You have just mended a foolish woman's broken heart.'

She took a sip from her drink and then a deep breath.

'Now, I expect you want to know what this is all about?'

Eunice and Laura had exchanged several emails via the website, but they had only covered sufficient details to establish that it was actually Eunice who had lost the ashes.

'Are you sitting comfortably?' she asked Laura. 'I'm afraid it's rather a long story.'

Eunice began at the beginning and told Laura everything. She was a natural storyteller and Laura was surprised that she had never written anything herself. The abduction of Bomber's ashes from the funeral directors had Laura in tears of laughter, laughter that Eunice could at last share, now that she had got Bomber back.

'It all went splendidly until I got on the train,' she explained. 'At the station after I got on, I was joined in the carriage by a woman with two small children, who had obviously overdosed on sweets and fizzy pop, judging by the tide marks around their mouths and their uncontrollable behaviour. Their poor mother could barely keep them in their seats, and when the little girl announced that she 'needed a wee right now!' the mother asked me if I could possibly keep an eye on her brother while she took the little girl to the toilet. I could hardly say no.'

Eunice took a sip of her drink and hugged the biscuit tin closer to her side as though she might lose it again.

'The little boy sat in his seat poking his tongue out at me just until his mother was out of sight and then leapt to his feet and made a run for it. Sod's law helpfully ensured that this was just as the train was pulling into a station, and I wasn't quick enough to stop him jumping off the train when the doors opened, and so I was forced to follow him. I had my bag over my arm, but by the time I realised I had left Bomber in his seat it was too late.' Eunice shuddered at the memory. 'I'm sure you can imagine the pandemonium that followed. The mother was beside herself, wildly accusing me of kidnapping her son. Frankly, I was only too glad to give the little bugger back. I was absolutely frantic about leaving Bomber on the train and reported it straight away, but by the time the train had reached Brighton he was gone.'

Laura topped up their glasses. 'It's an unusual name, Bomber.'

'Oh, that wasn't his real name. His real name was Charles Bramwell Brockley. But I never knew anyone call him that. He was always Bomber. And he would have loved you,' she said to Carrot, gently stroking his head, which was by now resting in her lap. 'He loved all dogs.'

'And he was a publisher, you say? I wonder if he ever crossed paths with Anthony. He was a writer; short stories in the main. Anthony Peardew.'

'Oh yes,' Eunice replied. 'That's a name I remember well. His is a great story, you know: Anthony and Therese, the study full of his collection, the website. There has to be a book in it.'

Laura thought about her schoolgirl dreams of being a writer and smiled wistfully. Too late for all that now.

Eunice was still hugging the biscuit tin tightly to her side.

'Do you still work in publishing?' Laura asked her.

Eunice shook her head. 'No, no. My heart wasn't in it after Bomber . . .' Her voice trailed away. 'But if you're ever interested in giving the book a go, I'd be very happy to help. I still have contacts and I could recommend you to some agents.'

The two women sat in silence for a while, enjoying their drinks, the scent of the roses and the peace and quiet of a sunny afternoon.

'And what about you, Laura?' Eunice finally spoke. 'Do you have someone in your life – someone you love like I loved Bomber?'

Laura shook her head. 'I did, until a few days ago. But we had a fight.' She paused, thinking about what had *actually* happened.

'Okay – *I* started an argument; a pathetic, ridiculous, puerile argument. Well, it wasn't even an argument, because he didn't argue back. He just stood there listening to me rant on like a hysterical halfwit before I flounced off. I haven't seen him since.'

Laura was slightly surprised at the relief she felt from simply saying it out loud. 'My name is Laura and I've been a complete bloody idiot.'

'You're very hard on yourself, my dear.' Eunice squeezed her hand and smiled. 'But you love him?'

Laura nodded miserably.

'Then talk to him.'

'I've tried. But he never answers his phone and I can't say I blame him. I was *spectacularly* horrible. I've left messages saying I'm sorry, but he obviously isn't interested any more.'

Eunice shook her head. 'No, that's not what I meant. Talk to *him*, not his phone. Find him and tell him to his face.'

Suddenly Eunice reached inside her bag and took out a small box.

'I almost forgot,' she said. 'I brought you something for the website. I found it all those years ago on the way to my interview with Bomber. I've always kept it as a sort of lucky charm. I never really gave a thought to the person who must have lost it. But now it seems only fair that you should have it. I know it's a long shot, but maybe you might be able to find whom it really belongs to.'

Laura smiled. 'Of course, I'll try. I just need to make a note of any details you can remember.'

Eunice didn't even need to think about it. She rattled off the day, date, time and location without hesitation. 'You see,' she said, 'it was one of the best days of my life.'

Laura took the box from Eunice.

'May I?' she asked.

'Of course.'

As Laura took the medallion from the box, she knew for just a moment what it felt like to be Sunshine. The object in her hand spoke to her just as surely as if it had a voice of its own.

'Are you all right?' Eunice sounded as though she was very far away, speaking down a bad phone line. Laura scrambled to her feet, unsteadily.

'Come with me,' she said to Eunice.

The door to Therese's bedroom swung easily open and Laura placed the communion medallion, with its tiny picture of St Therese of the Roses framed in gold, on the dressing table next to the photograph of Anthony and Therese. The little blue clock, which had stopped, as usual, began ticking again of its own accord. Laura held her breath, and for a moment the two women stood in silence. And then downstairs, in the garden room, the music began, softly at first and then louder and louder.

The very thought of you.

Eunice watched in astonishment as Laura punched the air with joy, and through the open window there blew a swirling shower of rose petals.

As Laura walked Eunice to the garden gate, Freddy pulled up outside the house in his battered Land Rover and jumped out. He greeted Eunice politely and then looked to Laura.

'We need to talk.'

Eunice kissed Laura on the cheek and winked at Freddy. 'That's exactly what I said.'

She closed the gate behind her and walked away, smiling.

50

The five of them walked together along the promenade, Eunice and Gavin arm in arm carrying Bomber, Douglas and Baby Jane in a striped canvas shopping bag. Eunice had been going to go alone, but Gavin wouldn't hear of it. When Bomber had first been forced into Happy Haven he had asked Gavin to keep a friendly lookout for Eunice, but Gavin hadn't known how to without offending Eunice's notoriously independent spirit. However, since the memorial service when Eunice had made her full and frank confession, Gavin had found a chink in her armour and was using it to keep his word to Bomber. It was a perfect seaside day: bright and breezy with a sky the colour of blue Curaçao. Gavin had left the Audi at home and they had travelled by train so that they could both toast soon-to-be absent friends thoroughly and with impunity.

Eunice wanted the entire day to be a proper memorial for Bomber, and so they were following the time-honoured itinerary. As they strolled towards the pier they met a young couple walking a pair of miniature pugs wearing his-and-hers diamanté collars. Eunice couldn't resist stopping to admire them. The two little dogs submitted to appropriate fuss and compliments before trotting happily on their way. Gavin looked at Eunice's downcast face and gave her arm a squeeze.

'Chin up, old girl. It won't be long before Bill Bailey comes home.'

Eunice was finally permitting herself to adopt a dog. She had always intended to after Bomber died, but then, when she had lost his ashes, she somehow felt she didn't deserve one. She had to honour her obligations to old friends before she could allow herself a new one. The black and white collie with a white blaze and black spots had been kept on the end of a chain outside a shed for most of his miserable life, and the staff at Battersea had not been optimistic about his chances of rehabilitation. But the little dog had a big, brave heart and was willing to give the world another chance. The staff named him Bill Bailey after the song for luck, in the hope that he would find the perfect person to come home to. And he had. Eunice. As soon as she saw him, she fell for his pointy ears and his big, dark eyes. He was wary at first, but after a couple of visits he had decided that Eunice was the one for him and deigned to lick her hand. Next week, he would be hers for good.

Eunice and Gavin took it in turns to carry the shopping bag. To start with, Eunice had been reluctant to part with it, but the combined remains of her three friends were surprisingly heavy and she was glad for Gavin to take a turn.

'Bloody hell!' he exclaimed. 'We should have put them in one of those tartan shopping trolley affairs that old ladies push instead of carrying a bag.'

Eunice shook her head emphatically.

'You must be joking! And make me look like an old lady?' she retorted.

Gavin winked at her. 'Don't worry. You don't look a day over forty, old girl.'

Inside the amusement arcade it was hot and noisy and the air was thick with the smell of hotdogs, doughnuts and popcorn. By the expression on Gavin's face he thought Eunice had lured him into Babylon. The coloured lights spun and flashed in frantic synchronicity with the buzzers and bells. The money clinked into the machines and clattered out, although the former much more frequently than the latter. As one of Gavin's best brogues slipped on a squashed chip he looked ready to flee, but Eunice filled his hand with coins and nodded towards Bomber's favourite machine.

'Come on, you – get stuck in! Bomber loved this one.'

As Eunice posted a coin into the slot, she remembered the confusion on Bomber's face the last time they were there; but then how quickly it had been replaced· with a smile when she had come to his rescue. Today was for happy memories, not sad ones. Eunice made Gavin stick it out for almost half an hour, by the end of which he was almost enjoying himself. Against all the (most likely fixed) odds, he won a small and very ugly teddy bear on a claw-game machine, which he proudly presented to Eunice as a gift. As she inspected the lopsided bear's comical face, she had an idea.

'We should buy a souvenir for each of them,' she said, holding up the striped bag.

In one of the kiosks on the pier, they found a key ring in the shape of a doughnut for Douglas. In a shop in The Lanes Gavin spotted an antique Staffordshire china pug.

'He looks like a boy dog to me,' said Gavin, 'but perhaps Baby Jane would prefer that.'

They had fish and chips for lunch and Gavin ordered a bottle of champagne for them to toast the contents of the striped bag, which had its own chair. Eunice was determined not to let it out of her sight for a single moment. The champagne gave Eunice the courage to face what she had to do next. She had to let them go. The pavilion sparkled white in the sunlight and its domes and spires seemed to billow and prick the sky.

In Xanadu did Kubla Khan / A stately pleasure-dome decree . . .

It always put Eunice in mind of Coleridge's opium-inspired verse. They went inside first. It was to be Bomber's last tour and Douglas and Baby Jane's first. Eunice carefully bypassed the kitchen where the dog-powered spit-roast was exhibited. In the gift shop she bought a snow globe containing a model of the pavilion for Bomber's souvenir. Just as Eunice was about to pay, something else caught her eye.

'I'll take a tin of those biscuits too, please,' she told the woman behind the counter.

'Feeling peckish already?' asked Gavin, as he offered to carry them for her.

Eunice smiled. 'I owe a lady called Pauline a tin of biscuits.'

Outside in the grounds, by the pond, they found a bench and sat. The pavilion hung upside down in the water's reflection like a collection of Christmas tree baubles. Eunice took a pair of scissors from her pocket and cut a hole in one of the bottom corners of the striped bag. She had thought long and hard about how she could carry out Bomber's final wishes. Once she had decided on the 'where', she had to work out the 'how'. She didn't even know if it was allowed, but she hadn't asked in case the answer was 'no', so stealth was essential. Eventually, inspiration had come, as ever, from one of their favourite films: *The Great Escape*. If a dozen or so men could scatter the dirt excavated from three tunnels via their trouser legs in full view of armed guards, then surely Eunice would be able to scatter the ashes of three dear friends through the hole in the bottom of a shopping bag without drawing unwelcome attention. She was about to find out.

'Would you like me to come with you and keep a lookout? I could whistle the theme music if that would help.'

Eunice smiled. This part she really was going to do alone. Gavin watched as the small figure walked determinedly across the grass, back straight and head held high. At first, he took her path to be random, but it soon became apparent that it was anything but. When she rejoined him at the bench the striped bag was empty.

'Bomber was right about this place,' he said, staring at the reflection in the pond. 'It is utterly fabulous. By the way,' he added, 'what did you write?'

'Chocks away!' she replied.

51

The cursor on the screen in front of her winked encouragingly. The star sapphire ring on the third finger of Laura's left hand was still an unfamiliar weight as she lifted her hands to begin typing. Freddy, her fiancé of just three days, was in the kitchen making the lovely cup of tea with Sunshine, and Carrot lay sleeping at her feet. Laura was finally ready to chase her dream. She had found the perfect story and no one could describe it as being too 'quiet'. It was a sweeping story of love and loss, life and death, and, above all, redemption. It was the story of a grand passion that had endured for over forty years and finally found its happy ending. Smiling, she began to type. She had her perfect opening line . . .

The Keeper of Lost Things

Chapter 1

Charles Bramwell Brockley was travelling alone and without a ticket on the 14.42 from London Bridge to Brighton . . .

Loved *The Keeper of Lost Things?*

**Feeling bereft after saying goodbye to Anthony,
Laura and Sunshine?**

Keep on reading . . .

From Ruth Hogan's beguiling imagination comes
another irresistible novel of unexpected friendships,
second chances . . . and dark secrets.

THE PARTICULAR WISDOM OF SALLY RED SHOES

Masha is an intelligent, independent woman in her
early forties whose life has been irremediably changed
by a tragic event twelve years before.

Unable to share her grief, she finds solace in the local
Victorian cemetery and in her town's lido, where she
seeks refuge underwater, safe from the noise and the pain.

But a chance encounter with two extraordinary
women – the fabulous Kitty Muriel, a convent girl-
turned-magician's wife-turned-seventy-something
roller disco fanatic, and the mysterious Sally, a bag
lady with a prodigious voice – opens up a new world
of possibilities, and the chance to start living again.

Until the fateful day when the past comes roaring back . . .

A story of empowerment, hope and redemption.
A book about ordinary people hiding extraordinary pain,
and the small acts of joy that rescue them.

#SallyRedShoes

Acknowledgements

The fact that I am writing this means that my dream has finally come true and I am now a proper author. It has been a long journey and there have been some strange diversions, frustrating traffic jams and many bumps in the road. But here I am. There are so many people who have helped me to get here and if I were to mention all of you it would be a novel in itself, but you know who you are and I thank you all.

My parents are, of course, to blame. They taught me to read before I started school, enrolled me at the children's library and filled my childhood with books, for which I am eternally grateful.

Thank you to Laura Macdougall, my incredible agent at Tibor Jones, for believing in me and *Keeper* from the very beginning. We first met under the John Betjeman statue at St Pancras (it was definitely a sign) and within minutes I knew that I wanted to work with you. I thank you for your unstinting support and enthusiasm, your unfailing professionalism and determination, your expert guidance in my initial forays with Twitter and Instagram and your lemon curd.

Thank you Charlotte Maddox at Tibor Jones for all your work with my foreign rights deals and for being such an enthusiastic cheerleader for *Keeper*, and to the whole team at Tibor Jones – undoubtedly the coolest agency on the planet – for making me feel so much at home with you guys. You rock!

Thank you to Fede Andornino, my editor at Two Roads and founder of Team Sunshine, for taking a risk on *Keeper*. Your humour, patience and boundless enthusiasm have made working with you an absolute joy. Yay! Thanks also to the whole team at Two Roads, especially Lisa Highton, Rosie Gailer, Ross Fraser, Aimee Oliver, Hannah Corbett and Jess Kim for welcoming me so warmly and for all your hard work in turning *Keeper* into a real book. Thank you also to Amber Burlinson for her brilliant copyediting skills, Miren Lopategui for her careful proofread, and Laura Oliver and Susan Spratt for actually *making* the book; and Ben Gutcher, Lizzi Jones, Olivia Allen, Ellie Wheeldon and Sarah Clay for making sure it reached the hands of readers. Thank you to Sarah Christie and Diana Beltran Herrera for bringing Padua's rose garden to life and creating a beautiful cover.

Thank you to Rachel Kahan at William Morrow, another member of Team Sunshine, for your invaluable editorial input and for the humour with which it was imparted. Thanks also to all my foreign publishers for taking *Keeper* all over the world!

Huge thanks to Ajda Vucicevic. You were there at the start and your faith in me has never faltered.

Peter Budek at The Eagle Bookshop in Bedford has been my friend, mentor, and shoulder to cry on through good times and bad. He has also provided me with endless cups of tea, invaluable advice and heaps of wonderful research material. Pete, you are a legend. Now finish writing at least one of your books!

Tracey, my mad friend, you died while I was writing *Keeper*, and I am so sad that you are not here to share this with me, but you inspired me to keep trying when I was sorely tempted to give up.

Thank you to the staff at Bedford and Addenbrookes Hospitals for all your care and kindness, and for making sure that I was still around to finish this book. Special thanks go to the staff at The Primrose Unit for your continued support and interest in my writing.

I should like to thank Paul for putting up with me. Whilst writing *Keeper* I have filled the house with all the lost things I found, left bits of paper covered in notes all over the place and generally allowed my 'stuff' to creep into every room. I have locked myself away for hours on end and then emerged grumpy and demanding dinner. And yet, you're still here!

Finally, I should like to thank my wonderful dogs. They have had to put up with 'We'll go for a walk as soon as I've finished this chapter' far too many times. Billy and Tilly both died while I was working on *Keeper* and I miss them every day, but Timothy Bear and Duke are asleep on the sofa as I write this. Snoring.

About Ruth Hogan

I was born in the house where my parents still live in Bedford. My sister was so pleased to have a sibling that she threw a thrupenny bit at me.

As a child, I loved the Brownies but hated the Guides, was obsessed with ponies and read everything I could lay my hands on. Luckily, my mum worked in a bookshop. My favourite reads were *The Moomintrolls*, *A Hundred Million Francs*, *The Lion, The Witch and The Wardrobe*, and the back of cereal packets, and gravestones.

I passed enough O and A levels to get a place at Goldsmiths College, University of London, to study English and Drama. It was brilliant and I loved it.

And then I got a proper job.

I worked for ten years in a senior local government position (Human Resources – Recruitment, Diversity and Training) I was a square peg in a round hole, but it paid the bills and mortgage.

In my early thirties I had a car accident which left me unable to work full-time and convinced me to start writing seriously. I got a part-time job as an osteopath's receptionist and spent all my spare time writing.

It was all going well, but then in 2012 I got cancer, which was bloody inconvenient but precipitated an exciting hair journey from bald to a peroxide blonde Annie Lennox crop. When chemo kept me up all night I passed the time writing and the eventual result was *The Keeper Of Lost Things*.

I live in a chaotic Victorian house with an assortment of rescue dogs and my long-suffering partner. I spend all my free time writing, or thinking about it, and have notebooks in every room so that I can write down any ideas before I forget them. I am a magpie; always collecting treasures (or 'junk' depending on your point of view) and a huge John Betjeman fan.

My favourite word is antimacassar and I still like reading gravestones.

ruthhogan.co.uk
twitter.com/ruthmariehogan
instagram.com/ruthmariehogan

About the cover

The cover design for *The Keeper of Lost Things* brings to life Padua's rose garden and was created by Two Roads designer Sarah Christie with Diana Beltran Herrera, a Colombian artist based in Bristol. Inspired by Anthony and Therese's love for roses, Diana has produced striking hand-made paper sculptures of the flowers: you can find out more about her creative process on her website dianabeltranherrera.com.

The design also features some of the lost treasures collected by Ruth Hogan during the writing process, and it's possible to explore the complete collection on Ruth's Instagram page: instagram.com/RuthMarieHogan (or simply search for #KeeperOfLostThings). It's growing fast, so keep on checking back for the latest updates.

Some of these objects are also scattered around the pages of the book, welcoming the reader at the beginning of each chapter: a visual reminder that even the most insignificant of objects can hold the most extraordinary of stories...

stories ... voices ... places ... lives

We hope you enjoyed *The Keeper of Lost Things*. If you'd like
to know more about this book or any other title on our list,
please go to www.tworoadsbooks.com

For news on forthcoming Two Roads titles, please sign
up for our newsletter

enquiries@tworoadsbooks.com

TwoRoadsBooks